NEXUS CONFESSIONS:
VOLUME SIX

D1638553

NEXUS CONFESSIONS: VOLUME SIX

Edited and compiled by
Lindsay Gordon
and Lance Porter

Always make sure you practise safe, sane and consensual sex.

Published by Nexus 2009

2 4 6 8 10 9 7 5 3 1

First published in Great Britain in 2009 by
Nexus
Virgin Books
Random House, 20 Vauxhall Bridge Road
London SW1V 2SA

www.virginbooks.com
www.rbooks.co.uk

Addresses for companies within The Random House Group Limited can be found at: www.randomhouse.co.uk/offices.htm

The Random House Group Limited Reg. No. 954009

Distributed in the USA by Macmillan, 175 Fifth Avenue, New York, NY 10010, USA

A CIP catalogue record for this book is available from the British Library

ISBN 9780352345097

The Random House Group Limited supports The Forest Stewardship Council [FSC], the leading international forest certification organisation. All our titles that are printed on Greenpeace approved FSC certified paper carry the FSC logo. Our paper procurement policy can be found at www.rbooks.co.uk/environment

Mixed Sources
Product group from well-managed forests and other controlled sources
www.fsc.org Cert no. TT-COC-2139
© 1996 Forest Stewardship Council

Typeset by TW Typesetting, Plymouth, Devon
Printed and bound in Great Britain by CPI Bookmarque, Croydon CR0 4TD

CONTENTS

Introduction

Who can forget the first time they read a reader's letter in an adult magazine? It could make your legs shake. You could almost feel your imagination stretching to comprehend exactly what some woman had done with a neighbour, the baby-sitter, her best friend, her son's friend, a couple of complete strangers, whatever ... Do real women actually do these things? Did this guy really get that lucky? We asked ourselves these questions, and the not knowing, and the wanting to believe, or wanting to disbelieve because we felt we were missing out, were all part of the reading experience, the fun, the involvement in the confessions of others, as if we were reading some shameful diary. And when Nancy Friday's collections of sexual fantasies became available, didn't we all shake our heads and say, no way, some depraved writer made all of this up? No woman could possibly want to do that. Or this guy must be crazy. But I bet there are readers' letters and confessed fantasies that we read years, even decades ago, that we can still remember clearly. Stories that haunt us: did it, might it, could it have really happened? And stories that still thrill us when the lights go out because they have informed our own dreams. But as we get older and become more experienced, maybe we have learnt that we would be foolish to underestimate anyone sexually, especially ourselves.

The scope of human fantasy and sexual experience seems infinite now. And our sexual urges and imaginations never cease to eroticise any new situation or trend or cultural flux about us. To browse online and to see how many erotic sub-cultures have arisen and made themselves known, is to be in awe. Same deal with magazines and adult films – the variety, the diversity, the complexity and level of obsessive detail involved. But I still believe there are few pictures or visuals that can offer the insights into motivation and desire, or reveal the inner world of a fetish, or detail the pure visceral thrill of sexual arousal, or the anticipation and suspense of a sexual experience in the same way that a story can. When it comes to the erotic you can't beat a narrative, and when it comes to an erotic narrative you can't beat a confession. An actual experience or longing confided to you, the reader, in a private dialogue that declares: *yes, if I am honest, I even shock myself at what I have done and what I want to do.* There is something comforting about it. And unlike a novel, with an anthology there is the additional perk of dipping in and out and of not having to follow continuity; the chance to find something fresh and intensely arousing every few pages written by a different hand. Start at the back if you want. Anthologies are perfect for erotica, and they thrive when the short story in other genres has tragically gone the way of poetry.

So sit back and enjoy the Nexus Confessions series. It offers the old school thrills of reading about the sexual shenanigans of others, but Nexus-style. And the fantasies and confessions that came flooding in – when the call went out on our website – are probably only suitable for Nexus. Because like the rest of our canon, they detail fetishes, curious tastes and perverse longings: the thrills of shame and humiliation, the swapping of genders, and the ecstasy of submission or domination. There are no visiting milkmen, or busty neighbours hanging out the washing and winking over the hedge here. Oh, no. Our readers and fantasists are far more likely to have been spanked, or caned, feminised into women, have given themselves to strangers, to have dominated other men or women, gone dogging, done the unthinkable, behaved inappropriately and broken the rules.

Lindsay Gordon, Winter 2006

Symbols key

 Corporal Punishment

 Female Domination

 Institution

 Medical

 Period Setting

 Restraint/Bondage

 Rubber/Leather

 Spanking

 Transvestism

 Underwear

 Uniforms

Eva's New Customer

When you work in the service industry, one of the first things you learn is discretion. It's part of that mantra: 'The customer is always right,' I suppose. I'm sure you know the sort of thing I'm getting at: smiling politely and playing along when a woman asks to buy a corset for her 'sister', or nodding understandingly when a gentleman wants to purchase a wig for a 'fancy dress party'. It's all discretion.

I'm pretty liberal anyway. I think people should just do what they want and go to whatever lengths they want to go to, to look the best they can. Even if that means squeezing yourself in the middle like a toothpaste tube, or wearing a patch of fur on your scalp – as long as you pull the look off, best of luck to you.

I've been working in retail outlets for nearly twenty years now. I started small, leaving my management job in a famous clothing shop chain to open a fashion shop in one of those niche-market arcades. At first I sold a mix of production clothing, locally made character items and rare gems picked up from charity shops and the like. My customers were mainly students and trendy studio-flat dwellers in the city – I'm sure you can picture the look they go for.

It was a nice little concern, most enjoyable, but it didn't really bring in enough turnover, so I thought about branching out. After a year or so I started a line in expensive shoes. That certainly helped. They seemed to attract the right sort of clientele: those glamorous wives, who would pull up in their soft-top cars and glide around the shop in their sunglasses and tight knee-length skirts before buying a pair of knock-out leopard-print courts or black equestrian-style fuck-me boots. The great thing about expensive shoes, compared to retro-chic, is that the mark-up is so much higher.

But that wasn't all: things got busy – as can happen when word gets about that there's a delightful little shop off the beaten track selling beautiful and unusual garments to die for. And you can bet your cashmere shawl that they'll be the envy of all and sundry at the next soiree (especially that Claudia, who will go a sickened green at the very sight of you). We all know how women work in these circles: items need to be stylish and unique – and the ladies certainly seemed to like it when I was able to guarantee that they had the only pair of these shoes, or those boots, in the whole city.

It came to the point when I had to start stocking whole outfits. Customers were asking for matching skirts and matching hosiery and I found myself turning this auxiliary business away to nearby stores, which really stuck in my craw. So, I cut down on the anti-cool student and yuppie stuff, and brought in underwear, hosiery, blouses, skirts and accessories.

The thirty-forty-fifty-something wives and business-women beat a path to the door after that and I had to hire help and look for larger premises. Some were even offering me cash to put together a holiday ensemble for them. Me? A style guru? I'd never considered myself in that mould, I must say.

The lead-up to Valentine's Day? Well, I saw some pretty glorious sights behind the changing-room curtain during that month, let me tell you, and some pretty respectable women in some pretty racy attire. But like I say, you learn discretion early on in this business.

The other bonus for me was that I had to change the way I dressed from the casual workaday outfits to the slinky, high-heeled, tight-skirted, silken-bloused look that matched my customers' aspirations. It made me feel so powerfully sexy to slip on those stockings, zip that skirt tightly up around my buttocks, and slip on those patent heels. I revelled in the admiring glances from builders and car-drivers on my way to open up and, of course, the jealous glances of my naturally bitchy customers!

I got such a buzz from dressing up that I actually took to changing into another outfit at lunch-time. What can I say, completely by chance I had discovered the thrill of squeezing one's curves into a girdle, rolling a pair of light silky stockings up one's legs, exposing one's rump as one bends over to fix the clasps, slipping one's feet into a pair of killer heels, and now I couldn't get enough of it. By the time one is checking one's look in the full-length mirror, one's pussy is positively gushing. Dressing-up once a day just simply wasn't sufficient.

Indeed, adoring myself in provocative attire was so exciting I could not leave things there, and I began to close the shop for the full lunch hour, to really enjoy my midday outfit-change. I invested in one of those thick, realistic, rubber vibrators (I'm sure you've seen them, with the authentic penis-shape, the veins, the bendiness – more like the real thing than one of those rigid classic dildos) and let my pussy spend a climax upon it before re-opening the shop again for the afternoon.

I also began to play host to the suited and tanned husbands of my sophisticated new clientele, looking to buy something for their wives' birthdays, or maybe to get one of those unexpected gifts that help to keep the romance blooming. I gladly helped them out with their questions about sizes and styles and sent them on their way with an outfit that was sure to please them both (let's be honest here, it was usually lingerie and hosiery they were after – very few went for any outfits intended for public consumption).

3

Consequently, I became used to serving men in my women's clothes shop, but it was at least a few months before my mind was awoken to the real agenda. I played host to what turned out to be my first transsexual customer. On his/her first visit he came in casual male attire, although he was sporting a very florid, camp demeanour. He was accompanied by a female friend and after a tour of the racks and a lot of giggling and chatting between the two of them – I could tell they were very good friends – they both approached my desk.

'Hello,' said the short-haired female. 'I know it's unusual, but I wonder, would you mind if my friend tried a few items on?'

I think I betrayed a look of surprise at first, but after a quick glance at the slim young man I could not think of a reason why not.

'Sure,' I shrugged.

'Thank you,' he said. 'I have to be careful the first time I try a new shop, that's why I bring my wee pal along with me.'

'Of course,' I smiled, not really sure what he was getting at exactly.

They picked a few of the outfits from the racks and he took his tall, slim frame behind the curtain. His friend waited outside, chatting to him through the curtain as though he were one of the girls. Momentarily he came out, looking resplendent in a short green dress with a high neck, we discussed the look, and he went back behind the curtain to try another. They bought three outfits from me that day, and a pair of shoes – in the largest size I had available. I must admit when I started out I never considered that I would start to get transgender customers, but then again, why shouldn't I?

'Do you stock any wigs?' he asked as he was paying for his purchases. I had to disappoint him and reply that I did not.

'You should get a few in,' he winked. 'And larger sized shoes: it'll bring you extra custom – I guarantee it.'

The incident was an eye-opener, and it certainly changed my attitude, for, now, all of a sudden I was seeing my male customers a little differently. I no longer believed them when they told me they were buying outfits for their wives – I was always a little suspicious that maybe, just maybe, the outfit was for thcm.

I did take that gentlewoman's advice and I did start to stock larger sizes in shoes and I had a shelf put in, high on the back wall, to display a selection of wigs.

As the months rolled on, I became a dab hand at divining who were the genuine customers buying for wives and who were buying for themselves. The lack of a wedding ring was a big giveaway, obviously, but there were other, more subtle clues: when I asked what size, they always said, 'About my height,' and when they bought shoes, it was never below a size seven.

I never said anything. Discretion, I felt, was paramount. But I did wonder if the fancy, silky, sexy women's clothes appealed to them for the same reason they appealed to me. I was so tempted to ask, but knew that if I did I ran the risk of being seen as indiscreet. Nothing scares away a customer quicker than lack of discretion.

I tried to think of the way I feel when I dress in sexy clothes: the snug silkiness of my shiny stockings, the tight skirt that makes me so aware of my own shape and curves, the feel of my breasts pushed against each other. I feel feminine, I feel powerful, I feel desired and admired. And I wondered if perhaps my cross-dressing customers were trying to tap into this feeling.

My attention began to focus in on one customer, Simon Cassell (I got his name from his credit card), who seemed to be very generous about buying his wife outfits; he would come in every month, just about, and buy 'her' something slinky or sexy.

He seemed a little vain, sporting his orange-brown tan, neat haircut and usually wearing tight polo-neck top with a jacket and expensive shoes. That side of him, at least, fitted in with my little piece of amateur profiling of the typical cross-dresser – a need to be loved, to be admired.

The real giveaway with Simon was when his wife accompanied him, to genuinely purchase underwear for her birthday. The first thing that put a smirk on my face was that she was not 'about his height', but some six inches shorter. I also got a good look at her feet, which were petite sweet little things and nowhere near the size eights that Simon's previous visits had indicated she tended to wear. I said nothing of course to either of them, maintaining my professionalism. Discretion.

My suspicions aside, I had a very enjoyable hour or so with Mr and Mrs Cassell. Mrs Cassell wanted to try everything on before buying, but was very insistent that Mr Cassell should not see her in the outfits in the shop as it would ruin the effect on the night, so I was drafted in as a critical pair of eyes. I did enjoy myself peeking through the curtains to give her my opinions. It was hardly like being at work at all really, watching a sexy woman trying on underwear. The first thing she tried was a diaphanous red nightgown, with a matching red basque and some red high-heeled sandals. She certainly got into the spirit of things – I could see through the tiny gap in the curtain that she was stripping off completely before climbing into the basque. She seemed to be giving a show for herself in the mirror as she slipped on the negligee and placed the shoes over her pointed toes.

'What do you think?' she called out to me.

I poked my head in to see and my mouth watered at the sight of her. The basque top followed the curve of her waist and the heels accentuated her ankles perfectly. The stocking clasps dangled freely on her thighs (they had to dangle as I can't allow my customers to try on stockings I'm afraid – not without buying them, the same goes for panties). Her naked bush poked out from under the basque and the faint outline of her pussy-lips peeped through the curls. I tried not to look.

'Well,' I said encouragingly, 'if I were a man, I'd definitely shag you!'

It was, perhaps, a slightly misleading thing to say, as I would be quite happy to have shagged her as a woman. Or at the very least, buried my tongue amongst the undergrowth.

Agitated and frustrated, Simon hung around in the shop, banished to the other side of the counter where he was unable to sneak any unlicensed peeks of his wife in her resplendence.

'You're in for a treat,' I said to him with a smile.

He just laughed.

Next she tried a black bra and suspenders set, which we had matched off the racks with a long nightgown and black shoes. The same ritual again: she stripped off naked and, deliberately and elegantly, donned the bra, suspender belt, gown and shoes as she watched herself in the mirror. I was called in again to give my opinions.

'Glorious again,' I told her, trying my best not to concentrate my gaze on her lovely little bush for longer than would be polite. Difficult as that was.

After a short discussion we were both agreed on the red outfit and, adding a pair of red lace knickers and sheer seamed stockings, I packaged the ensemble and punched through the purchase on that very familiar credit card of Mr Cassell's. I wished I could see his wife in the full kit, I really did. That was the only disappointment of an otherwise wonderful experience.

Now I was just about one hundred percent sure that Simon must be getting off in private by dressing himself up as Simone, and I had other customers who I wasn't quite so sure about. Obviously I had my suspicions now whenever any male walked in unaccompanied and started to buy suspender belts or stockings, or asking for dresses for a wife the same size as him, but, frustratingly, none of them gave themselves away like our Simon had by bringing in his wife.

* * *

7

About a month later a striking, tall, slender woman walked into my shop with big hair and angry heels on. She hardly needed the three inches' height they gave her, she seemed quite tall enough already. She gave me a very friendly hello as she strutted into the shop and proceeded to browse the shelves and racks. I watched her wiggle as she walked past the counter and found myself tingling in my pussy in a way that the sight of a woman's arse had never brought about before.

I watched her some more, just out of the corner of my eye, and admired her slim, fit-looking legs – not thick or muscular but you could see the definition in them as she moved. Then I noticed her dress. Its bottle-green colour and high-necked style was strangely familiar to me, as, for that matter, were the black sandals she was gliding around on.

Then it dawned on me. I had stocked both the items in this very shop. I had probably sold them to this woman! Well, what you have probably already guessed by now did not then occur to me until a good few moments later: this was the transsexual who had come in with the short-haired woman and bought the three dresses and the pair of shoes from me.

'I remember you now!' I said to her.

'Oh, did you not recognise me? I'm sorry, I would have said,' she replied in her husky, but feminine, voice.

'Well,' I commented, 'you do look stunning, I must say. And you have a lovely arse, if you don't mind me . . .'

'No, I don't mind at all, thank you, Honey,' she replied.

I walked around the counter to speak with her more closely. I had so much to ask, but did not know where to start. The biggest question on my mind was why she was turning me on so much, but I could hardly start there.

'So, tell me, I'm interested, how much time do you spend as a woman?'

8

'Oh, practically all of my time really. I only revert to being a boy for special occasions, you know, such as certain family gatherings and social events. But I'll phase it out completely in time.'

'You don't mind me prying, I hope.'

'God no! I wish people would just ask me what they want to know, rather than whisper about me or laugh across the street. I'm Jade, by the way.'

'Nice to meet you. I'm Eva,' I replied, softly shaking the hand she had offered.

It seemed a shame, after all the questions I had been asking myself, not to take advantage of Jade's presence by doing some research into all this cross-dressing that seemed to be going on out there.

'Seeing as you don't mind, I have many more questions,' I warned her. 'First of all, have you any idea how many men actually do cross-dress? My shop seems to be full of men whom I can't help suspecting are buying for themselves.'

'Ah yes, well, it wouldn't surprise me. Most of those are a bit different to me of course, I dress this way because I feel that I am a woman. Your customers do it because it turns them on in one way or another,' she told me.

'I see, yes, I should have realised that. I'm sorry.'

'Not at all, anything to help. The usual reasons are that they like to feel humiliated, or pretty, or vulnerable, or dainty, or even imagine that they're being lusted after. Much more than that I can't help you I'm afraid, it's not really my scene. I would just let them get on with it!'

She was right of course, after all, it wasn't harming anyone and I did fancy myself as the liberal type.

I thanked her generously for her advice (before selling her something slinky, naturally). The conversation had been a great help, but I had lacked the courage to ask her the other question floating around in my mind: why did it turn me on suddenly? Why did watching Jade's male arse in a short dress make me moisten? That particular mystery went unanswered, but I did resolve from then on not to be quite so concerned about the wannabe sissies and tarts that frequented my boudoir. Just let them get on with it, and don't bother them, I said. And so I continued to be the soul of discretion for the next three or four months.

It was the return of Simon Cassell that snapped my resolve in two. He came one afternoon as I was close to thinking about flipping the sign and popping off home for the evening. I caught his eye as he came right over to the desk to speak to me.

'Hello again. I trust the outfit you bought a few months ago was satisfactory?' I said.

'Oh yes,' he confirmed. 'So much so in fact I'd like to buy another one. Can you help me put one together, as a surprise for her?' he asked.

I nodded. I was smirking of course on the inside.

'Certainly, remind me what size she is again?'

'Oh just a little smaller than me,' he lied.

We both knew that was not true, but I really think he thought I had forgotten how diminutive his gorgeous wife was.

'Of course she is, now I remember. Shall we start with a dress?'

I showed Simon a number of dresses, some long, some short, some revealing, some more modest. He seemed to enjoy feeling the fabric with his fingers as his eyes danced over them. For my part, I could not help but try to imagine him in each and every one as I displayed them over my arm for him. I began to undress him in my mind, imagining how firm his thighs and arse might be under those conventional clothes.

He selected something short, another red number, with a high neck and open back. It was not obvious to me at the time, but of course the high neck is chosen in order to completely conceal the false cleavage.

'Lovely.' I congratulated him on his choice. 'Shall we select some underwear?'

The underwear had to be matching of course, and he loved the very first thing I showed him: a three-piece set consisting of a little red bra, knickers and suspender belt, all with the same lace pattern. I placed them on top of the dress, which I had draped over the counter.

'What sort of stockings do you think she will look best in?' I asked.

'I'm not sure,' he replied.

I heaved the big box of packaged stockings from behind the counter up onto the till.

'Those on the rack are just for show, I've got the full range here,' I told him.

We flicked through the collection, and I drew his attention to a few red pairs, one sheer, one fishnet, one seamed, but to his credit – and my surprise – he selected a pair far more suitable: champagne in colour, with a red band and red seam, the heels were fully fashioned too; they were gorgeous. Why, the little darling has an eye for this! I thought to myself.

I eyed him up and down as I tried to imagine his fit body in that underwear, the cut of his quadriceps in those stockings, his hard buttocks in those knickers. I shook my head in an attempt to come to my senses. It seemed to bring my head back round, but you can't shake your pussy to stop it juicing I'm afraid – I had no remedy for that.

'You really are obsessed with turning her into a scarlet woman, aren't you!' I joked as I placed them on the pile.

'I suppose I am. Em, speaking of which, I think I'd like to change her hair for the day, how do you think an auburn wig would go down with her?' he asked me, pointing to the row of wigs up on my highest shelves.

I didn't really consider how I thought his wife would react to being asked to change her hair colour, as I knew it was irrelevant. I simply suggested that it would be a

11

good idea. I fetched the ladder up to the shelf and brought down all the auburn, red and ginger wigs in my new range. I did not bother to see if my kinky customer would look up my skirt while I was up there, I knew he would.

After some deliberation, he chose a shoulder-length dark auburn one, with some highlighting in the front. I placed it in a net, and it too joined the pile on the counter.

'Shoes?' I said. He nodded.

I had a few red pairs on the rack, and, continuing the scarlet theme, he picked up each one, holding them like they were injured animals in the palms of his hand, and then turning them to look at the heel. He ran his finger along the arc of the sole, possibly imagining his foot following the contour.

'These I think,' he said, handing them to me. 'Size eight if you have it.'

I slipped through the curtain at the rear and quickly located the style in the right size, bringing the box to the counter. He took out his wallet and handed me his credit card as I totalled the purchase.

I had been enjoying myself, watching this little sissy buy himself an outfit, and I was rather sad that it was all over. There was also the overriding feeling that perhaps my lot as the discreet shopkeeper was not a particularly good one, and after all these months of equipping cross-dressers and dutifully keeping their secrets and sparing their blushes, surely I had earned the right to see the final effect – especially when the customer was so well-formed.

I handed him back his card. I knew what I wanted to ask him, but was I brave enough?

'Would you like a bag for all this?' I said, stalling. I took a deep breath.

He nodded. My heart was pounding now, but I tried to maintain a calm and aloof air.

'Or would you like to try them on first?'

Oh the relief of finally asking that! I can't tell you.

Simon froze where he stood. He gasped and his mouth fell open a little.

'Sorry?' he asked.

'You heard. Would you like to try them on before you leave?' I pressed, my nerves now calming themselves as I sensed I had the upper hand.

'But . . .'

'Oh come now. We both know these are for you.'

He was silent.

'Come on – I bet you make a sexy little tart,' I teased him, eyeing his figure to punctuate the comment.

He never said a thing, only releasing a very shaky, nervous breath and nodding his head. I led him to the dressing room and pulled the curtain right back. He followed silently, breathing slowly and softly. His head was bowed and I noticed he was avoiding eye contact with me. Was this his female persona? I wondered. A submissive little tart? If so, I supposed I should have to take charge, shouldn't I? I had no idea really.

I flipped the 'CLOSED' sign on the door so that we wouldn't be disturbed.

'You'd better take off your clothes first,' I said to him. He reached for the curtain, but I held it open. 'No, I want to see.'

Silently, Simon's shaky, nervous fingers removed his conventional clothes, folding them neatly. There was a bench set into the wall of the little curtained alcove and he rested them there. I smiled as my pussy wept: he certainly was a pert thing and his semi-erect penis hung in the air in front if him with a pearl of pre-come at its tip. I do like to see that. I brought the clothing over to him and handed him the suspender belt, which he hurriedly stepped into, pulling it up to the waist.

Something wasn't quite right, however.

'Take it off again,' I said thoughtfully.

13

He did so.

I think the problem was that I was watching a man put women's clothes on. That wasn't really the idea that was turning me on. No. The prospect that was exciting me, and goodness knows why, was turning a man into my own little scarlet harlot.

'Do it again,' I said, 'only it needs to be more feminine, more dainty. Point your toes,' I suggested.

He tried again, this time pointing his toes as I had said for him to do, and slowly drawing the belt up his legs and over his hips. It was a huge improvement, and yes, it turned me on.

'Much better. Now these, take your time.'

I threw the packet of seamed stockings to him and sat back on my chair to watch my naked man, with his cock twitching and dribbling, take out the fresh new nylons and draw them slowly over his pointed toes up to his thighs.

'Now cross your legs when you fasten them.'

He kept his toes pointed as he crossed each leg over to fasten the four clasps to the light, caressing fabric of the stocking. He seemed to be a natural.

'You have clearly done this before, you little tease,' I joked with him.

At least, I had intended the comment to be a joke, but when I noted the effect the comment had on him and his cock, I realised that perhaps the things I was saying to him had much more significance to his fetish than I had imagined. I passed him the knickers.

'You had better hide your arousal with these,' I told him. 'We wouldn't want all the boys to know how this little whore enjoys her job so much.'

It was certainly a thrill for me to talk to him like this, but when he gasped at what I had said and tried to rub his cock with his forearm (no doubt thinking I wouldn't notice) I knew I was onto something with him.

Now he stood before me, his fine leg muscles encased in champagne-coloured nylon, a pair of knickers hiding

14

and holding trim his erectile bulge, and a suspender belt tightly around his waist. I felt powerful and horny at the same time, and let me tell you it is an addictive combination.

'I bet you'd look even prettier with this on,' I said as I passed him the high-necked dress on the hanger. 'And I want to see you wiggle into it when you put it on.'

Simone, for that seemed like the right name at the time, unzipped the dress and, still remembering to point *her* toes, stepped into it, letting it slide up her stockinged legs. I had to help her get her broad shoulders to fit into the arms and the zip needed some persuasion, but eventually the skimpy little number was on my tart and I watched with real relish as *she* wiggled like a fish and smoothed the fabric down with her hands to remove all the creases. The dress was too short to cover her stocking-tops: the red bands poked out from under the hem. I marvelled at what a slut I had created and actually caught myself stroking my own clitoris right in front of him. I composed myself.

'The boys will love that wiggle,' I goaded, handing her the shoes. 'Remember to point your toes – it turns me on.'

Simone slipped into the shiny red shoes and tottered in front of me, waiting for her next instruction. I was amazed to see the way she held her hands: out to the side as though about to curtsey, very lady-like indeed. Did that come naturally? I wondered, or was it rehearsed in front of the mirror? No matter, it was making me feel so dominant and horny, I didn't really care.

'Now while you straighten the wig, I'm going to apply some lipstick from my handbag.'

At last my scarlet harlot was completed and I stepped back to look at my creation. It was quite beautiful, and it made me wonder why male dress-codes did not display the form in this way more often. I made her twirl for me and was surprised to feel my pussy tingling with excitement as I humiliated her for my visual amusement.

'Is this what you like? To have a woman turn you into a slut?' I asked him.

'Yes,' he whispered, almost inaudibly.

I lusted for more of this heady erotic drug coursing through my clit and pussy so I made her perform some more for me, insisting she strut up and down across the shop as sexily as she could.

'Imagine you were trying to attract a horny customer to fuck you,' I suggested.

Simone's cheeks reddened and blushed as she paraded herself up and down for me (and the imaginary audience) and I found myself becoming more and more aroused by my role; I was now unashamedly rubbing my clit through my clothing in front of her, swimming in power, pleasure and a perverse delight.

To me, there seemed only one way to finish this exercise, and I hoped that my little slut was up for it. I reached into the bottom drawer behind the counter where, right at the back, I kept my rubber cock. I placed it on the counter where Simone could see. She was still strutting her stuff for me and, judging by the prong sticking out of her crotch and ruining the line of her short dress, still enjoying it. She stopped when she saw my dildo. I tried to stay in some sort of character, as I had noticed how Simone seemed to like it, but I must admit to feeling a little silly at the time.

'Oh, what's this? A customer for "Simone" the wee slut?' I mocked. 'What a lucky girl, perhaps she had better lean over the counter and stick her arse out,' I added, raising my eyebrows suggestively.

To my surprise, Simone silently complied, leaning herself against the counter, just as though she was being frisked by the police, and lifted her dress, exposing her bum to me. As I moved round, wetting the end of the cock in my mouth, just like I do for myself, Simone shamelessly reached down to her crotch and began slowly masturbating her penis, closing her eyes in anticipation.

Slowly but firmly I worked the end in. The head of it slipped in past her sphincter reasonably easily. This was not the first polymer penis to find its way inside this anus, I surmised. I worked it inside, listening to Simone's gasps as a guide to help me know when she could take more.

'Yeah, take that cock, you slutty girl,' I told her in whispers. She gasped and moaned some more, so I kept repeating it – it seemed to be working on her.

Her rubbing on her penis quickened and, as it did, I quickened the thrusting of the rod until just about the whole shaft had been devoured by her arse. A mix of pleasure and discomfort was written on Simone's face and appeared to be working together to excite her uncontrollably – she was now masturbating herself as fast as she could and wriggling on my 'lunch-time lover' like a porn star.

'The cock is going to come, can you feel it? Its going to come soon,' I said to her. I knew the comment was ambiguous and hoped it would help Simone's fantasy as she built to orgasm. It seemed to have the best effect of anything I had said so far, so I kept repeating it.

'Yes, yes!' she yelled and I knew climax was not far off.

I gave her two especially deep thrusts and watched as her buttocks gripped the dildo and her cock spurted three big lumps of spunk, all over her hand and dress.

I don't know why but I found myself congratulating her and clapping my hands.

'Oh well done, well done, that was fun!' I said.

Simone (or maybe Simon had made a return now) said nothing, trying his/her best to savour what seemed to be a very deep orgasm.

Once he had come round he was very embarrassed at first, but I did my best to allay his discomfort as I helped him clean up and dress as himself again. No one should feel bad about their fetishes, I insisted, and I hoped to see him back.

17

I still have my bad lunch-time habits, by the way and, once a month, Simon comes by to spend his disposable income on my expensive clothes and, as long as he's phoned ahead to let me prepare, I let him strut around for me and do his stuff.

I'm still very discreet with all my other secret cross-dressers, but you never know, maybe one day I'll slip, and challenge another one of you at the counter to make you parade your new ensemble for me.

– *Eva, Glasgow, UK*

Big Girls

The only reason I said anything to her was because I was drunk.

I'd seen Sue at other parties. Considering her size it was hard not to see her. Call it a fetish of mine, if you like, but I have a thing for big backsides and I make it a point to notice them. When I first saw Sue a month earlier, I'd wanted her in that instant. However, it took a month, a chance meeting at a different party, and a couple of bottles of Grolsch before I found the courage to say what was really on my mind.

She'd squeezed her 54A hips into a miniskirt for the party. The tops of her stockings were visible below the hem line and, because the fabric was stretched so tight around her broad thighs, I was nursing an erection as soon as I saw her. But I didn't dare approach her because I knew I would say the wrong thing and mess up my chances of ever getting close to her.

However, as the evening wore on, I found myself standing closer to her, and drunkenly leering at the vast swell of her rear.

Eventually, Sue noticed me and she seemed suspicious of my interest. 'You keep staring at my arse,' she snapped. 'Is there something wrong with it?'

'No,' I gasped. 'It looks like the most perfect arse in the whole wide world.'

She glared at me, as though she thought I was being

19

sarcastic. 'If it's so perfect,' she asked, 'why do you keep staring at it?'

I responded without thinking and said, 'I keep staring at it because I'm trying to imagine how good it would be to have that perfect arse of yours sitting on my face.'

It was the sort of chat-up line that should have earned me a slap across the cheek. Even though I was worse the wear from beer, I knew as soon as I'd said the words that I'd gone too far.

Sue turned her back on me and went to get a drink from the kitchen.

I followed, apologising as I ogled her massive, swaying hips.

'I didn't mean that to sound rude,' I told her. 'I was just being absolutely honest with you. You really are the sexiest woman I've ever seen.'

She turned around suddenly and put her hand against my crotch. Before I even realised she was facing me she had her fingers wrapped around the shape of my erection.

'Something's certainly exciting you,' she agreed. Her voice was briefly warm, promising and seductive. Then she seemed to change her mind and shook her head. 'But I couldn't sit on your face. I'd smother you.'

I shrugged. 'I'd die with a smile on my face.'

That made us both laugh. She squeezed my erection just a fraction too tightly, and then she was holding my hand and leading me back through the party toward the stairs. I didn't know the hosts well enough to feel comfortable taking advantage of their bedrooms but, because I was being led there by Sue, I couldn't bring myself to complain.

Outside the bedroom door she stopped and faced me. 'Don't go thinking I'm a slut,' she whispered. 'I don't do this with every guy who looks at my arse.'

Our mouths were so close I had to kiss her. Her ample boobs pushed against my chest. As I put my arms around her broad waist my fingers slipped downwards to touch the huge swell of her rear and my erection strained with fresh enthusiasm. I squeezed her buttocks through the miniskirt and said, 'I wasn't thinking you were a slut.' But, at the back of my mind, I silently admitted I'd been hoping she might be one.

We pushed into a bedroom, squashed together as we continued to cuddle, kiss and grope. Falling onto the bed I found myself crushed beneath Sue's enormous weight. The pressure of having so much woman on top of me almost squeezed the climax from my cock.

'Are you sure you want this?' she asked.

'God! Yes,' I groaned.

She rested on my chest and crawled over me. Raising her skirt a little, giving me a glimpse of the tops of her stockings and her pale thighs, she giggled and asked again, 'Are you sure you want this?'

The black bands of her stocking tops cut tight into her flesh. Each thigh, nearly as wide as my waist, ballooned out from above the fabric. The pale flesh was rippled with cellulite and I couldn't respond to her. I knew, if I said a word, I was likely to lose control and spurt in my pants.

Sue seemed to have seen my enthusiastic expression because I could hear her smiling when she spoke again. 'You want this arse on your face?'

I nodded.

She hitched the skirt higher.

I got my first glimpse of her bare buttocks. I found out later she was wearing a thong but, because she was so large, the string had disappeared between her cheeks and it looked like I was being presented with a big beautiful bare arse. The cheeks were pockmarked and dimpled with ripples of excess fat. The sight was so exciting I had to clench my teeth for fear of coming on the spot.

'Kiss my cheeks,' she whispered. 'Kiss my cheeks and worship my arse.'

I started to lean forward but she was backing her rear onto my face. I held myself still as she pushed her mammoth cheeks closer. Stroking them, touching the enormous swell of her flesh, I was touched by the thrill of excitement that I had been anticipating since first seeing Sue. Placing my lips gently against each cheek, savouring the light musk of her perspiration, I revelled in the pleasure of holding and kissing her huge arse.

'Beautiful,' I murmured.

'Do you really want me to sit on your face?' she asked.

I caressed the massive curves of her hips, trailing my lips over the dimpled flesh of each cheek. 'God! Yes,' I told her.

'Then tongue my arsehole,' she insisted. 'Tongue my arsehole and, if you do it right, I'll sit on your face.'

I swallowed and acted without hesitating. I had to urge her cheeks apart, spreading them open, which was when I discovered the thin black band of her thong. Teasing that to one side I took a moment to admire the tiny, taut ring of her anus, and then pushed my mouth over the hole.

Sue stiffened. As I pushed my tongue into her rear, urging the little hole to grow wider as I tried to get it deeper, I heard her groan.

'You filthy bastard,' she grunted. But I knew it wasn't a complaint. 'You really do like that, don't you?'

I didn't bother answering. I was lost in a world of bliss as I pushed my tongue deeper and devoured her sweaty dark taste.

'I hope you're going to tease my pussy that well when I'm sat on your face,' she gasped.

I tried to promise her that I would do my best, but it was impossible to articulate the sounds with her sphincter gripping my tongue. Squeezing and kneading the vast globes of her backside, worshipping her rear as I urged my tongue deeper, I basked in the pleasure of having her backside eclipse the bedroom light above me.

'Go on,' she said suddenly.

I could hear the breathlessness in her voice and knew she was aroused. If my nose hadn't been pressed between the cheeks of her arse I suppose I would have caught her scent earlier. But, when she pulled her anus from my tongue, I was treated to the rich fragrance of her wet pussy.

'I'm going to sit on your face now,' she told me. 'And you'd better do a good job down there.'

I promised her I would and lay back on the bed as her cheeks loomed over my face. From the edges of my vision I saw the dark bands of her stockings were still pressed tight against her broad thighs. I could see she was kneeling, preparing to half-squat over my head. But my main attention was focused on the rich dark curls that covered her split and the moist pink lips that were about to engulf my mouth.

It's hard to say how long I was trapped underneath Sue's huge bulk. As I drank and licked and relished my position beneath her, I lost track of time. I could hear her making groans and sighs of pleasure from above me. But I wasn't thinking about her satisfaction. I was only thinking of my own personal bliss from being suffocated beneath her cheeks. My mouth worked against the split of her sex and her juices poured over my jaw and trickled up my nose.

It's impossible to describe the suffocating pleasure of being beneath her. Tasting every drop of her excitement, drinking her wetness when she climaxed, and being forced to breathe all the air from in and around her pussy was a divine experience. I know, when Sue finally levered herself away from me, I was exhausted and I'd come in my pants during the experience.

She kept grinning at me and insisting that we would have to do it again.

I've seen Sue at a couple of other parties since then. Each time, when we've acknowledged that the other is there, we've found ourselves upstairs and she's spent a happy hour sitting on my face while I've spent my time enjoying my position beneath her humungous backside. One day, if I ever pluck up the courage, I might ask her out on a date so we can do more.

– *Neil, Blyth, UK*

Good For Only One Thing

I bet many guys would call me fortunate. I'm married to an attractive woman who earns such insane commissions as an investment broker that when I lost my post as a college instructor eighteen months ago she took me out to a fancy restaurant, ordered a $300 bottle of champagne and told me not to bother finding another job. All she expects me to do is take care of the housework, which for a grown man and his professional spouse rarely amounts to more than a couple of hours of cooking and cleaning each day. With so much time on my hands I could sit down and write the Great American Novel – and, believe me, I have tried. But for some reason or other I just can't get started. There's something about staying at home all day and worrying your head over laundry, ironing and what to cook for dinner that steadily drains a man of self-belief and worldly ambition. Before you know it you've become the live-in maid and fuck-toy of your bread-winning better half.

Take the other day, for instance. Instead of shutting myself in the den with the laptop, I spent the whole afternoon preparing a dinner that would put any housewife to shame. You see, since losing my job, I always feel the urge to impress my wife and prove to her I'm making a contribution to our marriage. But when seven o'clock came around and my culinary masterpiece was ready to serve up there was no sign of her, nor any message to say when she'd be home. Calling her at work was out of the question. She's made it very clear that I am never – repeat *never* – to bother her with my 'petty housekeeper talk' while she's cutting deals with her filthy-rich clients. So what did I do? Same as I always do – I waited for her. Yes, 'Waiting for June' is the sorry refrain of my stay-at-home life.

I sat down on a stool near the door and chewed at my fingernails. Here I am, I thought, watching myself in a nearby mirror and not liking what I saw; here I am, a guy with a Master's degree from Brown University, and a former English instructor, listening out for the click-clack of my wife's high-heeled shoes coming up the hallway. Yes, you could say I was craving to hear the imperious tattoo of her sharp stilettos, like some droopy-eyed hound pining for its mistress.

That sweet staccato hymn did eventually reach my straining ears – and, boy, did I feel my spirits rise! I sprang from the stool and opened the apartment door before she even had the chance to insert her key.

There she stood – my beautiful blonde wife, the money-earner, the mistress of the house – looking every inch the power-dressing career woman in her designer jacket and pencil skirt, ultra-sheer stockings and black fuck-you high heels. The force of her presence rendered me speechless and I was visibly trembling as I stepped aside to let her come in. What I saw was a strutting example of the aspirational career woman so beloved of the high-end glossy magazines – the success-focused glamazon who makes your cock hard and your balls shrivel up, at one and the same time. It was difficult to believe this figure of intimidating beauty and corporate power was my wife of three years. Her rich blonde locks were sternly combed back, forming a smooth glassy sheen against her head, and gathered in an abundant French plait. A rose-pink gloss made her lips look sweeter than sugar candy – those smirking Cupid's bow lips which sealed million-dollar deals, while I stayed at home hand-washing panties.

'Hi, babes,' she said. 'You miss me?' Her eyes sparkled, their bewitching green enhanced by a subtle combination of mascara and pastel shading.

I closed the door and fought to contain my excitement; I had to show her how upset I was by her late return. 'You could at least have called me,' I said sulkily. 'Another ten minutes and dinner would have been ruined.'

Silently, I helped her remove her jacket, beneath which she wore a white silk blouse, provocatively tented by her breasts. The hourglass curve of her figure, running from bust down to cinched waist and ending in the full female flare of her hips, drew an involuntary sigh of admiration from me. Her assessment of my appearance was far less rapturous.

'I see you're wearing your apron,' she said.

Her unabashedly sexual grin made me blush. The apron she was now surveying so knowingly was made from shiny black PVC and consisted of a bib, and a skirt section which reached down to my knees. Printed on the front was a mortifying cartoon image: a life-size carica-ture of a naked female torso and thighs, rendered in a gaudy-pink flesh tone. Thus two saucer-sized tits with large red nipples rested above my own chest; an impos-sibly slender waist made a mockery of my paunch; and a shaggy brown triangle representing pubic hair rested directly over my semi-hard cock. My wife had presented me with this 'slut apron' on my last birthday as a joke. 'Marcia's husband bought her one just like it,' she'd said, seeming to relish my embarrassment. 'So we girls thought it would be so funny if I got one for you.' She likes me to wear it around the house when she's home.

I shuffled over to the kitchen intent on serving dinner. I was determined to get some recognition for the hours of work I'd put in. As I bent down to the oven, she came up behind me and stroked my ass.

26

'Please,' I protested sharply. I turned around to face her. I had to show her I was not a complete pushover. 'Let's just eat, shall we?'

She responded by dragging me towards her and mashing her lips hard against mine. Her kiss was hot and possessive, her long tongue stretching into my mouth and taking my breath away. Raised up on her high heels she was inches taller than barefoot me, and I instinctively tilted back my head to keep my mouth against hers. I always melt under her kisses, but she pulled her lips away just as suddenly as she'd used them to attack. I put a hand on the hob to steady myself.

Instead of taking a place at the table, she sauntered over to the couch, swaying her beautiful round ass. She lay down with her back against the armrest, stretched her stocking-tinted legs across the cushions. Looking over at me, she patted her thigh where her clinging skirt had ridden up in creases.

'Come to me, honey,' she said and she licked her lips.

Just a kiss, I told myself as I approached her. She parted her legs to make space for me on the cushion and I couldn't help stealing a glimpse of her black stocking tops and the pale flesh in the shadow of her skirt.

As soon as I sat down she grabbed the bib of my apron and once again I was pulled towards her and a hungry female mouth took possession of mine. Cock swelling and stiffening inside my pants, I ran my palm up her inner thigh to where the friction of stocking gave way to smooth flesh. The temptation was strong and I was almost hers at that point. But suddenly recalling my promise to myself, I pulled away. I would not yield so easily.

'No,' I managed to gasp.

She dragged my hand back under her skirt and jammed it against her crotch. 'Feel how wet my panties are,' she said. She ground her sex against my knuckles as, half-heartedly, I tried to pull free. I could feel the pucker of her warm sex lips through the satiny fabric, a hungry hidden mouth kissing at my fingers.

'Please, June,' I cried. I was fighting my own desire as well as hers, my base urge to tug aside the damp gusset, plunge a digit or two into that voracious sex and finger-fuck a big appreciative grin onto her face. Drawing on all my willpower, I managed to gain control. I pulled my hand free, stood up and straightened my apron. My cheeks were burning. 'How was your day?' I asked hoarsely, trying to divert her mind to other things and take my own thoughts off her exposed panty crotch and the wet patch spreading from its centre.

'My day was just fine,' she snapped back. She did not close her legs or try to pull her skirt straight as she spoke. 'I finally closed the Barker deal.' The Barker deal was worth more millions than I felt was ethical to pronounce; but I wasn't surprised by the news. In all the time I've known June she has never failed to get what she sets her mind on achieving. 'With the commission I'll earn I'm going to put down a deposit on that town house I talked about.' She informed me of this unilateral decision with her thighs parted and the plump crotch of her panties insolently on view. 'If the new place is too much work for you' – she swung out a stiletto-shod foot and with the toe she prodded the front of the apron directly above my cock – 'I'll hire a maid to help you out.'

I was hurt by the insinuation that I would be unable to cope with the housework and stared down at the pointed toe of her shoe as it casually traced the contour of my beating erection. The firm strokes were excruciatingly arousing but I refused to give in to my craving. I had to show disapproval. I really had to. What would I be reduced to if a maid took over my household chores? I'd be no better than a whore – a kept male whore.

'Come on,' I said, trying to sound disapproving. I took hold of her ankle and carefully lifted her foot away from my crotch. 'Let's eat dinner.'

'Get Tyrone,' she ordered.

'What? Now?'

She nodded slowly and fixed me with an unblinking deal-closing stare. I've learned not to contradict her when she has such a determined look in her eyes, so I agreed to fetch Tyrone; but I insisted we had to eat before anything else took place.

'Just go and get him,' she said impatiently, folding her arms behind her head and stretching out her legs.

Tyrone is June's pet name for a black nine-inch strap-on dildo which she keeps in our bedroom. Just the sight of this potent monster, as I slid open the top drawer, was enough to make my insides drop. There it lay on a bed of her expensive underwear, boldly veined down its length like the real thing and complete with balls – a big man's cock engorged with lust. The exposed glans was shaped like the proverbial fireman's helmet and as fat as the end of a truncheon.

I carried dildo and harness through to the living room and handed them wordlessly to June; then I went over to the kitchen, determined to serve the meal. 'It's almost ruined,' I complained, sounding bitchier than I'd intended. I couldn't shake the image of the thuggish cock from my head.

June remained on the couch while I worked. I knew exactly what she was doing. She was inspecting and admiring her cock. And each time I leaned across the table I had the shameful feeling she was studying my ass and remembering all the times she had fucked me in that very position.

'Honey, come over here and fix on Tyrone for me.' She was holding up the enormous thing by one of the leather straps and dangling it in front of her face.

I begged her to let us have dinner first, although the weak core of me was screaming to be filled up.

'Just tie him on, honey. Won't it be so sexy if I wear him while I'm eating?'

29

The thought of June sitting at the dinner table with nine inches of thick ebony cock sprouting from her crotch made my legs shake and I gripped one of the chairs for support. She continued to grin at me and swing the dildo like a treat until, trained dog that I am, I scuttled across.

'Good boy.'

As always, the dildo-fitting ritual was performed in silence. Without a word passing between us, June stood up from the couch and I sank down onto my knees as she turned her glorious round ass to me. My first task was to undress the lower half of her body. I tugged open the zip on her skirt and eased the tight-fitting garment over the generous swell of her hips and buttocks. Her lacy thong panties were soon fully exposed and I feasted my eyes on the pussy-cradling crotch panel as I slid the skirt all the way down her long legs and guided it over her high heels. She stepped away from it and proceeded to unbutton her blouse, which she handed to me, still without speaking. I quickly took care of both garments, folding them and draping them over the arm of the couch.

She was facing me now, squeezing her heavy breasts though the cups of her bra. Still on my knees, I moved my hands down towards her shoes.

'No, leave them,' she instructed. 'Put Tyrone on now.' She took a step closer, bringing her plump panty crotch up to my face and giving me her sex scent to breathe in.

I picked up the dildo from the cushion and with well trained fingers I fastened the attached leather belt around her waist. Her newly acquired male member jutted out before her, angled upwards from her crotch, boasting its erect and ready status. Long, thick and black, it made a stark contrast against her pale skin. She turned her ass to me and stood with her legs slightly apart.

'Make sure he's tight,' she said, looking down over her shoulder.

I reached for the strap hanging from the base of the dildo, pulled it between her legs and fastened it to the buckle on the back of the belt.

'Tighter,' she ordered.

I managed to tug another notch through the buckle. The leather strap cut deep into the cleft of her buttocks, drawing the gusset of her panties in with it. I heard her sigh – a sigh of pleasure which told me the base of the dildo was wedged tight against her crotch and squeezing her clit. The big false cock would stay in place now, however vigorously she rolled and jerked her hips. Her creamy round ass cheeks, split by the thin line of black leather, faced me like dear old friends. I planted a light kiss on each one, the mute sign that my task was complete.

As she turned back around, she inadvertently pistol whipped my cheek with the head of her new appendage. 'Gee, sorry, honey bun.' She stifled a girlish giggle with her hand. 'I forgot how big he is.' She stood admiring herself, pleased with her large breasts and her long legs in their classy stay-ups. But the dark erect phallus was her pride and joy. How confidently she wears that cock, I was forced to admit to myself as I watched her stroking it with her slender manicured finger. Her cockiness – that was the only word for it – aroused and dismayed me at the same time.

I felt I had to resist this cock-endowed virago, this fast-rising star of investment brokering who took sadistic pleasure in beating men at their own game. I started to get up from my knees, resolved to go the kitchen and serve dinner. But she pushed me down again.

'Suck on him for a bit,' she said. 'I love to see your lips around my cock.'

'Then can we eat?' I pleaded.

'Eat this.' She pressed her cock roughly against my lips.

My mouth was already full with saliva. I was cravenly eager to do her bidding and suck that big lady-cock; and from the smug way she was looking down at me and gripping her shaft with one hand, I'm sure she knew it. I opened wide and immediately the fat head was shoved

31

inside. I sucked and slurped on the hard imitation glans and stroked the backs of her nylon-sheathed thighs, just the way she liked.

'That's good,' she sighed. 'Suck me, honey bun. Suck me like the little slut you are.'

She fed me more of her unnatural organ until my tongue was squashed flat beneath it and the round head filled the back of my throat and brought on my gagging reflex. But I loved her rough treatment despite the awful noises she was forcing from me. My own cock had grown to full and aching stiffness in my pants beneath the apron, though it would have been a pitiful comparison were it laid beside the one my wife was making me choke on.

'Oooh, I can feel that against my clit,' she groaned. 'Don't you dare stop.' She clutched my hair between her fingers and guided the back-and-forth movement of my head, forcing me to take more and more of her thick length into my mouth and grinding the base of the strap-on against her clit and pussy lips. I endured this rough usage for as long as I could, before pulling my head away, coughing and gasping for breath. The huge plastic cock bobbed before my eyes, dripping with my spit.

'Good boy. You got him all lubed up.' She smeared my juices along the full length of her shaft using a deliberate wanking motion; then she rubbed the spit-glazed head with the underside of her thumb, reminding me of a horny freshman who can't wait to rip open some pink. 'It would be such a shame to waste all your hard work. Take off your pants, honey bun.'

'You said we could eat first.'

'I'll only put the tip in, honey bun. I promise. I just want to give you a taste of what you're having for dessert.'

I got to my feet and obediently removed my clothes. Naked, I stood facing my wife, my puny erection no match for hers.

'Put your apron back on,' she said.

I stared at her blankly.

'I want to fuck you while you're wearing the apron.'

Once again I gave in to her. I picked up the degrading novelty apron and slowly tied it on. She watched, jerking her cock obscenely, as I imprisoned my own inferior erection behind the cartoon female bush.

'You'd better suck on him again,' she suggested. 'The wetter you get him the easier he'll go in.'

I got back down on my knees in front of her cock, swallowed the head and bathed it in my saliva. Then I used my wet tongue to lubricate the shaft all the way to the big fake balls. I gazed up at my wife as I worked and she nodded down approvingly, watching my drool dripping from her sex toy.

'OK, that will do,' she said finally, snatching her cock away from my mouth. 'Get in position.'

I turned to face the couch and rested my elbows on the cushion. I could feel my heart pounding hard against my chest as I arched up my naked ass.

'Lift it higher,' she ordered, stepping behind me.

I presented myself to her like a bitch in an alleyway.

'Good boy.' She knelt down on one knee and shifted my ass into her preferred position.

'Not hard,' I murmured into the cushion.

She leaned forward and purred into my ear, 'I won't hurt you, honey bun.' She began rubbing her cock between my buttocks. Shamefully, my own ass juices provided additional lubrication and the plump head slid easily in the slick furrow. She repeatedly nudged my asshole, which I kept clean and shaved for her, sending delicious thrills running through my body and gradually opening me up.

'We should eat first,' I protested shrilly, hating myself for surrendering so easily.

Slowly but firmly she began to squeeze the head of her cock inside. I had taken her cock in my ass countless times before, but my trained muscles still tensed with pain and I bit down on my bottom lip as the bulging glans stretched me open.

'Good boy,' she said. 'I've almost got him in.'

I let out a grunt as she broke through the last trace of muscular resistance.

Once the first inch of cock was embedded, she spread my cheeks, digging her thumbnails into my ass flesh. I wondered how I looked to her, slumped over the seat of the couch, my anus skewered on her thick black tool.

I grunted again as she fed me another inch. She was pitiless, forcing her stiffness deeper into my tight channel as if it were her right. I chomped into the cushion as she began to thrust from her hips and drive my body to her rhythm.

Then I heard the raucous sound of her clearing her throat and suddenly something warm and wet splattered between my wide-stretched cheeks. June was spitting on me! And she did it again and again, hocking thick loughies down at my reamed asshole as if it were her spittoon. This added a shocking new dimension to our marital buggery, each contemptuous gob of spit she landed on me a reminder of just how low I had sunk.

The extra lubrication did the trick, however. Her cock slid into me easily now and the fiery pain in my bowels melted into pure pleasure. I felt giddy. Her skilful fucking was stirring maddening sensations that burst from the rim of my asshole and flooded my cock and balls. My bowels opened wide for her, inviting the intrusion of her perverse cock, begging for each squelching thrust. Soon it felt as if she were ramming the whole nine inches into me.

'Oh, God,' I moaned into the cushion. 'Don't stop. Please don't stop.'

'Never say I don't give you what you need, honey bun.'

Her swaggering tone frightened me. She was servicing me like a stud would service one of his regular sluts. The week before, as I knelt under her desk in the den, lapping at her pussy, I'd heard her talking to Marcia on the

34

phone, as if she'd forgotten I was there; and even now, even as her stiff girl-cock was lancing me towards climax, her cruel words rang in my ears. *I just keep him around because he's cheaper than a housekeeper. And fucking his slutty ass is a great stress reliever.*

I twisted my head around, seeking reassurance. Her sweet pink lips were pursed in concentration but other than that she showed little sign of exertion. I gazed up into her eyes which narrowed and became almost savagely thin. I wanted to speak, but all that came out was gibberish and grunts, animal noises shaken from my throat by her relentless pounding.

'Easy, honey bun, easy.' She stroked my head, raking strong fingers through my hair. It made me feel good, good enough to believe she cared about me, and I let myself relax and enjoy being fucked. She pressed her fingers to my lips and I kissed them appreciatively until she gently pushed my face down into the cushion and kept it pinned there with a firm hand on my neck.

I stopped worrying about my masculine pride – it didn't matter any more – and I surrendered to the skill of my beautiful and multitalented wife, an alpha female who had mastered life and, unlike her stay-at-home husband, always came out the winner. She increased the intensity of her thrusts, penetrating me from different angles, sliding stiff inches in and out of my slippery wet and, by now, gaping asshole. She seized the apron strap like a harness with her other hand, dragging at it as she sired me, rubbing my sweat-slickened body back and forth against the inside of the plastic apron.

I felt myself reach the point of no return. She knew just how to fuck me and with each thrust she brought me ever closer to the brink of orgasm.

'Don't stop,' I begged her.

Her cock was stabbing a secret place inside me. Bolts of pleasure shot through my body. I grunted at each hard thrust. I wanted her to go on forever generating those magical sensations inside my asshole. She made my whole body feel joyfully alive.

'Oh, please don't stop,' I whimpered. Why shouldn't I admit it? At that moment I was hers. She owned my ass and I was her bitch.

I felt her stroking my back and smoothing her palm over my flesh like a rider coaxing a horse. Then she dragged her fingernails down the groove of my spine, all the while fucking me with deep regular thrusts.

'You can't get enough of this, can you?' she said, laughing.

'Yes, June! Yes!' I cried. 'I'm going to come.'

Then the thing I most dreaded happened. Her thrusts became slower and shallower until they were a tormenting tickle in my bowels. She slapped my ass cheek, hard enough to make it sting.

'I'll finish you off later,' she said.

I tensed my needy ass muscles around her big cock, but I could not hold it. I was too stretched and too lubricated and she slipped it through my grip with a teasing slowness. I wriggled my tail end in pursuit of her withdrawn cock, begging to be stuffed full again.

'Please, I was almost there.'

'Beg me,' she said.

'Please, June. I need it.' I was shameless in my desperation as I pleaded for the huge black cock worn by my wife.

'Beg me to fuck your ass.'

'Fuck my ass, June. I beg you to fuck my ass.'

'Whose ass is it?'

'It's your ass, June.'

'The next time you try to play hard to get I won't fuck you for a week, understand?'

Even as she taunted me, I was stretching back my buttocks and gifting her my gaping asshole. All I could think about was feeling her stiffness back inside me, stretching me, filling me up and nudging that pleasure spot.

'You're a real slut, you know that?'

I cried out in joy as she entered me again, burrowing smoothly into my passage with her long erection. Once more she was fucking me hard and fast and I could feel the callous sentiment in each thrust.

'Is this what you want, *slut*?' She leaned forward and hissed that last word hotly behind my ear, ramming her cock inside me up to the hilt and holding it there. 'Well, *slut*, is it?'

'I want it, June,' I croaked. 'I want your cock.' Bright colours were swirling behind the lids of my closed eyes.

She held my cheeks apart and powered into my receptive hole. The unmanly shrieks she was fucking out of me were beginning to arouse her. The only way I can sexually excite my wife these days is to squeal like a violated bitch as she takes possession of my ass – and, sure enough, behind me, I could hear her joyous moans of conquest. The forced awareness that I could never be more to her than a fuck-toy, a receptacle for her plastic cock, was shattering in its intensity. Each thrust drove home my abject status – and beginning deep inside my ass tunnel pulses of pleasure ripped through my body. My balls were swollen to bursting point with the molten lust that had accumulated inside them.

'Oh, God! Don't stop, June. Please don't stop.'

This time she didn't stop. She continued to screw my grateful ass, pushing me down onto the couch and driving me towards climax. My cock, stiff and aching for release, was pressed against the cushion's edge, spilling juices into the plastic apron, which was already slick with my own sweat and sliding against my belly and thighs. She laughed as she prodded my hidden pleasure spot and with each thrust forced my cock and balls to rub towards climax.

'I'm going to count to ten,' she said.

I doubted I could last half that long. Before she had even reached three, my bowels went into a spasm and my balls shot their foaming contents into the apron. But while my body quaked with joy around her solidly lodged cock the countdown continued.

'Ten,' I heard her say.

I tightened my ass muscles, but as before I could not prevent her cock's slow and teasing withdrawal and I felt it slipping through my grip with dismal ease.

'Please, more,' I begged, clenching at the last inches of her organ. 'Fuck me again.'

But she took no heed. She cruelly extracted her whole cock and, when the big rounded head popped from my hole, the blissful feeling inside my body poured out in its wake. I groaned in despair; it felt as if my insides had collapsed.

I looked back at her through watery eyes and saw she had already stood up. Her handsome black cock stuck out from her crotch and I felt a crippling desire for it. It bobbed stiffly as she lowered her arms to straighten her stockings. 'A Wall Street entrepreneur got in touch with me today,' she said, relishing my torment. 'He's taking me out this evening.'

I whimpered something about the dinner I'd prepared, but she was oblivious to my words. Her mind was on more important matters: her entrepreneur and how she would exploit the meeting with him. She quickly unstrapped the dildo and tossed it onto the couch next to me; then she picked up her skirt and blouse as if I no longer existed for her.

I watched her getting ready to leave, still sprawled forward over the cushion, buttocks raised sluttishly, the streams of come I'd shot inside the apron growing cold against my belly. I could not ignore the strap-on which lay beside me, abandoned by her now, used and dirty, and more forcefully than ever a reminder of my low sexual cravings and my wife's absolute dominance over me.

Just before leaving, she turned to face me, dazzling me with an image of crafted beauty and executive power female-style – high heels, stockings, skirt and mocking pink lips. I looked hopefully into her distant eyes, longing for a few words of affection before she departed for the evening.

'Make sure you clean up Tyrone,' was all she said. 'I've a feeling I'll have something to celebrate when I get back.' She blew a kiss at me, smiled dryly and strode out of the apartment, leaving me to close the door.

Yes, on the surface I've got it all. I'm married to an attractive 31-year-old blonde who is about to set up her own brokerage firm in New York. Once my daily chores are done I've got so much time on my hands I could sit down and write a novel. But all I've come up with in eighteen months is this confession. Perhaps June's right when she says a slut like me is only good for one thing.

– *'June's husband', Colorado, USA*

Beaches

You get to see a lot down on beaches, especially when you live there. I do and I seen it all. Bums and tits and cameltoe like you would not believe, some of them in tiny little bikinis you wouldn't think would hold it all in and some of them right out of their bikini, bare naked like they just don't fucking care. I like bikinis but I like bare naked best. Best of all I like to watch 'em change but you got to be sneaky for that. There are lots of ways I do it. Like pretending to go bird watching so nobody cares about my binoculars. Or there's pretending to be asleep so they don't worry about what they're showing. You get the best peeps of all when they don't know you're there.

I'm not going to tell my favourites but there's always good places if you use a bit of imagination. There's some places where the Germans were there in the war. They built what they called the Atlantic Wall, all the way along the coast of France and that. I call it the Peepers' Wall. There's bunkers you see, with slits for the guns and if you look out of them you get to see a different sort of slit, a lot. Girls like to change next to them, 'cause they're out of the wind and that. If you go inside and look out through the gun slits you can see it all and they never even know you're there.

This one time I was doing it, just waiting, 'cause if you're a peeper you got to be patient. I got in the bunker real early, before the beach started to fill up and before long this absolute babe turns up. I knew she was going to be special right from the start. Long legs she had, and long blonde hair, with big sunglasses and freckles. Just in some torn up jeans and an old T-shirt she looked great, and her jeans were so tight on her little round arse I swear it was like they were painted on her. And she's got cameltoe – pants' crotch tucked right up her slit so you can see her cunt lips.

First she fools around for a bit, like girls do, putting her towel down and checking for stuff in her bag and that. Then she has a quick peep around to make sure there are no dirty bastards watching – or maybe hoping there are, you never know – but one thing's for sure. She never guessed the dirtiest bastard on the whole island was almost close enough to touch, tugging his nadger and enjoying the sight of her arse in her blue jeans.

Then she starts to strip. Fuck me but that was good. First the top comes off and I'm a bit disappointed to see she's in her bikini top underneath so no titty show, it doesn't look like. Then it's her jeans, and she does it with her bum stuck right out at me, so close I could have reached out and goosed her, I swear. She looked even better out of those blue jeans than in them, nice and firm and bouncy, but with enough meat on her to call her a real woman. I don't like scraggy-arsed girls. They look like blokes.

So there she is, in this little bikini, most of her bum cheeks sticking out around the sides and the cunt piece so tight up she's got more cameltoe than the fucking Arabs. And she's shaved. That what did it for me, when she turns round and flicks out her towel, with her little titties hanging down in her bikini cups and her nips poking up, then straightens up and you can see she's shaved her cunt, with her bikini pants right up her slit and her lips showing, nice and pink and smooth. I did it over that, 'cause I know that you get the best peeps when their clothes are coming off, most all of the time, and once

41

they're sunbathing you don't get to see so much, unless they're bare naked and she wasn't.

I had another one on the same island, not so close but full nudie. There's a beach right under this big cliff, all big round stones and rock, no sand at all. Families don't go there 'cause of the climb and the rock, but there's flat bits just right for sunbathing so a lot of babes go there so they can strip off without having to worry about who sees or getting hassled. Me, I like to watch, but I never hassle a girl. It's like a game I reckon, and a lot of the time I reckon they don't mind being watched as long as they don't think I'm going to hassle them. Some of them get off on it, I reckon.

So anyway it's a good place, with a bunker right up on the cliffs at either end, 'cause they weren't stupid those Germans and they knew they might have to shoot some poor bastard anywhere on the beach, which means the gun slits can always see everything, and I do mean everything. She was nice this girl, fat little tits and an arse like a peach in cut-down shorts, and you could see she had no titty holster on under her top 'cause her nips poked right out. You could see that from right up on the cliff where I was looking.

She had no idea. Thought she was all alone. I watched her strip, right down to the buff. I love it when a beach girl pulls her top up or takes down her trousers or whatever she's got on and you see bra and knicks instead of a bikini, 'cause that way you know they're coming off and you're going to get a proper eyeful if you're lucky. I did with her. She just didn't know anyone was looking. Off came her clothes, every fucking stitch, like she was in her own bedroom with the curtains shut.

I knew she had nice titties, but I swear they were like fucking footballs, and as her top comes off she gives 'em a little squeeze, holding one in each hand like she's in Tesco's checking out the melons. Maybe she didn't like 'em, 'cause they were so big, or maybe she was proud of herself. I don't know, but I'd have loved to have given 'em a squeeze for her. Anyway, once she'd got her tits out she stayed like that for ages, walking up and down and enjoying the sun, before she decided to go in the water. Now I reckon her shorts are coming down, maybe her knicks too, so I start up the old rhythm, hoping to get there just as she's bending down with her titties swinging and the whole of that gorgeous arse on view, maybe even with the lips of her cunt peeping out behind. I love that.

She doesn't do it, but goes in the sea instead, shorts and all. You know how I feel, fucking frustrated, with a hard on like the Post Office Tower and I know her titties are still on show only it's all under water so I can only see her head. I could've finished off just thinking about her, but like I said, a peeper's got to be patient. I tell you, I thought she was training for the Olympics the amount of time she spent in the water, splashing around and giving just a peep of titty now and then, then swimming right out to this big rock. I couldn't see the other side, and nor could anyone else or so I thought and her and all. She disappears and I reckon she's going to strip right off and sunbathe there, maybe even get up to something dirty all on her ownsome, 'cause girls do you know, more often than blokes think.

Talk about frustrating. I can't see her at all but I know she's there and I'm imagining her stripped right off, bare naked, playing with her titties and rubbing her cunt until she gets herself off. Another thing with being a peeper is you got to be hopeful, an optimist, or you miss a lot of the best sights, and you got to believe in your luck. I've got it, me, the luck of the Irish.

Maybe five minutes she'd been out of sight when this boat comes around the point with three blokes in it, fishing for crabs in pots. I reckon she'd been at it, 'cause you never saw anyone move so fast when she saw. Back in the water she goes and back to the beach where she splashes around again until the boat's gone. Then she gets out and that was a sight to see. She's all wet and her nips are sticking out like corks and her shorts are plastered on so tight, with a lot of cheek on show.

I reckon she's had a bit of a scare with the boys on the boat and will probably pack it in, but of course she's got to get out of her wet shorts hasn't she? So down they come, only now she's all nervous 'cause three guys have just seen her tits. She pushes 'em down real fast, wriggling her bum to get them off over it, 'cause she has got a lot of meat. And then it's all bare and she's bending to pull 'em off her feet and I can see it all, big fat dangling titties, her bum all white and round and peachy, and her cunt, right between her thighs, all pink in the middle like she's ready for cock. That was all I needed, you can believe me.

Those were the best two I got off the bunker trick, but the problem is you got to go a long way to get there and half the time it's a wasted effort. Crowded beaches are better if you're OK with just cameltoe and bum cheeks, maybe a bit of bare tit, and you do get the odd couple who'll fuck on a beach if they reckon they can get away with it, but if you want the really dirty stuff you got to go somewhere the girls feel safe.

Not that I mind just cute peeps, specially if I can get pics for later, but that's not always easy. You got to be cunning, like putting a camera in a bag with a remote to operate it, but you need a lot of techie stuff to get good shots and it's expensive and risky. Then there's vids but you get the same problems only worse 'cause it's more obvious. Course, once you got some nice stuff you can put them on the net now, which is good, and see what other peepers have been up to. There a lot of us about.

Trouble is, most of it's nudist beaches and stuff and for me that ain't the same. It was great when it first started and it was a big thrill to see a girl with her tits out on the beach, or sunbathing face down with her bikini strap undone and wondering if she'd turn over and flash it, but now that a lot of 'em do it and it's all over the net as well

44

so it's no big deal any more. I always did get a bigger kick out of seeing what I'm not supposed to, right from the start. That's human nature I reckon.

For the best stuff you want somewhere lonely and you got to be clever and lucky too. Sometimes it's just luck, like when I was walking along this one beach down on the south coast, not even looking out, 'cause there was nobody to look out for. There was sand breaks all along the beach, and as I climbed over one there she was, just the neatest little babe you ever did see, on a little patch of sand with some old geezer, lucky bastard. She was bare naked, and down on all fours, crawling so she could look for shells or something. I don't care what she was doing, I care what she was showing. She just didn't care, or more like she thought she was all alone 'cept for her old man, 'cause her knees were wide open and her little tight bum was stuck up in the air so I could see right between her legs and between her cheeks, the sweetest little cunt you ever did see and an arsehole like a little rosebud. I wonder if that old bastard got to stick his tongue up her. I would've done.

That was luck but you get the best results when you're clever but you got to be a bit of a dirty bastard to really get off on it. I'm talking about watching 'em pee, 'cause everyone's got to, and a girl on a beach in the middle of fucking nowhere has to go in the end, so it's all down to being in the right place at the right time. Sand dunes are best, where they're overgrown with that spiky grass you get, or bushes, and you can settle down with your binoculars or a camera with a nice long lens, watching a likely spot.

You got to do a recce first, to make sure there are no proper toilets anywhere near and some decent girls about, and then wait. Nine times out of ten it works and not just once. On a good afternoon I had six babes in my sights, knicks down and showing everything, cept their tits of course. It's no good for tit. What it's great for is bum,

45

'cause they got to stick it right out and you see it all, cunt, arsehole, the lot, and I'm not a pervert or nothing but I love to see the piss squirt out of a pretty girl's cunt, not 'cause of what she's doing, but 'cause you know it's something she don't even show her boyfriend. And it gets better.

This one time I was at a favourite spot on a beach that's just miles of sand with these big dunes at the back. It's always good for a show and a lot of the girls go topless so you get some tit and all, but there's a problem and that's all the local gay guys. I don't mind gays, and they're not usually into a bloke like me, but they can be a pain, specially if they realise what I'm up to and get shirty about it. I mean, what's going on there? They've come there to blow each other and fuck knows what other dirty stuff and they have a go at me 'cause I'm peeping!

Anyway, sometimes the girls get a bit nervous knowing there are a lot of blokes about. Fuck knows why, unless they're scared they'll get taken up the arse, but there it is. So I'm waiting, in this nice cosy place with my camera trained on a likely spot and who should come along, not one girl, but three. I knew they were going to do it, and you can bet I had the old nadger out quick as winking, and sod the gay guys.

They're babes these girls. A little hottie in what look like her knicks and with her tits out, what she's got of them, another with a wriggly little bum and a nice pair but strapped up in a red bikini and another quite a bit older but still nice, with a big round arse and tits that look like you could milk 'em and get enough for your cornflakes.

They take it in turns, same routine, two of them looking out while the third does it, knicks down, bum out and out it comes in the sand with me taking photos. I can see every wrinkle of her arsehole. The older one goes first, and just to see her push those bikini pants down over that big round arse is enough to get me hard. She does plenty too and I could have come on that, but I'm in no hurry. The next one's even better. She must be maybe eighteen, no more than twenty, but she's got it all, gorgeous tits and the roundest, firmest bum you ever did see, nice and meaty but not fat. To watch her drop her bikini was just fucking heaven, and I don't know whether to take the pics or wank my cock while she's pissing, 'cause she's got her bum struck right out and her feet cocked apart in this funny way, so fucking cute. She's embarrassed too, and keeps looking around to see she doesn't get caught with her knicks down, but she has been, and fucking then some!

Then there's the topless hottie, the one I've been waiting for. She's already tits out and that would be enough on another day, but not now. I'm taking photos for later and I'm hammering away as she sticks out her bum and I see she really is in just her knicks, little white ones nice and snug on her little peach of an arse. They don't stay up though, they come down, nice and slow like she's doing it to give her boyfriend a cheap thrill but really 'cause she's dead scared someone'll see.

I get every detail on camera, lots of shots of her bum as she gets it bare, and then everything as she squats down with her back pulled in and her bum stuck out her, little pink arsehole showing and her cunt, so fucking cute you wouldn't believe it, and as her piss starts to come so have I, all over the fucking place. There, you wanted a confession, now you got one, and if you ever see a guy on the beach with a pair of fuck-off big binoculars, girls, remember he's only bird watching and don't be scared to show your tits.

– Howard, Chichester, UK

Foot Feeding Frenzy

I'd never have dared attempt it – a very public foot
seduction – if the hot sun and the sparkling water and the
two margaritas I'd had with lunch hadn't all simulta-
neously gone to my head. A dizzy blonde head already
spinning from the mere sight of that sexy redhead's long,
smooth, pale, gleaming legs, her elongated, high-arched,
exquisitely-curved peds sporting ten plump, supremely
suckable, crimson-tipped toes – dangling there in the
heated water.

She was sitting on the edge of the hotel pool, leaning
back on her hands and baring her body to the blazing sun,
thighs spread and splayed, legs dripping off over the side
and into the water, shin-deep. She was wearing just a
neon-green bikini, a floppy straw hat, and a pair of
oversized white-framed sunglasses, her skin gleaming
porcelain under the sun and sunscreen. Soaking up the hot
rays like the five other tourists lounging around the pool.

Only her feet and lower legs were in the water.

And I was in the water.

In the deep end, treading water, transfixed by those
narrow, hard-shelled knees gently rocking back and
forth, those lightly-muscled white thighs flexing taut and
soft, those slender, elegant shins churning waves. Watching, whetting my primal instincts to the salivation point.

I stopped treading, and sank underwater. And peered
through the crystal-clear, sunlit liquid to watch the

mushroomed toes and the curvaceous feet, the slim ankles and the long, calf-backed shins, swish back and forth in the silence of the water. I could hear them, though – those luscious feet and legs – calling out to me like a siren's song.

Calling out to me like women's gorgeously sculpted feet and legs have been calling out to me ever since middle school gym class, when one day I suddenly became aware of all those lithe lower limbs spilling out of my classmates' short-shorts. Became aware and aroused. From there, it had been a long, lovely stroll into a lifetime of lady leg and foot fetish.

And now my sexual sonar was pinging full blast, ringing that little pink bell in between my legs, as I gazed at those perfect peds and sublime shins in the water. I wettened with something more than just chlorinated dampness, too turned on not to attempt a strike. A ravenous *ped*ator desperately hungry for those highly edible leg offerings.

I shot forward in a powerful breast stroke (I'd been on my college swim team, naturally), my brown eyes locked on the twin, unsuspecting targets of my overwhelming desire. Surging through the water, underwater. The playful feet idly kicked back and forth, toes wiggling unconcernedly, innocent of the danger that was steaming straight for them, intent on devouring them whole, and then individually. The only thing missing was the theme from *Jaws*.

I was within fifteen feet of the pair of feet, and closing fast, arms pushing, legs pumping, hair streaming. Ten feet; the peds suddenly stopping their sluicing, arching, perhaps sensing the danger. Five feet; the peds moving upwards, racing for the safety of the surface of the water. The leggy redhead had obviously spotted the underwater outline of the blonde footivore streaking towards her exposed lower limbs. Her right foot breached the water, dripping, her left foot rushing to meet it.

And I struck. Lunging forward in one final burst, I caught the big toe of the left foot in my mouth and sank my teeth into the tender skin, sealing my lips around it. The toe wriggled, the foot jerking, but there was no escape from my greedy mouth. Unless the woman screamed, of course.

But she didn't scream. Rather, she pulled my head right out of the water on the end of her big toe. Her sunglasses were off, and I stared into her widened green eyes, not letting go of one centimetre of scrumptious foot-digit. The legsome lady didn't know what to do. She looked around for help, but the pool was empty now (it was the dinner hour), so it was just her feet and legs and me. I sucked on the bulbous tip of her big toe.

She opened her mouth to say something, but she couldn't find the words. So I used her hesitation to snake a hand up out of the water and grab onto her foot, lace my fingers around her delicate, tendon-cleft ankle. She was well and truly caught now, and she knew it. If only she *wanted* it.

I urgently sucked on her big toe, anxiously scrubbing its fat bottom with my tongue. At the same time I rubbed her breathtaking arch with my free hand, caressed the curvy underside of her beautiful foot and willed her to want this as badly as I did – or, at least, to indulge me, let me pamper her precious peds with my loving hands and mouth.

And then my heart leaped, when her bum touched back down on the tiles and her arms lost their rigidity. She ceased her foot-struggle and looked meaningfully into my misty eyes, telling me she was willing to experience this new sensation far from home. My foot-feeding dreams had come true! Right out there in the open pool water under the glaring tropical sun.

'My name's Helen,' she informed me, smiling nervously, her foot gone limp in my hands, toe in my mouth.

I didn't open my mouth to reply. I couldn't risk losing that ped to any sudden second thoughts. So I just sucked on her toe and caressed her foot, nodding up at the woman.

Her big toe was long and luxuriantly full-bodied, but there was plenty of room in my mouth for more. I deftly captured her next toe in line and sucked on the pair of them. Helen bit her lip, watching me, her breasts bobbing up and down on her chest like me in the water. I ran a hand up her calf, revelling in the mounded feel of the smooth, bunched muscles; sucking and sucking on her two toes.

She wiggled them around in my mouth, biting their nails into my tongue, getting into what I'd been immersed in since puberty. I popped the two toes out of my mouth and quickly engulfed the entire cluster on her tapered foot-tip.

'Oh ... my,' she murmured, all five of the delightful toes on her delectable left ped now caught in my wide, grinning maw. Her leg trembled beyond her foot in my mouth.

I sucked on her set of toes, lips straining, throat working, saliva spilling out of the corners of my obscenely stretched mouth. I wanted to swallow up the pretty woman's entire foot. But I had to make do with only about half.

I sank my teeth into her silken arch and baby-smooth sole, at the same time caressing her ankle and shin and calf and knee, running my quivering fingertips all over the hot, glistening skin of her lower leg. Then I pulled back on her ped, disgorging the heavenly foot-tip with its angelic toes, reddened and dripping. I sunk deeper into the water and stuck out my tongue and licked the bottom of her foot from rounded heel to forest of toes, painting the exhilarating curves of her sensitive sole with my wet velvet brush of a tongue.

She moaned, her leg vibrating in my hands. She stole another look around the deserted pool, and then dipped her right hand into her bikini bottom and began rubbing.

I flushed with even more shimmering heat, at the erotic sight of what I was doing to this fine-footed woman. And what her exquisite peds and legs were doing to me, my own pussy tingling as wildly as the tips of my breasts. I lapped at Helen's sole, overjoyed when the taut flesh went crinkly under my heated strokes, riding the rollercoaster-thrilling contours of her foot-bottom with my exuberant tongue over and over again.

She urgently rubbed herself, and extended her other foot. I quickly and gratefully grabbed onto it, stroked its vulnerable, concave bottom with my dragging tongue. Licking her one sole, the other; Helen shuddering, rubbing faster.

I tilted her peds back down and positioned them side by side, pointing them directly at my open mouth. I briefly admired all ten of her adorable toes all together, before excitedly sucking on them – a big toe, the other big toe, both big toes; each toe in turn up and down the line, right foot, left foot. Moving my head back and forth and sucking on her squirming foot-digits.

I slithered my tongue in between them, one foot to the other, washing the wriggling piggies with my eager tongue. Licking and sucking and biting – feasting on the frenzy of toes. Until I squeezed her slickened foot-tips tightly together and plunged all ten of her toes into my mouth at once, inhaling a full half of both of her feet.

She gasped, staring in amazement at the ends of her arched peds where they disappeared into my stretched-out mouth. Her hand flew in her bikini, and she shivered with orgasm, shocked to ecstasy by my wanton foot-lust.

I looked up her arches and along her shining shins and over her rounded knees and up into her quivering thighs, desperately sucking on her jumping feet, my own pussy primed for fingertip explosion. My head bounced around with the force of Helen's orgasm transmitted through her lovely peds, and I almost reluctantly dropped a hand into the water and into my own bikini bottom.

And, sure enough, as soon as I made contact with my swollen button, I came. Hard and hot and heavy, like Helen. Trashing about in the water as heated wave after wave of pure pleasure washed through me. But never once letting those feminine foot-ends, that were the cause of it all, fall out of my mouth.

Helen and I never did get a chance to really pussy-foot around, unfortunately. Because both of our vacations ended that day. By nightfall, we were legging the long miles back to our respective hometowns.

But just the memory of that one swimming pool foot-feeding frenzy kept me warm and moist throughout the rest of that long, cold winter

– Felicity, Winnipeg, Canada

Tail

We were at my house, Neil was out and my best friend, Carmel, was helping me pick what I should wear for a party we were going to at the weekend. Well, I *say* helping – we were having fun going through everything in my wardrobe and Carmel would either get me to model it or try it on for herself. Carmel is a little taller and slimmer than I am and most of my stuff looks better on her, though my trousers hang short and she doesn't fill out the fitted clothes so nicely. But with her sleek black hair and sharp cheekbones she's got this dark elegance that I'll never have. I'm more the cream and honey type.

So I was in a minidress, all shimmering pale-blue scales, when the doorbell rang. And I had to go down to answer it like that because Carmel insisted. She waited at the head of the stairs in her cami-top and knickers, peering through the banisters and sniggering into her hand as I opened the door.

It was my neighbour Mr Allen, who is sort of elderly and beardy and very proper. He definitely looked a bit shocked when he saw my bare legs. He was holding a brown cardboard box which he shoved into my arms saying, 'The postman left this at our house for you while you were out.' Then he backed off down the path. I shut the door quickly but Carmel was laughing so loud he probably heard her hoots anyway.

'Do you think he liked the dress?' she asked, running downstairs. 'Should we ask him?'

I blocked the door with my back because Carmel was the sort who would do just that. But thankfully the sight of the parcel distracted her.

'What is it then? Have you been shopping online? Let's have a look!'

I mumbled that it was just some things I'd ordered as a surprise for Neil, but she wouldn't let it drop. She can be right pushy when she wants, can Carmel. Eventually I admitted that it was some stuff from a lingerie shop – and then of course we had to go back up to the bedroom, open it up and have a look.

I was careful. I got the top item out and tucked the box away as I handed her a red PVC bustier to examine. Carmel liked it – well, actually, she squealed with laughter and insisted I try it on. There was a lot of giggling and dirty talk about how much Neil would go for it, as I twirled in front of the mirror. I felt a bit weird wearing something so tartily sexy while my friend watched, but she was really complimentary about how well it suited me. And I did like the way it looked – the shiny red plastic stretched tight over my skin, my creamy boobs bulging up out of the half-cups.

'Is that the only thing you ordered? It was a big box for one piece of clothing.'

It was impossible to throw Carmel off the scent. I had to admit nervously to another new purchase. This was black and came in a plastic wrapper. It looked like heavy silk but when I got it out she could see straight away that it was a rubber miniskirt. With a great squeal she spotted the selling-point: a hole cut out where the wearer's bottom would be.

'Perv! Is Neil into rubber then?'

'He likes bums – you know that.' I'd gone pink. 'It's just a joke thing, like.'

'Try it on!'

So on went the latex skirt. It was very tight and smooth as I eased it over my thighs, and cool against the skin. It was the first time I'd tried this material. I'd imagined it would have a sticky texture and maybe smell of rubber, but it was talced so it was silky-smooth and it felt really nice to handle. It was very snug and I could feel my bum cheeks bulging through the hole. I twisted, trying to get a look. 'Is that in the right place?'

'Well, your thong looks silly. You'd look better without it.'

I struggled to pull off my panties under the rubber skin, leaving my cheeks bare. The skirt was tight enough to actually lift my bum, making it jut out even more than usual. 'So, what do you think?'

'Neil likes spanking you, doesn't he?'

'Sometimes.' I tried to look casual. 'He's not weird about it or anything.'

'He won't be able to say no to that target.'

I hobbled off for a look in the mirror. I had to agree, my bum cheeks and crack were framed by the black latex, making a perfectly round white target for a hand to land on. I could see already how eager he'd be to turn that target a burning scarlet. Just the thought made me tingle. But while I was admiring myself, Carmel was sneakily examining what remained in the cardboard box.

'What's this then?' She waved the third item I'd ordered, her delight at my wickedness printed all over her face. Plastic-wrapped, it looked at first glance like a short stainless steel carrot, but instead of leaves it had a whisk of long black hair. 'Is it a whip?' she asked, ripping the packaging open and trailing the hairs across her palm.

'Uh . . .'

She flicked her bare thigh experimentally.

'Carmel!' I'd gone hot all over.

'Oh my God!' The truth dawned on her. 'Oh my God! It's a dildo, a dildo with a – with a tail!'

'It's a butt-plug.' My expression dared her to disapprove.

For once she went quiet and her eyes opened wide. 'No! *You* do that?'

'It's a toy, that's all. It's fun.'

'You'd stick something this big up your . . .' But the look in her eyes expressed admiration. Trust Carmel.

I squirmed, proud and flustered and a bit turned on all at the same time. 'I don't see why not.'

She grinned at me. 'Think it'll go in?'

'Not easily,' I admitted with a giggle.

There was a glint in her eye now. 'Go on. This I've got to see.'

I bit my lip. Part of me was shocked. I mean it's not the sort of thing you'd expect a friend to ask, is it? But then Carmel had never been shy. And I did want to get my hands on that plug with its long tail of real hair. I'd been looking forward to this delivery so much. Even seeing it in her hands had started a warm wet trickle that was in danger of escaping from inside me. I tried to laugh my way out of the situation but she was having none of that.

'Scaredy cat!' She bounced onto the bed, waving the plug threateningly at me.

'Go on. I know now, so you might as well. I want to see what you look like with a tail.'

So I agreed, though I made her wash it and I got the lube out of the bedside drawer – that thing wasn't going anywhere without lube. Carmel drizzled the clear jelly out of the tube like she was pouring raspberry topping onto an ice cream. The steel plug glistened. When I took it from her she was reluctant to let it go.

'You're going to wear it through the hole in that skirt, right? That's how it should look?'

'Yeah, OK.' I knelt on the mattress, feeling very self-conscious, my thighs pushing against the latex skirt that was trying to keep them closed, my bum stuck out. Reaching behind me I carefully slipped the metal head between my cheeks, holding my breath as I did so. The metal and the lube felt really cold, and I managed to smear the gel down my bum crack. The hard nose of the plug bumped my tight sphincter, meeting a lot of resistance.

'Sorry,' I giggled, all too aware of how weird and dirty this must look: my best friend watching me take it where the sun don't shine. But she wanted to see and, yes, I wanted to show her. 'It's not easy finding the angle. Neil usually does this for me.'

'Let me help.' Carmel pulled the skirt down another couple of inches to make it easier for me. Her long nails scratched my cheeks and her breath tickled my bare shoulders. She stared down into the split of my cheeks. 'Wow. Is that thing really going to go in?'

'Well,' I said, 'we usually work up to something this big. Small things to start with.' I was using shallow probing thrusts, like the pecks of a beak. My pussy was so juicy I was oozing onto the latex.

'His fingers?'

'Yeah.'

'His cock?'

I flashed on Neil's smooth latex-skinned dick sliding into my arse. 'His cock's bigger than this, Carmel.'

'Let me get some more lube on, then.' She squirted it down my crack and I squirmed at the cold slipperiness of it. The point of the plug was starting to make headway despite the awkwardness of the situation. I let out a little grunt. It was hard work, this.

'Does it ever hurt?' She was still sat there, almost touching me. I could smell her perfume and feel her body heat.

'A bit. I usually fiddle with myself, you know . . . That helps.'

'You do that then and I'll do this.' Without warning she pushed my fingers aside and took charge of the plug. My aching wrist was grateful, even if my rear muscles tightened anxiously.

'Careful!'

'I will be.'

I moved my hand down to my mound, giving it a task it was more used to. Round the front there I didn't need extra lube, and the pressure of a fingertip on my neglected clit was instantly soothing. I shifted forward onto my knees and one hand and lifted my bum up.

'That's better.'

It was. The smooth metal moved in and out nudging my bum-hole open further and further, as hot and cold flashes ran up and down my spine. The ring of tight muscle relaxed slowly under my friend's gentle pushing. My own juices were running freely now too, coating my fingers, and my face was burning. I tried to lick my lips but my mouth was dry because I'd been panting softly without realising it. My pussy lips were swollen beneath that black rubber skirt.

'It's going!' Carmel whispered – just as the whole broad shoulder of the plug slipped right into my arse. My muscles closed around the narrower stem, holding it all snugly inside. I couldn't help letting out a long moan. There's something about the sensation of a full, stretched bottom that makes me so hot and horny. It really brings out the slut in me. Carmel pulled her hand away and I nearly begged her to put it back. I didn't want to stop what my fingers were doing to my clit.

'That looks so pretty.' Her fingers stroked my bare cheeks, tracing the circle framed by the rubber. They brushed the tail, stroking through the long horsehair, fanning it over my bottom, and I let out a whimper as each little touch stirred the nerves inside me. I heard her soft chuckle. 'OK.'

She knew what I wanted. She took the tail in her hand and used it to stir the plug inside me from side to side, then in circles, then spun it. She tugged it, threatening to pop it out, then eased it in deeper. My supporting arm gave way and my front end dropped to rest on the bed. I pressed my face into the duvet but kept my bottom pointing at the ceiling. I found I liked it best when she wiggled the plug back and forth quite sharply. It felt so dirty – and so good – letting my friend plunder my bum-hole. My own fingers danced on my clit. I could feel my bottom surrendering to the big cold mass of the plug, sucking at it when it tried to pull out, quivering with delight when Carmel stroked me between my cheeks. I shut my eyes as I began to come in lovely warm spasms that rippled out from the centre of my bottom through my whole body. I squealed into the crumpled duvet, screamed something about fucking my dirty arse, fucking me right up the arse, but I wasn't really aware what I was saying.

That was more or less the moment Neil came in through the front door and it all went totally crazy.

Sometimes it's good to have a pushy friend. Though I guess Carmel is a bit more than just a friend now, to both of us.

– *Erica, Leeds, UK*

Party Girl

I don't know why I'm here boasting about this. I'm not even proud if it. Or maybe I am, I can't decide. I guess I must be or I wouldn't write about it. Then again, I'm not giving my full name, and I'm not letting them put what town I'm from, so . . .

Parties. That's where my bother starts really. There's so much going on: there's pressure to impress, there's the flirting, obviously, and then there's always rivalry, and the jealousy. And I like to feel that I'm the belle of the ball: the funniest, the prettiest, the wildest.

Some egghead once tried to tell me it was because I was insecure or something like that. I don't think he knew what he was talking about. I mean, me? Insecure? With everyone watching me, taking notice of me, loving me? Utter rubbish. I just told him he wasn't making much sense to me and his silly degrees weren't worth a thing and that was that.

Anyway, I was talking about me and parties. I suppose I'm not so bad earlier on in the evening. I turn up, make my entrance, mingle here, mingle there, have a laugh and a giggle with my gang. That would make for a good evening I reckon, if I left it there. It must be the drink, because I start to feel that I need to be the centre of attention. Soon I find myself talking lewdly with the boys, or dancing in ways I shouldn't be. The appeals and admonishments of my friends fall on deaf ears – and soon they're disowning me!

Many is the time I've been shown pictures of myself gyrating on tables, knickers peeking out under my skirt, bumping and grinding with some guy or girl I never met before. Most of the time I'm quite proud of my antics and I think the people showing me these photos are quite taken aback when I completely fail to turn red at the sight of myself letting it all hang out. Perhaps, the next time I'm shown a picture of myself unbuttoning a stranger's jeans with my teeth, I should start to feign embarrassment. It was for a bet, by the way.

I reckoned I had the art of spicing up a party all stitched up. But I really had to take stock and think again when Miranda came along.

I first spotted her at a house party in the West End. We arrived late because Terri, who is always disorganised, came out without her purse and we had to go back for it. This got me pretty agitated and I'm afraid I had a good moan at her. That earned me some rolled eyes from my other friends, but I had good reason to feel annoyed.

The timing of the entrance is very important, you see. I can drive my friends mad fussing over what time a party starts and planning the arrival. You need to be a good time after the start, in order to make your appearance, but not so late that other guests get the chance to grab all the attention before you've even got in the door.

So it was that my face flushed when we arrived at an already busy flat, too full to allow us a proper audience for our arrival. To make it worse, another girl appeared to be capturing an audience for herself in the living room: a handful of guys were crowded round laughing and joking with her, and even a couple of the girls about seemed taken with her. You should have seen the way she eyed them, girls and boys alike, all flirty and simpering, the tart.

To make it worse her looks seemed to be the exact opposite of mine. Whereas I'm a petite blonde, she was tall, dark, exotic and athletic. I sneered inside as I saw her glance in my direction.

After we had sorted our coats and drinks out, I did my best to mingle, but I wasn't finding it easy. I couldn't really help myself from watching her out of the corner of my eye and the distraction kind of got in the way of things socially. I found myself nodding vacantly at many a line in a conversation that I had just been too preoccupied to listen to properly.

Left on a sofa across the room with Terri and Sharon, two of the girls I had arrived with, for company, I tried in vain to attract the eye of the three boys and two girls who seemed utterly enthralled by this dark, sultry, gorgeous . . . bitch. Sorry. I can't think of a better word that sums up how I felt about her right then. They hung on her every word (she was way too loud, by the way) and acted like some sort of hired posse or entourage for her.

Casually I pulled my skirt up my leg and swung my shoe as I coolly sat on the three-seater discussing the punch with my two friends. I got the odd glance from bystanders, but my aim had been to catch the eye of one of the lads across the room, and break up the little rally this girl was running over there.

Gradually, the music got going and the dancing wasn't far behind. I perked up a bit, getting lost in a tune here and there as Terri and Sharon dragged me up to dance. I even noticed a few eyes turning in my direction. I was starting to feel more like my usual party self and my hips responded in their usual way, adding an imprudent gyration here and there when the mood took me.

I should have thought of it earlier. There was a large square wooden coffee table in the centre of the room; it had started to collect beer bottles and a few glasses but things had not yet reached that ridiculous party stage of total clutter on every flat surface. I leaned over and started to move a few glasses and bottles onto other items of furniture.

'What are you up to, Kirsteen?' Terri asked.

'Do you fancy a dance?' I answered.

'Don't be daft,' she answered, 'Not up there.'

I didn't give her a choice. I grabbed her hand and stepped onto the makeshift podium and began to move to the R & B on the sound system. Terri maintained her reluctant stance down on the floor, but eventually she had to relent. It was a bit mean of me to take advantage of the fact, but I knew she would never leave me up there on my own.

I'm sure you've noticed that two straight girls do not dance like two straight girls; we're not averse to doing a bit of dirty-dancing with each other – we know the boys can't resist it, after all. And that's how I made sure Terri and I danced. She rolled her eyes at me again at first but soon we were grooving it. I allowed myself a glance around the room, and, yes, we were being watched all right, by just about everyone, including the guys with Miss Popular, who suddenly didn't seem so mesmerising to them. I felt good again.

I wanted to press home the advantage, really steal the show, so I'm afraid I may have gone a little far. I allowed my right leg to inch nearer to Terri, until my standing foot was between hers. She could not retreat, being on an improvised podium, and so now we were dancing very closely indeed. I did not bother to check if the boys were watching, I knew they would be. Keeping rhythm to the music I incorporated a move with my arms which allowed me to imply that I was brushing my friend's breast through her top. She gave me one of those looks – an eyebrow, and a sardonic smirk – but there was no direct objection, so I carried on with the show. It felt very good to know that I had beaten off the competition and become the focal point of the room and the feeling took over, I think.

So I pushed my luck with poor Terri and allowed my hand to brush the side of her breast a couple of times. She looked daggers but kept dancing. I didn't stop there. I wanted us to be the talk of the flat by the time we stepped down, and driven by that wish I allowed myself to fondle her unambiguously as we danced.

Terri is used to my nonsense, and puts up with a lot, but she showed a bit of resistance to my antics, leaning back slightly, so I did not try it again. I remember thinking it was a shame she had such a thick bra on under her top, otherwise her nipples might have been giving everyone quite a show by now. It was that thought that gave me another idea.

'Come on, brush mine as we dance,' I said into her ear.

She looked at me again with the same expression.

'Go on, I need you to,' I insisted.

She shook her head and shrugged her shoulders in defeat. Bless her, she did it! As we rocked and gyrated she let the palms of her open hand rub down from my shoulder over my breast down to my waist. It felt good. Another song started and we kept on dancing.

'Happy now?' she said.

You see, I was wearing a silky dress, with a loose, but pretty short, hem. And no bra. I knew if she did as I asked, my nipples would start to show through my dress. Now that *would* attract attention. That *would* make me unforgettable. The talk of the night.

'Keep going, just for this song,' I told her.

I am pleased to say she did. I offered my chest to her as we danced and, with a look of suffering admittedly, she plied the light brush of her hands over the silk that covered my nipples. I felt them tingle and harden as though trying to poke through the material.

Out of the corner of my eye, I noticed nudging and whispering travel around the room as the guys observed our activity and tried their best to get word about without earning the withering looks of their female friends. I noticed heads poking around the door to get a glimpse of us. Mission accomplished, I thought.

After the song ended I stepped down and we returned to our seats next to Sharon. There were a couple of humorous claps of appreciation.

'Feeling OK again now?' Sharon asked as we sat either side of her, referring perhaps to my agitation at us running late on the way there.

'Yeah, not too bad,' I replied. 'I'm going to see what drink is in the other room.'

I stood up and went for the door. As I rose I managed a very smug smile in the direction of my dark-haired pretender. She kind of half-returned it. I considered her dealt with and strutted out of the room, putting on my best wiggle.

My nipples were still erect and it was with great delight I noticed bystanders staring at them over their drink-filled glasses as I passed by. I knew this party would be remembered for my presence by many, and for a long time. That's all I ever want from a party really!

I went to the kitchen, smiling to myself as I caught boys admiring my nipples and heard them whisper about me as I made my way. It felt so good for so many reasons, but the chief one was that my teats were throbbing and tingling where my dress rubbed over them. I stuck them out as I smiled politely at the lads hanging around in the kitchen and fetched myself some more booze. I refreshed myself with a swig of vodka and then refilled my glass with some of the punch, then returned to the main room, once again enjoying the parade along the hallway. This time the whispers preceded me.

When I got back to the main room my positive mood took a bash. There was a Latin tune playing, which I didn't recognise, I'm not really into that sort of thing, and the name of it wasn't really important. What was important was that the coffee table had been moved up against the wall and in the space opened up in the middle of the room the dark-haired girl was teaching a group of guys some of those salsa dancing moves. The boys were standing in a rough circle and there she was dancing with each one in turn, rubbing up against them, pressing herself to them, hooking her leg round them and then spinning onto the next boy. Obviously everybody was looking and my erect nipples and my lesbian dance with Terri had been forgotten. I sat down with a slump on the sofa between Terri and Sharon.

'This girl's more of a tart than you are, look at her.' Terri nodded at her, perhaps trying to get me back for pushing the boundaries of her natural bisexuality further than she wanted.

'Bitch,' I muttered.

We watched as she dirty-danced with the half-dozen guys who all of a sudden had decided one thing they had always wanted was a salsa lesson. They clapped and cheered her as she went and I felt my face redden.

It got worse as the song changed. The guest appointed with the music duties had obviously decided on a Latin scene for the next quarter of an hour, because he played another one.

A couple of boys came over to stand by our sofa and admire the girl in action, and it was then that I caught wind of her name.

'Miranda's great isn't she?' said one.

'Just a bit,' agreed the other.

I never turned round to look at them, I just continued watching this Miranda, who had taken the cue of a new song to get even worse. She was now teaching the five boys a new move, something a little reminiscent of the Lambada, if you remember that. Swaying to the music, she was now standing astride her partners' forelegs and pressing her crotch against it as she danced, riding each thigh as though it was a bucking bronco. It was more or less a group dry-hump to music.

I watched, my ears burning with jealousy (for the attention she was getting), as she worked her way around the circle to the guy standing nearest to us. I turned away in disgust as she rubbed the crotch of her knickers up and down his leg and looked over his shoulder to return the smug smile I gave her earlier. I stormed out to the toilet.

It wasn't quite a runny-mascara-in-the-loo moment but I was pretty upset. I seethed and hissed in there as I answered nature and touched up my make-up. When I had finished I just stared at myself in the mirror. I saw an angry, jealous me – a more ruthless and determined me. I stared her down, as though challenging her to act. And in response to that challenge, the girl in the mirror took off her knickers, put them in her handbag and strode out of the bathroom back to the main room.

The Latin music was still going and Miranda was still hard at it – and still gaining all the attention. But I reckoned I had the answer to all that. I strode into the circle of males, and grabbed one for a dance. Now I'm more of a hip-hop girl but I did my best to find the rhythm of the spicy music, and set about copying Miranda's moves on my surprised but eager dance partner.

My bare pussy rubbed and ground on the denim of his jeans. I felt the muscle on the top of his thigh clench and relax as he moved and I enjoyed the feel of his strong flesh on my clitoris. I had meant to shock, and completely forgotten that there might be the side-benefit of getting off.

The next guy I pressed nearer to me, so my breasts brushed him a bit as we danced, making my nipples erect as before. I ground my moistening pussy into his leg, this time making it quite obvious with the choppy movements of my hips that I was rubbing my clit directly on his leg. It tingled with a rawness I hadn't felt before. I found myself getting horny, but when my dance partner leaned in to venture a kiss, I twirled away to the next guy.

This guy had been dancing with Miranda only a few seconds before and as I pressed against him in dance I felt his still hard penis poke against my stomach. I met his eyes as I ground my soft cameltoe into his leg and began my little gyrations, letting my pussy and clit run back and forth on his thigh. I was wet now, noticeably wet, and must have felt so warm on his outstretched limb. I was pretty sure I had reached my goal and stepped back to see what I had been aiming for: a wet patch of my sexy juice on a stranger's trouser. He looked at it, I looked at it, we looked at each other, and I moved on to the next guy.

I heard laughs of disbelief behind me, and cheering and clapping from my previous dance partners, and saw Sharon and Terri shaking their heads at me. I just gave them a carefree smile and carried on.

My plan seemed to be having the desired effect – I felt I had, once again, eclipsed Miranda my rival, but as a side-effect I was really horny now and I was getting urges to kiss my next dance partner, urges which I tried to fight. I wanted to be outrageous, yes, but still remain in control. I pushed his face back as I think he sensed he could steal a kiss, but instead of running away this time I continued to stimulate my bare, juicing pussy on his leg. The music changed but I just didn't want to stop. I was now as frisky as a bitch in heat, and acting like one.

I did stop, however, when I was finally distracted from my self-pleasuring by the sight of Miranda, working her way round to my previous dance-partner. But instead of continuing the dance, she knelt down in front of him and, glancing to see if I was watching, which I was, she placed her lips over the patch of my pussy-juice on his leg, and began sucking and licking it up.

I stood there watching her in disbelief. Once again it seemed she had out-trumped me. She never once broke her gaze from my eyes, lapping on those so-very personal juices, and enjoying them. She stood and approached my current partner, whose hand I still held, and did the same to the glistening, sugary patch on his leg.

I could hear the same rowdy clapping and cheering over the music as the male revellers watched her in action, as she stared me down and supped my sweet oils from a man's trouser leg. The boys fell silent as she stood. It was anticipation I think; we all knew what they were hoping would happen next. My heart raced, my legs trembled, I felt all those eyes on me and I anticipated the impending excitement.

Miranda kissed me, pressing her soft tongue into my willing mouth and mixing those intimate secretions with my saliva. I tasted it on her tongue and supped on her kiss as my stomach turned somersaults there in front of all those horny guys, clapping and whooping at us.

Miranda cupped the back of my head, and scrunched my blonde hair between her fingers as I pulled away from the kiss. I noticed for the first time that she spoke with a slight Mediterranean accent.

'You know, if we leave for the bedroom now, then we'll *both* be the talk of this party for years to come.'

She was right, but I think, as I took her hand and we headed down the hall, for the first time that night I wasn't acting out of the need to feed my ego. This time it was to fulfil the need of my soaking wet pussy – although perhaps it was wet because of all the attention we were getting. Does it matter?

The bed was covered in coats, as is often the case at parties. We shut the thick panelled wooden door behind us, muffling the music. There was a small, old-fashioned iron key in the door, which Miranda locked, placing the key on the side. We heaved and kicked the coats onto the floor and clutched in another wet kiss, our bare legs intertwining and rubbing each other. She brought her knee up so her thigh split mine, and allowed it to rub against my naked pussy. My hem rode up beyond my waist as I shamelessly writhed on it.

I pulled the straps of her dress over her shoulders and kissed and licked at her dark nipples as she nibbled at the back of my neck. And there we wriggled and rubbed for what seemed like quite a while – I certainly know the music changed a few times. It wasn't like being with a guy that way: she was quite happy to keep doing the same thing for as long as it felt good, not always rushing to the next thing.

Eventually, I wanted more, so I reached down and started to pull at her knickers. She carried on pressing her smooth leg against my pussy lips and neither helped nor hindered my efforts to expose her. Eventually they were far enough down her legs that she stopped kissing me and reached down herself to loop them over her heels and throw them onto the floor. I took the opportunity to lie on my back and open my legs to her.

She took the hint, diving in with her tongue and fingers. I felt her tongue first press to my clitoris and then lap at it, quickly but firmly. I buried the back of my head into the pillow. Still plying my love-bud with the tip of her tongue, and pressing her fingers gradually ever deeper into my pussy, she inched herself round towards the inevitable sixty-nine position. I bit my lip as I realised I was about to drink from my first pussy.

As her rear came nearer to me I reached out to lift up her skirt hem and rub her smooth olive-coloured buttocks. They felt cool and soft on my warm hand. My fingers crawled towards the furry flesh that protruded from between them and pulled delicately at her soft vulva. Having come this far, having crossed this barrier, I was eager to go all the way. A finger poked inside her entrance and I felt it wet and warm, just like when I start to finger myself. She swung around some more, and I pushed in further with my finger, just like I like to do it to myself: rubbing her clit with my thumb at the same time. She really liked it, pushing back on me a dozen or so times before she finally lifted her nearest leg over my head. Now I was staring directly at her pussy. I licked it tentatively.

She buried her face once more into my moist entrance, flicking and pressing her tongue onto my button and inserting a finger into my tunnel slowly but firmly. I think it was an instruction from her on how to do her, so I copied.

71

We lapped and writhed and rolled and licked and finger-fucked each other there on that bed. I felt myself being licked and toyed with in just the way I would do myself, if only I could, and I rode the wave of pleasure wherever it took me.

She was very wet and yielding and she hummed with pleasure, vibrating my clitoris as she did so; I pressed more fingers inside her, increasing the pace and force. I used her reaction as a cue to judge when to slow or quicken, to take it easy, or to place another finger inside her. Her elastic pussy eventually took four of my fingers up to just above my knuckles, squelching inside her. She moaned again on my clitoris, making it tingle and tickle.

I responded by quickening the pace my fingers invaded her soft tunnel and soon she was moaning and gasping into my pussy. Her hips jiggled and thrust back onto my fingers and I knew she was climaxing on them. I quickened the pace again to let her come. It felt good to know my first attempt at getting a girl off had been so successful.

'Relax. I will do you now,' she said to me as she caught her breath.

I lay back, and once again she nuzzled her face into my soft flesh, the tip of her tongue pushing its warmness and wetness into my pink, swollen clitoris, filling me with waves of pleasure. She slowly poked the entrance of my vagina with her middle finger and I found myself surfing those waves again, towards an orgasm.

She listened to my moans and as I got more excited I felt her push another finger inside, increasing the sensation. The firm but slow penetration continued, as did the pleasure. I looked up as she adjusted her position slightly.

'Relax to it,' she said.

I let my head loll back onto the pillow again and felt her ease three fingers inside me, parting my pussy-lips even more. Her change of position meant she was now able to curl her fingers up towards my G-spot. I thought

I was wet and feeling good before that, but this sent a shudder of pleasure right through me. I could hear my pussy squelching as her hands pushed deeper, millimetre by millimetre. It was like my G-spot was a tap, and every time the tips of her fingers curled over it more fluid seeped into my tunnel. My stomach juddered with the sensations.

Then, just as I thought I had reached a point when orgasm was inevitable, Miranda knelt bolt upright and looked at me. I looked back.

'What?' I whispered.

'You will be famous now,' she said.

I laughed. 'I know, they're probably still talking about us out there.'

'It's worse than that,' she said to me, batting her eyelids.

'What do you mean?'

She did not answer, instead she pulled me by the legs to the edge of the bed so I was sitting up with my legs either side of the corner. She knelt down on the carpet holding one of my legs firmly with her arm, and reached into my pussy with her other hand. I leant back on my hands and savoured the feeling of her three fingers parting my lips and then my walls.

'What did you mean?' I asked again, once I had recomposed myself from the initial rush of penetration.

She didn't answer me at first. She just laughed. I felt another finger inserting into me and heard my pussy squelching even louder as she reached again for my G-spot.

'Oh yes!' I gasped. 'Do it like before.'

She pushed her four fingers inside me with jabbing, chopping motions, and curled her fingers up to ply my spot every few thrusts. I'd never had so much flesh in there. She really knew what she was doing, this Miranda, as this filling I was getting would have been most uncomfortable without all the preparation she put into it:

softly stimulating me with the single finger as she had played on my clit, then plying my opening with two, then three fingers, before targeting the sweet-spot to fill my tunnel with juice and make me want more. I was now putty in her hands.

'How would you like to be known as that girl who got fisted at the party?' She didn't look up as she spoke, focusing on fucking me with her fingers and rubbing my clit with her thumb.

It was a question that threw up a few of questions of my own. For example: Was I about to be fisted? Could I take it? But the one I chose to ask was: 'Why, are you going to tell everyone?'

'I don't have to,' she smirked. 'Someone is looking through the keyhole.'

'What the fuck?' I said, shaping to roll over and get out of sight. I was sitting with my legs astride the bed and my filled pussy facing directly at the door, and didn't take the news that someone was out there staring right at me too well.

Miranda was ready for the protest, she had me pinned by my pussy anyway, and before I could get away she had shot up off the floor and sat herself right on my leg to stop me moving. She kissed me.

'Just think how good it will feel, the thrill of knowing they're taking turns to watch you out there, and then when you go back out you can party knowing everyone is talking about you. Is that not what you want?'

I looked at her and thought about it. I thought about how my pussy felt, how horny I was, how the adrenaline was shooting through me, how near I was to orgasm, and how I love to get attention. Most of all, I asked myself if I was ashamed of what I was doing and if I cared if everyone knew. I wasn't ashamed, and I didn't care.

'OK, but gentle, it's my first time,' I told her.

'I know,' she said, biting my ear.

She took up her position and spat all over the backs of her fingers so that they glistened in the low light. Once again I enjoyed the sensation of each finger easing its way in as her saliva mixed with my juice, lubricating me. I found myself staring at the darkened keyhole as I received those fingers; I could not see that eyeball enjoying the show, but just knowing it was there filled me with adrenaline and made my genitals tingle with excitement.

'Ah!' My head went back as I felt the thumb squeezing its way in for the first time. There was a tiny needle of pain as my vagina stretched to accommodate it. Now she was pushing slowly, but relentlessly, in.

Her hand was like a wedge being driven inside me, widening out to the knuckle and I felt more tiny needles of pain as we worked our way towards the knobbles of those joints. The discomfort just increased the adrenaline and therefore the pleasure.

'Just endure it a bit more,' she whispered. 'Once you're past the worst bit you'll never want to stop this.'

I steeled myself against the invasion, and she helped by using her free thumb to softly rub my clit. Ecstasy mixed with pain, and I was loving it.

The moment came and suddenly all the pressure around the entrance to my pussy melted away as her hand slipped inside me. I groaned, in relief and pleasure. She stopped, allowing me time to get composed. Feeling her hand sitting there inside me was tremendous, especially in the knowledge that a lucky guy was seeing me like this.

'Well done.' She grinned. Then she slapped my leg.

'I don't even know your name, you tart!' she joked with me.

'Miranda, meet Kirsteen,' I said to her.

'I would shake hands, but . . .' She shrugged with a grin on her face.

I could see why the boys liked hanging with her – she was a joker all right.

'Are you ready for more?' she asked.

I nodded.

She began by softly thumbing my clitoris again and I leaned back to savour it. Then I felt her slowly clench and unclench her hand and the walls of my pussy went crazy with the pressure. The wetness started anew as one knuckle repeatedly pressed up against the right spot. I never felt so much going on in there and I moaned and groaned uncontrollably, whether I was being watched or not I could not control myself. I lost it.

The pleasure spread, I felt the closing and opening hand press down through my body and my anus started to tingle and twitch. My stomach knotted up. I can't really remember any other specific sensations as they all melded into one engulfing orgasm that washed over me. I looked down as the climax rocked through me. I saw two or three strands of pussy juice squirt out of me, squeezing past Miranda's hand. She had to dodge one which narrowly missed her eye, landing on her cheek. Gleefully she scooped it with her finger and licked it up.

'Did you know you were a squirter?' she asked.

I did not answer for a while. I couldn't.

'No,' I admitted, eventually.

'Well, everyone does now.' she grinned.

We spent about half an hour cuddling, kissing, whispering and coming down before we neatened up and emerged from the room. My friends had already left. I wasn't looking forward to their comments when next I saw them; I had surpassed even myself at this party. Lucky they are not the judgmental types.

Miranda and I went for a dance together, wallowing in the longing and admiring glances of the guys, and also in the scowls of the girls – jealous of the attention no doubt. I still get those looks and see people talking about me now, almost a year later, so I think we can safely say I was definitely the talk of that party – even if I did have to share the limelight.

– *Kirsteen, Midlands, UK*

Educating Rupert

I have to admit I felt like a pervert the first time I thought about Rupert in that way. He wasn't just young enough to be my son: he was my son's best friend. The two shared a flat rent at university. My son, Danny, had first introduced us when I'd called down to visit him on campus. I met Rupert again several times over the first year of their degree course, usually when Danny brought him to our house during term holidays. Rupert's family had just moved overseas, so it was prohibitively expensive for him to visit them during holidays.

He seemed like a pleasant enough lad, looking a lot like a young Johnny Depp, and he was always so polite it made me feel decrepit. During the term holidays he would called me *Mrs Smith* and, when we were eating dinner it would be, 'That was lovely, Mrs Smith. Thank you, Mrs Smith. May I help with the washing up, Mrs Smith?'

I tried to get him to call me Lydia several times but he couldn't manage it.

And, when I caught myself masturbating one night, and thinking about how nice it would be to have Rupert's cock inside of me instead of my vibrator, and hear him call me Mrs Smith while he fucked me, I felt like a pervert for having such salacious thoughts about someone who was so young.

That didn't stop me from climaxing with the thought.

Actually, once I'd got Rupert's face in my imagination, I masturbated repeatedly and found myself creating the most lurid fantasy situations where his boyish face was pressed against my vagina while I educated him with lessons that the university would never have on their curriculum.

I kept telling myself it was just a fantasy, and I knew it would never go any further than that. But, every time I knew Rupert was going to visit, I would make sure I was wearing my sexiest underwear sets, and I'd always forsake jeans or sweatpants so he could see I was wearing stockings and showing off my legs.

On those nights when he was visiting, after hungering after Rupert so hard, I could masturbate to three or four climaxes while still wearing my stockings and heels. I'd have to press my face into the pillow so that my screams didn't alert Rupert or Danny as to what I was doing.

So I suppose it was inevitable that something was bound to happen when we were left alone.

It happened on a weekend when both boys were staying with me. Danny's estranged father called on the Saturday morning and invited Danny to visit him for the day. The invitation was extended to include Rupert as well but Rupert said he had to catch up on some reading for his coursework. He said, if it was OK with me, he'd prefer to spend the weekend in the guest bedroom while he pored over his books.

I said that was definitely OK with me.

I'd like to say that I never gave a thought to the idea that I would be spending all Saturday and part of Sunday alone in the house with handsome young Rupert. But the truth is I was instantly wet and I was desperate for something to happen between us. I drove Danny round to his father's, told him to call me on Sunday if he needed picking up, and then I went straight back home to spend the day with Rupert.

Needless to say I was disappointed to find Rupert was genuinely locked away in his bedroom and appeared to be studying hard. I knocked on his door, and told him if he needed a drink or a sandwich, or anything, he should let me know. And, while I wanted to place a special emphasis on the word 'anything' I didn't dare make myself too obvious.

I saw Rupert briefly around lunch-time. We had a coffee and a sandwich together. Then he disappeared back into the guest bedroom and I didn't see him until we were eating dinner together. I asked him how the studies were going and he said they were pretty tiring but manageable. I was quietly cursing the fact that he'd spent all day in his bedroom with his books when I'd wanted him to be in my bedroom with me.

Telling him that he needed to spend some time relaxing so that the information had a chance to sink in, I poured us both a glass of wine and suggested he should think about just relaxing for the rest of the evening. Rupert looked a little reluctant but I could see from the way he said, 'If you think that's best, Mrs Smith,' that he didn't want to argue with me.

It felt strange to be leading the conversation while we sat down in front of the rubbish on Saturday night television. Before I discovered my husband was having an affair, I'd been used to the man in my life taking control of things and urging the conversation toward sex. Sitting opposite Rupert in the lounge, asking about girlfriends and being vaguely suggestive, made me feel like the dirtiest slut in history.

I said I thought universities nowadays were all drugs and sex and he laughed and said it was nothing like that – at least, not for him and Danny. I asked him if he had a girlfriend and he said he wanted to concentrate on getting good results before he thought about girls. I began to wonder if he might be gay but he said there were lots of girls he fancied, he just didn't show any interest because he didn't have the time to waste. I was beginning to think I was wasting my time when Rupert said girls didn't excite him much: he preferred women.

The atmosphere was getting pretty intense. My clitoris was throbbing inside my panties and I was very aware that the crotch was sodden. When I asked him what the difference was between a girl and a woman he said he preferred the confident maturity of older women rather than the self-conscious narcissism of girls his own age. Then he said, while he preferred older women, he had never dared approach any of the ones he fancied in case they rebuked him.

I could have pounced on him there and then. Instead, I played it cool and rested back in my chair. Shifting so I was facing him, allowing my legs to part so he could see the tops of my stockings, I said, if there was an older woman he really fancied, he should tell her he found her attractive.

Rupert sat back in his chair and said, 'I find you attractive, Mrs Smith.'

We talked a little more.

Rupert explained he was a virgin, and he had a real thing for older women. He said he'd fancied me since Danny had first introduced us but he hadn't dared say anything. And he said that he needed to masturbate two or three times a day each time he stayed with us because I excited him so much.

I told him he wouldn't need to masturbate that night.

I joined him in his chair and we kissed at first. And, while that was arousing, I was desperate for more. Rupert had one hand on my knee and I had my fingers on the huge bulge in his trousers. I wanted to find out what he had for me but I was determined to be the perfect 'older woman' so I played it ultra-cool and forced myself to be patient.

'Tease my breasts, Rupert,' I whispered.

As he reached for them, he said, 'Yes, Mrs Smith,' and I squirmed. I thought about insisting he call me Lydia, and then I figured it was a huge turn-on hearing him call me Mrs Smith. I remembered my fantasy about hearing him call me that while he was fucking me. The thought of that happening really soaked my crotch. I kept hissing commands, telling him how to touch me and what I wanted. When he got my breasts out of my bra I had him kissing the nipples at first, then sucking them gently, and then holding them lightly between his teeth. I got him to alternate from one to the other and, each time I told him what to do, he said, 'Of course, Mrs Smith.'

After an hour he'd stripped me down to my stockings and heels. I could see his pants were still straining at the crotch and, before I let him go near my vagina, I said it was time for me to do something for him. Unzipping his jeans, teasing the shape of his young cock with my fingers, I pulled his cock out of his boxers and marvelled at its size. I was delighted that he was a virgin but it seemed such a shame that such a huge and impressive tool hadn't been put to good use before. While Rupert sat and looked terrified in his chair, I put my mouth around his cock and sucked on him.

'You don't need to do that, Mrs Smith,' he insisted.

I told him I wanted to do it, and that it would be better for us both if he'd come once before we moved on from the foreplay. It didn't take much to convince him and, within moments of my sliding my mouth around him, his cock was throbbing and a jet of semen was shooting from the massive tip.

I made a show of swallowing, and then licked my lips as I smiled at him. Then I told him it was his turn to return the favour and I stepped out of my panties. Taking his place in the chair and then guiding Rupert's head between my legs, I told him how to lick me and what I wanted him to do.

I was so close to orgasm I had to whisper every word.

Rupert kept calling me Mrs Smith.

I began to understand why he was such a good student at university. He obeyed every instruction I gave him and showed some startling initiative in the lessons on cunnilingus. I had his mouth pressed against my vagina, and

I was telling him to stroke his tongue against my labia and then tease my clit. But Rupert was also using his fingers and showing a surprising aptitude for pleasuring a woman. He teased a finger inside my vagina while his tongue slid against my clitoris. Then he slid his tongue deep inside my vagina while his fingers brushed against the muscle of my anus. I had thought it was exciting enough to have the handsome young stud showing an interest in me and eagerly obeying my instructions. But having him excite me with his fingers and tongue was incredible.

I came while he was licking me.

My scream was loud enough to make the double glazing shake. Rupert looked a little scared and asked if he had done something wrong. I assured him he had done everything just right and told him it was time for his final lesson.

That was when I took his hard length and slid it inside my vagina.

He didn't call me Mrs Smith while he was pounding into me. Or, if he did, I was so busy enjoying the moment I didn't hear it. He was young; his cock was thick and hard; and I was so relieved to have him filling me that I wasn't really thinking about what he was saying. I just rested back in the chair, parted my legs and let him repeatedly pound into me.

Afterwards I told him we would have to keep what we'd done secret and never tell Danny, and Rupert agreed. With painful politeness, he asked if we might be able to 'do it again' the next time he visited. I tried not to look too eager when I said we might just be able to do it again.

While I've been writing this, Danny has texted me to say that he'll be back home soon for another reading week. He's asked if it's OK if Rupert comes again.

I'm going to text back and say I'll be delighted if Rupert comes.

– *Lydia, Scarborough, UK*

Filfy Little Girl

My girlfriends were all, 'like, why don'tcha just blow off the geezer picnic and come to the beach with us?' But I just shook my little blonde head and grinned a sneaky grin. They were too clueless to realise that I actually *wanted* to mingle with all those mature men from my dad's company at the picnic; that I'd been a wicked little FILF-hunter since my eighteenth birthday.

Boys are OK, I suppose. If you're willing to settle for second best – drooling idiots who come in your mouth, hand, butt, or pussy after only a couple of strokes, leaving their girls bone-dry and wanting. Me, I prefer the trim, sleek silver foxes who know how to truly appreciate a fine young woman, using their years and years of experience to really bring her off, before they get themselves off. Ladies first, right? That's old-fashioned old school, for sure.

Trust me, I know. From *my* own experience. Just ask Mr Giardello, my former band teacher who could hit all the right notes. Or Mr Gibbons, the dirty dry cleaner down the block. Or any of the regular postmen who cruise my street (and always ring twice), for that matter. I've caught and gotten release from more foxes than an English gentrywoman in the last year or so. And I'm always on the hunt for more.

So, while my stupid friends took off for their childish beach-blanket games, I played responsible young adult and accompanied my dad to his company picnic. Dressed to kill in a pair of tight pink shorty-shorts, a white ruffled tube-top, and a pair of pink sneakers with bunny-tail white socks peeking out the back.

I looked the picture of teenaged innocence. If you didn't look too closely – at the acres of tanned flesh I was baring on my smooth legs and blonde-fuzzed arms; at the twin bra-free nipple points almost poking right through my tube-top; at my twin blonde pigtails which could easily be operated as handlebars by the correctly qualified gentleman.

Of course, the whole point was that men *did* look closely, as I eyed them up for possibilities. And they were everywhere in that sunny city park, the picnic loaded with enough man-candy to make me drool through my braces. Tall, handsome, well-seasoned men decked out in khaki shorts and polo shirts that really showed off their rugged, hairy arms and legs, the salt and pepper curls on their chests.

My mouth and cunny watered at one hunky specimen in particular – a muscular, silver-haired gent with a tanned, chiselled face and a pair of perfectly piercing blue eyes. He sort of reminded me of Harrison Ford, and I yearned for him to go all Indiana Jones on my little ass.

'Hi, I'm Brandi,' I piped up, extending a hand of invitation.

He took it and shook it, his huge hairy hand all warm and firm. 'Blake Comeau.'

I tingled all over, especially where it counted. 'Um, I hear there's, like, a duck pond or something somewhere in this park. You wouldn't, um, happen to know where it is, would you?'

'Sure. It's just past the English garden – down that path there.' He pointed to a trail that led through the trees at the edge of the open field we were standing in.

I clasped my hands behind my back and swelled out my chest so that my titties and nippies stood out even more. 'Um, you couldn't, like, show me, could you? I don't wanna get lost or nuthin'.' I grinned at the man. 'You look like you know your way around.'

He smiled back at me, showing off his straight, white teeth.

And off we went down the bunny trail, me lagging slightly behind my masculine guide – so I could watch his tight buns clench and unclench underneath his tan shorts. And halfway through the woods, I 'tripped' on a tree root and went down in the dirt. 'Ooowww!' I mewled, plopping onto my butt and holding my poor little knee.

Blake quickly bent down to help me, caring, compassionate adult that he was. He examined my knee with his tender, knowing fingers. 'Just skinned it a bit, is what it looks like,' he said, so close my brain fogged up with his musky aftershave. Grinning, he added, 'Want me to kiss it better?'

'Would you!?' I blurted.

He stared at me, his Paul Newman eyes boring right inside me, making my pussy moisten even more. Then he bent his silver head down and kissed my scratch, his lips all warm and soft.

He helped me to my feet, and I needed his help. Needed a lot more of his kind of help. So, I accidentally-on-purpose stumbled up against the man, pressing my brimming bod into his hard body. I flung my arms around his neck and gazed up into his eyes, and my head went all dizzy and my stomach did cartwheels. Then I kissed him right on the mouth.

His strong arms instantly closed around my charged-up bod, his moist lips pressing against mine. I practically swooned in his rugged arms, really feeling his heat and inhaling his scent, my buzzing boobs squishing up against his manly chest.

He sure wasn't any dumbass boy you had to tell what to do, or how you felt. He knew exactly what to do, moving his lips on my lips, consuming them. Thrusting his thick tongue into my mouth and bumping it up against my tongue. We were full-on making out, frenching like it was language class.

His big, sure hands travelled down my shimmering bod and onto my bum, grasping and squeezing my buns. Just about lifting me right off the ground and into his mouth. I moaned my appreciation, riffling my sparkly-tipped fingers through his silvery mane. I could feel something hard – and getting harder, and longer – pressing into my belly.

We finally broke apart, both of us gasping for air.

'Maybe we'd, uh, better be getting back to the –'

I put a stop to that foolish gallantry by grabbing the guy's hand and dragging him off the beaten path and into the woods. There was this certain well-hidden spot of open grass I knew about, deep in the forest.

When we arrived at the tree-lined bed of grass, I pushed Blake up against a birch and literally tore his green polo shirt out of his shorts, ran my sweaty hands all over his hairy, muscle-humped chest. Then I fastened my glossy lips onto one of his hardened man-nipples and sucked.

'Christ!' he grunted, staring down at me excitedly feeling up his chest and sucking on his nipples.

I was a grrl on fire, the birds and the bees and that studly FILF right in front of me setting me ablaze with passion. I teased his rubbery nips with my tongue, sucked on them, bit into them. Then I clawed his shorts open and dropped down onto my knees in the grass, bringing his shorts and boxers right down with me.

His huge cock sprang out into my beaming face, hard and veiny and longer than any boy's I'd ever seen, or handled. I had to wrap both my hot little hands around it to get a good hold. Then I tugged.

'Yes, Brandi, yes!' the big man groaned, grabbing onto my pigtails and pulling my face closer to his snake.

'It's sooo big!' I marvelled, for his benefit and mine. I

opened up my mouth as wide as it would go and took his humungous purple hood inside.

He jerked against the tree, as I tugged on his cap with my lips. Still stroking his throbbing shaft with my hands. I could smell the sweat of his hairy balls, taste the salty pre-come leaking out of his slit, as I earnestly sucked on his hood. I gulped air into my lungs through my nose and closed my eyes and went deeper, gobbling up almost half of his pulsing pole in one huge swallow.

Blake bucked, banging his cap against the back of my throat. I gagged, and snot bubbled out of my nose, the man's awesome cock filling my mouth like it'd never been filled before. I started moving my head back and forth, sliding my lips, my mouth up and down on his prick, blowing the guy.

He tightened his grip on my pigtails and started pumping his hips, fucking my mouth. And I didn't gag any more when he boinked the back of my throat, although tears started streaming down my face – tears of joy. The guy tasted absolutely yummy! I could hardly wait to get his great big cock inside my cunny.

I held onto the base of his pumping shaft with one hand and played with his balls with the other. They were huge and heavy and furry, and he groaned when I squeezed them, stuck his cock almost right down my throat.

Then he suddenly pushed me back, and his gleaming pipe flopped out of my mouth with a wet pop. I tumbled over onto my back in the grass, my mouth and heart feeling all empty. I was worried maybe the guy was having second thoughts or something, 'cause I was so young and he was so old.

But I should've known better. Like I said before, men – real men – aren't just in it for their own pleasure; they know that if they want to keep a girl coming back, they've got to keep her coming, period. Blake wasn't about to just blow and go. He was going to return my lovin' – with interest!

He stripped off his shirt and stepped out of his shorts and underwear. Then bent down and hooked his fingers into my teensy shorts and pulled them off of my legs and away from my sneakers, as I arched my bum off the ground. My cunny was bare and smooth and wet, and Blake stared at it for a second before draping his hot naked body over mine and sliding his cock inside me. Smooth as silk and twice as sensual.

'Yeah, fuck me, Mr Comeau! Please, fuck me!' I squealed in my little-girl voice, thrilling at the feel of his big cock deep inside of me.

Blake yanked my tube-top down and my titties sprang out, pink nipples buzzing like the insects all around. He grabbed and groped the shimmering flesh, twirling his tongue all around my swollen buds. I squeaked with delight. And when he started pumping his hips, sliding his prick back and forth in my electrified cunny, I screamed my head off, it felt so wonderful.

I thought I was maybe going to pass out or something. But I stayed conscious, clinging to Blake's neck and shivering with each powerful thrust of his pistoning cock, his heavy hands and thick, wet lips and tongue on my tingling boobs driving me wild. We were glued together by hot sticky sweat, my quivering bod gone molten.

Blake sucked my tits and fucked my cunny. And I let go of his vein-popped neck and grabbed onto his flexing butt cheeks, digging my fingernails into the hairy skin and urging him on. He covered my mouth with his mouth, jamming his tongue inside and right down my throat, pumping my pussy non-stop with his prick 'til I just couldn't take it any more.

One orgasm, two orgasms jolted me like lightning bolts. My first multiple ever! Wet, hot bliss welled up from my cock-churned cunny and tidal-waved through my shuddering bod, again and again and again.

I think I did lose consciousness for a second, the wicked sensations were so overwhelming; so totally adult.

The man was absolutely relentless, squeezing my boobs and kissing my mouth and pounding my cunny, taking this little FILF-hunter body and soul.

Until finally – finally! – Blake grunted into my open mouth and erupted his own lust inside my tunnel, hot jism coating my insides. Spurt after spurt after spurt. Pumping and spurting, my hands slipping on his sweaty cheeks, his hot breath flooding my burning face. Both of us moaning and groaning and humping out in the great outdoors like a pair of wild animals.

It took us about five minutes just to recover our strength. Then we came apart with a squishy, satisfied pop and climbed to our feet and put our clothes back on. I tucked Blake's slick dangling pleasure tool back into his shorts for him, giving it one final squeeze of affection before we headed back to the picnic.

Turns out, Mr Comeau was actually my dad's new boss. So I had to hook up with him a few more times, right? To make sure he treated my dad right.

Well, he treated both me and my dad great. For a while. Until his fat nosy wife came home from visiting her parents early one day and caught the two of us in the shower together. Blake had his soapy cock halfway up my bum, so it was kind of obvious even to his stupid wife that we were more than just friends.

Dad got fired. And Blake broke up with me. But I know dad can find another job – he *is* overqualified, after all. And you better believe I'm going to find me another FILF. Because once you've had man, you'll never settle for boy again.

– Brandi, Austin TX, USA

Waitress Service

During the long hot summer of 2003 I fell into a fling with a man who owned a seafront trattoria. I had a weakness for handsome lechers, and he was both handsome – with the standard Italian-stallion fixtures and fittings – and a lecher, bending down over my chair to whisper into my ear that probably nobody else had noticed, but did I realise that the elastic in my hold-up stocking had snapped and it was sliding down my thigh? I need not have affected the modest panic that I did; he smiled at my discomposure and remarked, 'Legs like yours should be shown off.' His cheap compliment, coupled with the predatory gleam in his eye, was enough to reel me in and we went to the neighbouring nightclub after closing, ending up on the beach with my skirt around my waist and his hand in my knickers.

For a while after that we fell into a pattern of meeting up after closing three or four nights a week. He was a masterful, somewhat possessive, lover and it soon became clear that he had a particular penchant for showing off his acquisitions. If we went to a nightclub, much of our time on the dance floor would be spent with one of his hands inside my top and the other on the taut seat of the short tight skirt he liked me to wear. At first I baulked, took a step away, looking around to ascertain how many of the swaying patrons had spotted us, but he pulled me firmly back and, despite the initial prickle of shame, I had to admit to myself that I found it arousing, often imagining continuations of the scenario when I was alone in bed. Once our smoochy dancing was over, usually ending with his hand nudging the hem of my skirt gently upwards so that the lacy top of my stockings were visible to all, he would find the corner of the club most accessible to the security cameras and push me up against the wall there, tongue down throat, knee shoved between my thighs, fingers creeping upward until they found the elastic of my knickers and slipped inside. That was when I was wearing any knickers, of course. For the first week, I would furiously avoid the eyes of the doormen as we left, but later on I would deliberately take in their knowing smiles and offer one in return.

Three weeks in, I was bent over the restaurant counter recovering my senses after being banged halfway to oblivion. Despite the late hour, a few people drifted up and down the esplanade outside and, had they thought to look through the uncurtained picture windows, they would have seen me, red in the face, breasts pressed against the counter with my lover standing four square behind me, pounding into me with his hands on my shoulders. He liked to point this out during sex: 'Do you think they can see you? Do you think a crowd is gathering outside, watching you and talking about what a slut you are, how much you love to take my big hard cock inside you so much that you don't bother to close the curtains? Eh? Eh?' – each insistent 'eh' punctuated by a thrust so hard I would gasp, or try to grip the ledge tighter for purchase, upsetting the tip jar in the process.

On this occasion it was taking longer than usual to recover my breath and I flopped raggedly, conscious of my lover readjusting his clothing to the side of me. He began to tidy up the paraphernalia on the counter, fussing and tutting a little as if the cause of the disarray were nothing to do with him, and then returned to a subject he had jokingly brought up a few times.

'You know, you really should work for me. I could use a waitress like you. Bring the punters in, eh?' I resisted the temptation to point out that he was already using me to the fullest extent and thought seriously, for the first time, about his proposition. I was doing odd office temp jobs, waiting to start my Masters at the end of September. My evenings were free and the extra money might be handy. I pushed myself up from my prone position and accepted his offer, rather to his surprise. But as soon as the words were out of my mouth, I could see the calculations ticking away behind his eyes. He had plans for me that would go beyond the scribbling of orders and uncorking of bottles.

When I arrived for my first shift, I felt a little awkward. The kitchen and waiting staff all knew about my relationship with their boss; indeed, some of them had heard the muffled sound of our couplings in the tiny backroom he used as an office. They were mostly friendly, in a curious sort of way, but one of the waitresses looked down her knowing nose at me. Probably jealous, I thought. My lover was a catch, in a certain way, though I knew it would never be serious between us.

The waiting staff wore traditional black-and-whites, and my lover had instructed me to go and collect mine in his office. The girls wore white cotton blouses, knee-length black skirts, black tights and black pumps with a low heel. I was somewhat startled then, when my own uniform turned out to be quite a variation on this theme. My blouse was white, but it was not cotton – it was a semi-transparent cheap nylon, buttoning up to the point where my cleavage started, leaving a small area of my white lace bra visible over the top. The skirt was substantially shorter than the standard version, its hem brushing the tops of the sheer seamed stockings I had been ordered to wear, so that the slightest tilt forward would reveal the suspender snaps and a flash of white thigh. The black pumps were of glossy patent leather and boasted four-inch stiletto heels. Stepping into them, I felt my arse and chest thrust rudely outwards, and as the skirt was a size too small for me, its shiny polyester fabric almost split across my straining bum.

'My God,' my lover said admiringly. 'You must be careful with those shoes. If you stand the wrong way, they will reflect your pussy.'

Glancing down, I could see that he was right – the edges of my skirt and my staring face were reflected in the leather.

'Why can't I wear what the other girls wear? This makes me look like a hooker.'

'I haven't hired you to be a respectable waitress, *bella*. I want you to look like the slut you are, to get the men's attention and bring them back for more. I want you to flirt, to tease them. Especially the older richer men. Stay away from the tables full of women. You are selling your body.'

The idea was arousing. A whore by proxy, spending my evenings being fantasised over by middle-aged men who would have to cover their laps with the menus while they ordered. All the same, I was nervous of the prospect, and of the probable ridicule and opprobrium I might face from my colleagues and members of the public. Indeed, had this been my home town, rather than a stop-gap between graduation and further study, I would probably not have gone along with his scheme. But I had no reputation to preserve here and nobody to tattle on me to friends or family. So I let the full sensual potential of it captivate me and posed tartily in the mirror for a while, my lover looking on with a broad smile until he tired of watching, landed a ringing slap on my tightly-skirted behind and told me to put on my make-up. 'Lots of it. I want you to look like a prostitute.'

That first shift was difficult in some ways – there was a great deal of staring, of whispering behind hands and bitchy comments from female customers, not to mention the unfriendly waitress. But in others, I had never felt sexier or more powerful. I had the male customers in the palm of my hand; my Monroesque wiggle across the restaurant was followed by dozens of longing pairs of eyes and I relished my role, leaning forward over tables until my cleavage was inches from a nose while the back of my thighs and stocking tops were lewdly exposed to the tables behind me.

'You look like a very naughty girl,' murmured one elderly gent to me while I served him and his friend brandy to go with their cigars (this being long before the smoking ban).

'Oh, I am,' I winked, and the way he jerked in his seat confirmed that he liked this answer.

'I should take you over my knee and give you a good spanking,' he told me and I giggled, moving swiftly on. He left me a fifty-pound tip.

When I told my lover of this comment, he took it upon himself to administer the threatened punishment, bending me over his office desk and reddening my bottom while he described to me how he had spent the entire evening afraid to move from behind the counter, so turned on had he been by my performance. 'You hot little slut,' he snarled. 'Spread your legs.' He fucked me like a madman, pistoning his hard cock in and out of my pussy while his hand continued to smack away at my sore arse until I came harder than I could ever remember. Then he tucked a wad of banknotes into the crotch of my knickers, making me walk home with the dry paper scrunching against my wet pussy. It seemed this arrangement was working for both of us.

By the end of the first week, business had taken a definite upswing. The restaurant had always had a convivial atmosphere and was popular with large groups of revellers celebrating birthdays and stag nights and sporting victories, but bookings were now 30% up on the equivalent time last year, or so my employer told me.

And one noticeable feature of the parties we were hosting was that they were overwhelmingly male. I would hear the susurration of whispered comments early in the evening – 'Check out that arse', 'You can practically see her nips', 'Drop your fork and get her to bend over to pick it up' – then I would walk into the kitchen and hear a different tenor of remark, mainly in the slag-bitch-slapper vein. Later on in the restaurant all pretence of subtlety would vanish along with the sloppy spaghetti and chianti, and it would be 'Sit on my knee, darling', 'Nice pair! You got a sister?' and so on. The rule, however, was that they could look all they wanted, but they could never touch. My lover might like to show me off, but at heart he was the classic possessive hot-blood and any straying of strange fingers would result in swift ejection from the premises.

Despite this, he would up the ante over the course of the successive weeks, his seeming intention being to drive the horny punters over the edge. Before each shift I would be summoned to his office, where he may or may not issue a new variation on my uniform or demeanour. At first, he asked me to undo the top two buttons of my blouse, so that a full decolletage was visible between the scalloped lace of my bra. If anybody mentioned it, I was to act flustered, as if it had happened accidentally. The last time I did, one gentleman leaned forward and, ever so gently, ever so sweetly, buttoned them back up for me. That night, my lover took me up the arse for the first time, quite forcefully. He meant me to understand that I was not to allow such attentions. And yet his orders continued. I was to eschew my bra one night and serve tables with my nipples brushing against the staticky gauze of the blouse, which caused them to stand to attention rather visibly for most of the evening. On one memorable shift, he unfastened my blouse, cut off my bra and then sucked my nipples until they were rosy-stiff and sore, finally anointing them with two drops of red wine. I spent the next five hours with two blush-pink stains drawing attention to the swollen bullets; I had never been more stared at in my life. So far.

Satisfied that he had subjected my breasts to sufficient public scrutiny, my lover then went to work lower down. After the second week, I became resigned to the idea that I would be spending most shifts with no knickers on, but there would be differences in the quality of the nakedness. Sometimes I would be made to masturbate before starting work so that the aroma of my juices lingered and mingled with the cooking smells as I leaned across the tables. Sometimes my pussy and thighs would be slick with his spunk after a pre-work fucking, and one mortifying night he came all over my bottom and pulled the skirt straight down over it so that a large round damp patch showed through the straining fabric. I begged him not to do that again, even though it was one of the things I thought about most often while getting myself off in later years.

By the time September came around, I was addled by the intensity of it. The sex was outrageous and the restaurant was heaving every night with voyeurs. Some would be verbally abusive, but most were complimentary, overworking their charm to get an appointment in my non-existent knickers which was never forthcoming.

I suppose I was expecting it – almost waiting for it to happen, in a way – but one Saturday in September he finally went too far. Although the holiday season was in its final throes, there had been no slowdown in reservations, and on this particular night we were entertaining a football team, two stag parties and a variety of smaller male groups. Prior to the shift, my lover and I had our customary meeting in the office, which had consisted of bending me over the desk, easing up the fearfully tight skirt to my waist and lubricating my anus until it was able to take a medium-sized butt-plug, which I was to keep in place until the end of the night, when it would be removed and replaced with his cock. Once the skirt was back in place, there was a telltale protrusion that might or might not give the game away to the customers, depending how familiar they were with this kind of toy. I wriggled my bum in the mirror, trying to develop a walk that would make it less obvious, but no matter what, tonight my stilettoed sashay was going to be more like a waddle.

I had never done this before, and I found myself resenting my lover for making me do it. Much of what he usually made me do was humiliating to an extent, but at least I was able to look and feel sexy while I was being humiliated. The butt-plug made me feel vulnerable and ridiculous, as well as being very uncomfortable. I enjoyed the feeling of fullness that accompanied anal sex, but this was not the same. To make matters worse, as soon as I tottered out to the tables, I saw that That Guy was here again. That Guy was a startlingly handsome man whose cricket team ate at the restaurant fortnightly. He had never tried to pressure me, but had flirted with me in an understated way that nonetheless made my pussy tingle on each occasion. I did not want him to see me like this, but I bit down on my lip and tried to ignore the stretching intruder in my back passage as best I could.

I think he could sense my discomfort, and greeted me with a warm, supportive smile when I took the order and served the wine. As I bent down to place his Chicken Cacciatore before him, I felt the shock of his hand on my skirt, gently pressing at the base of the butt-plug. I could hardly breathe. 'Is this what I think it is?' he asked softly. I nodded, caught completely off-guard. 'Once I've eaten this, I want you to be waiting for me in the cloakroom. Is that clear?'

So this was the natural conclusion of our exhibitionistic games. Assumptions about me were being made, and I wasn't sure I liked them. I liked to show off, to drive the men wild, to please my lover in this way – but when it came down to it, I did not want to be the town bike, giving freebies to all and sundry because short skirt equals easy lay. It was like a bucket of iced water over my rampant libido, and I shook my head, red-faced.

'Are you playing hard to get, love? Because believe me, with that whore's get-up you almost wear every night, it won't wash. Don't pretend to be anything more than a slut who wants it badly.'

'You're wrong,' I hissed, but That Guy – clearly no gentleman – had his large batsman's hand all over my shiny rump, and what was more, he had an audience. The worst possible audience. My lover and the hostile waitress, both with arms folded, watching.

'See. Told you. Slut,' said the waitress, and at first I thought she was talking to my lover, but with mounting horror I realised that she was in fact talking to That Guy, who raised his eyebrows at her while he slapped my bum.

My lover pointed through to the office and I followed him there, pleading my case, assuring him that the advances had been unwanted, but he did not want to listen. Eventually the argument became heated, then passionate, and we had one last wild rut on the desk before I told him to screw his job and flounced out.

I was sent on my way that night with a ripped blouse, split-seamed skirt, one missing heel, spunk-soaked pussy, plug still in place. I made quite a picture, walking down the busy Esplanade to my bedsit. I suppose it was a shame we didn't part on better terms but I didn't take it to heart. Besides, I was leaving at the end of the month.

I passed through town again a few years ago and found myself walking down to the Trattoria. It is now a Thai takeaway. I like to think that the business never recovered from losing its sex-doll waitress, though I'll probably never know if there's any truth in that. All the same, I'm willing to bet I'm still talked about in certain locker rooms.

– *Abigail, Maidstone, UK*

98

Whose Cock Is It Anyway?

I'm not a slut or anything. This just happened because the mood was right that night. It started when my boyfriend, Tony, was supposed to be going out to the match with some friends. Including Tony there were five guys sitting in our front room – their plans had been spoilt because Tony's car died and none of the others were able to drive them all to the stadium. So, since there was a match being shown on the TV, and we had some beers in, they decided to stay at ours and watch the telly.

I was watching too, although I was also using my mobile to call a couple of girlfriends. It seemed like a fairly relaxed evening and I was sharing Tony's beer, which was probably what made me need to go for a pee.

When I got back from the loo all five of them were sniggering. I asked what was so funny but none of them would tell me. I have to admit, I was getting peeved until Tony told me to check the pictures on my mobile. I did as he said and found there were five new photographs on my mobile.

Each photo showed a different cock.

'What the fuck is this?' I asked.

'We thought you'd like some new pictures for your mobile,' Tony laughed. All his mates laughed with him.

'It's a guessing game for blondes,' his friend Alan told me. 'You've got to guess whose cock is which.'

I bristled at the remark about blondes. I said, 'I can guess which is yours, Alan. That would be the really tiny one.'

They all laughed at that – even Alan.

And while we were all laughing, I couldn't stop myself from scrolling through the pictures of five cocks. Two of them were hard, two were soft and one was sporting a semi erection. Looking at them, knowing the owners of those cocks were all sitting in front of me, watching me, was quite a turn-on.

'What do you think?' Tony asked. 'Do you think you can guess whose cock is which?'

I shrugged and said it should be easy enough.

'Will you pay a forfeit if you guess wrong?' Alan asked. When I asked what sort of forfeit he said, 'If you guess wrong, you've got to take off an item of clothing.'

They all laughed at the idea, and started to cheer enthusiastically. Tony was cheering loudest of all so I figured he would be cool with it and I said, 'What's in it for me?'

We haggled for a while and eventually decided I would get one shot at each picture. If I guessed wrong, I'd have to take off an item of clothing. If I guessed right that guy had to get his cock out to prove I was right. (There was money involved too but it's bad enough I'm sounding like a slut here without making myself out to be a prozzer too.)

So we all got another beer. The match was forgotten by this point as I sat in front of the guys, scrolling through the pictures on my mobile and trying to work out which cock belonged to which of the guests. It was really sexy looking at the pictures, knowing that I was seeing the cocks of the guys sitting in front of me. My pussy was oozing with excitement but I figured I would show them that I was in control. I pointed at Tony's picture and said that was his cock.

Alan said that was a cheat, and that I was bound to know what Tony's cock looked like since I'd been living with him for the last year. But Tony was good-natured about it. He agreed it was his cock, and stepped out of his jeans to prove it. That stopped the laughter.

Suddenly the mood became tense with anticipation.

I deliberately messed up the next two guesses. Seeing Tony standing naked had made me realise how much fun we could have with the evening and I wanted to exploit that to the full. I guessed that the short, stubby soft cock belonged to Jack. I could see that it didn't. The cock on my camera was almost hidden by a forest of thick black pubes and Jack is blond. When I then said the next picture belonged to Carl I was left sitting in front of our guests wearing only my bra and a thong. Apart from Tony, all the lads were fully dressed but they were shifting uncomfortably in their seats. I could see they were all trying to hide the bulges of the erections they were sprouting and I quietly sympathised. I have to admit I was very turned on by that point but I was trying to play the situation to my own advantage.

'Two left,' Alan pointed out. 'And I think that's the biggest and the smallest, isn't it?' He had this really smug grin on his face and asked, 'Do you still think mine is the tiny one?'

I scrolled to the picture that showed a thick, long cock being held in one hand. Aside from the cock and the hand there was very little else to see in the picture. The only other thing I could make out was the edge of a wristwatch that looked exactly like Alan's fake Rolex.

'That's your cock,' I told him. 'Now get it out and prove I'm right.'

'Are you sure?' he asked. 'Do you want to make the bet more interesting?'

I shrugged and said OK. 'If I'm wrong, I'll take off everything,' I told him. 'But if I'm right, everyone else here has got to get their cocks out.'

He didn't bother checking with the others. He just said OK and started to undo his flies.

Even though I was right, I learned that night that I would never want to play poker against Alan. He kept up the pretence that I was wrong right until the moment that he stepped out of his jeans and revealed his enormous hard on. It was almost double the length of some of those in the photos. It was a cock worthy of being in a porn movie. He leaned close to me, put one hand on my bare side, pressed his mouth against my ear and whispered, 'Well done.'

That would have been exciting enough, but the fact that his exposed erection was swaying between us made my pussy start to clench with hunger.

'I win!' I cried. 'Come on, boys. Show me all what you've got.'

There were a few protests from the remaining three guys but, when Alan and Tony insisted, they took off their clothes.

I hadn't thought it would be possible to feel over-dressed whilst only wearing my bra and thong. But, faced with five naked men, I felt a little uneasy. Tony put a hand on my backside and told me that we wouldn't do anything I didn't feel comfortable doing. That made me relax and I kissed him gratefully.

The other boys cheered at that and Carl asked if he could have a kiss too.

Alan asked if I was going to keep myself covered up and I told him I might lose my bra and panties before the end of the night.

Someone asked what I was going to do now I'd got all of them with their cocks out and I said I was thinking of fucking one of them. It was a totally outrageous thing to say and I have to admit I almost came from my own boldness when I said it.

'Which one of us?' Alan asked.

'Whichever one of you can perform best,' I told him. I wanted to reach out and squeeze his big thick cock whilst I was saying the words but I kept my hands to myself. Looking at them all, I said, 'I want you each to start jerking off. First one to come gets to fuck me.'

No one responded.

Carl said that I was unlikely to get the best performer by picking the guy who came first but I just told him he was wasting valuable time. That got all of them clutching their cocks and tugging swiftly. Alan asked if I was going to remove my bra and panties, to give them some inspiration. He was wanking himself quickly as he asked the question. I unhooked my bra, let it fall away from chest, and then stepped out of my thong.

Tony spurted.

A couple of the boys complained that it wasn't fair that Tony had come first, and that he got to fuck me regularly, but I ignored them. Getting down on my knees, wiggling my bare arse for the rest of them, I sucked Tony hard again so he was ready to fuck me.

'Is there any point us carrying on?' Alan asked.

I had my mouth around Tony's cock when I looked at him. He was still stroking his length. All the others were staring at me with their dicks in their hands. I was really excited by the control I had over them and I said, 'I might have a special prize for whoever comes next.'

Instantly, the four of them were jerking vigorously. I looked up at Tony to see if he approved of my idea but I already knew he approved. His cock had grown immediately hard when I mentioned the 'special prize' and I knew he was anxious to see me playing with at least one of the others.

With Tony hard I straddled him in his chair and began to ride up and down. The others were wanking furiously and I got a real thrill from seeing their hungry gazes stare at me while they jerked off. Alan had remained standing while he pulled himself. He came closer to me as I slid up and down Tony's length.

'Do you want me to come on your tits?' he grunted.

I didn't get a chance to reply before he was splashing a white load of come across my neck and breasts. I was surprised by how much he came. I also loved the sensation of his hot seed dripping down my bare flesh.

'You really want that special prize, don't you?' I laughed.

He was looking at his own come dripping from my nipples. Because I could tell the sight excited him, I rubbed my palm against my breast and smeared the come over them until they were glossy. Carl stepped over while I was stroking myself and sprayed his load across my breasts. He wasn't as good with his aim as Alan (or maybe he was better?) and some of it splashed across my face. Then Jack and finally David joined us and also spurted. I was dripping with come and I don't think I've ever felt hornier or more aroused. I rubbed their mingled spunk into my breasts, disgusted by the fishy stench of it, and loving the idea that I was being so dirty. In a voice that was loud enough for all of them to hear I told Tony, 'Hurry up and come, darling, I think Alan is desperate to have sloppy seconds when he fills my cunt.'

Tony came instantaneously. I had a rush of pleasure that was almost orgasmic. And I watched the four spent cocks in front of me start twitching back to life.

The evening came to an end an hour or two after that. I eventually took all of them – one after the other. By the time Alan was fucking me for the second time my pussy felt loose and stretched and greasy. Before leaving, Alan made everyone promise that we wouldn't talk about what we'd done – not to anyone. He said he wasn't just saying it for my benefit – a couple of the lads had girlfriends who would go ballistic if they found out what we'd been up to. And, although there have been a couple of rumours floating around, I think the majority of them stayed true to their word and kept the secret.

Tony and I are still together and the sex remains good, even though he's never mentioned that night since it happened. Not that I mind too much about the incident being a secret because I still have the photos of those five wonderful cocks stored safely on my phone. I occasionally look at them and remember what we did. And it always gets my pussy sopping wet.

– *Janine, Southampton, UK*

Pool Room Hustle

Us T-girls always have to work that little bit harder. Without a shorter skirt, a bigger bust, much longer legs and a perfectly made-up face, it's almost impossible for a tranny to seduce a straight guy, let alone have a proper relationship with one. I'm not talking about tranny admirers here. There are plenty of men out there – and God bless them for it – who'll sleep with any guy whose favourite apparel consists of stockings, heels and a baby doll. No, I'm talking about straight guys, everyday guys; the type who've never even met a crossdresser before. A tranny has to work really hard to get those guys, but some of us are convincing enough to succeed.

I suppose I have an advantage over most other trannies in that I'm only 5 feet 6 inches tall. My height doesn't give the game away as soon as someone sees me, although I'm not going to exaggerate – even though I make a good-looking woman, most people still quickly guess my secret. I've been taking hormones since my teens, and I've even had a boob job, but there are certain things I'll never be able to hide. They don't make me look any less pretty, I think, but they do suggest my previous life. Looking really close, he's in there somewhere – the little boy I used to be!

That's why I'll always have to work much harder – why I'll always have to be willing to dress like a slut. Heading to the pub last Tuesday, I knew it was hopeless turning up in just a T-shirt and jeans. No one fucks a tranny who turns up wearing just a T-shirt and jeans. A tranny has to show off all her wares if she wants to prove how much of a woman she is!

It was quiet that night, so my entrance made quite an impact. The five or so guys drinking at the bar and the couple canoodling in the corner all looked up as I walked through the door. I was wearing strappy heels, which were noisy on the floorboards, and which drew attention to my long slim legs. My fishnet stockings drew attention, too, as did my thigh-skimming pleated skirt and skimpy top. The top had a decidedly plunging neckline, from which my two prize assets were spilling out. (They'd cost me a fortune, so I was hardly gonna hide them!)

Happy to be the centre of attention, I strode to the bar and asked the barman for a glass of white wine. I could tell everyone was still looking at me, which meant one of two things. They were either thinking 'What a slut!' or 'Shit, that girl is really a guy!' The back of the bar was mirrored, so I could sneakily watch their faces in the glass and read the confusion in their eyes.

I like my power to cause confusion, to blur the genders wherever I go. I know my breasts are firm and my legs are long, which means most men feel a superficial attraction towards me. I like that I can unnerve them that way and even make them doubt themselves. Straight men hate it when they're made to feel attracted to another man. So what if that other man might look more feminine than the wife back home? The damage has been done – they fancied a guy!

I giggled as the barman poured my wine, because I could see the Tuesday night drinkers feeling all that self-doubt. They were magnetised by my outward appearance, which was totally female and highly sexed. With my breasts being implants, they have a perfect shape and pertness about them, the likes of which you rarely see outside of a porn film. And my stocking-clad legs and long blond hair completed the picture of a nympho slut. The kind of slut they would have all liked to fuck, if it wasn't for that confusing, *dangerous* even, hint of boy within there somewhere.

None of these guys seemed able to get past it, so I picked up my wine and went into the pool room. They watched me disappear through the door, half-disappointed and half-relieved. Their one chance of getting laid that night had just upped and left, but at least they could go back to being hetero now!

I had heard the pool balls clattering together, so I knew I was going to find some new friends to play with. They looked up when they saw me enter; two young guys with big, strong bodies. They smiled at me, then at each other, a deathly silence hanging in the air. They'd done what all guys do when I walk in. They'd seen a cute young girl they wanted to fuck, then guessed my past life and got confused.

'What's up?' I said, keen to break the ice. 'You scared of being beaten by a girl?'

I walked up to the table and laid a fifty-pence piece down on the side, which told them I wanted to play the next frame.

'We're not scared,' said one guy, but whether he meant scared of being beaten by a girl or scared of being in a room with a tranny, I wasn't sure. He and his friend were still glancing nervously at each other. Also, at me – they seemed to like my breasts!

'Rack 'em up,' said the same guy, who seemed to be the louder and brasher of the two. He was speaking to his friend, who took my coin from the table and racked up the balls for the frame against me. I told them I'd take the pair of them on, then made a joke about being easily able to handle two guys at once. The guys looked at each other, then started to laugh. They were beginning to feel at ease with me.

'You break,' said the louder guy, adding his name was Tom and his friend's was Ed. He handed me his cue and

107

then stood behind me as I bent across the table and prepared to split the pack. As I got into position, I knew my skirt would ride high up my thighs, exposing the tops of my fishnet stockings. It was the act of a slut, but then a T-girl can't afford to mess around. I liked these guys and would have been glad to go home with either one of them, but I knew that would only be possible if I could make them see what was sexy and female about me, so maybe they'd then overlook the few remaining bits that were male.

'Nice shot,' said Tom, as I smacked open the pack and managed to pot both a yellow and a red. I smiled at him and then wandered round the table, but I wasn't looking for an easy pot. Having already flashed him my stocking tops, I now wanted a shot that would allow me to lean right across the table and give him a view down my cleavage-crack. My tits are such a gender fuck! It becomes so much harder not to think of me as a genuine woman once you've seen my perfect breasts.

I got down into position, then looked up at both guys, who were now standing right beside each other. They blushed when I caught them staring down my top, but it gave Tom a talking point, a way of raising the elephant in the room.

'Whatever you paid for them, it was worth it,' he said, so I thanked him for the compliment, then played my next shot. I was so glad he hadn't asked me if my tits were natural. I knew he knew I was born a guy, and I hate it when men pretend they haven't noticed when I know for sure they have.

'So, how long have you known you wanted to be a woman?' Ed then asked, and I could see him start relaxing now the subject was out in the open.

'All my life,' I answered, then the slut in me kicked in again. 'Just like I've always known I fancied guys.'

I had missed my last shot, so Tom approached the table and lined up a red to the middle pocket. My previous comment was still hanging in the air. I had given them a teasing look as I'd said it, letting them know they were in with a chance.

'So, where do you go to meet guys?' Tom asked, then he took his shot, but hit it too hard.

'I come here,' I said, then I laid my cue down on the table. 'And I meant what I said earlier about being able to handle two guys at once.'

Sometimes I just can't believe the things that come out of my mouth. It's like I'm always having to sell myself, having to let people know exactly where they stand with me. That's why most trannies stick with admirers, because those guys understand that a T-girl should be treated just like any other woman. But other men don't know how to behave around us. Often they're even too scared to flirt. And as for seeing us just as regular girls to hug and kiss and grope and fuck, well, it's just too much for their heads to cope with. A chick with a dick? It just blows their minds.

Tom and Ed took another look at each other, like they were both still uncertain how serious I was. I seemed to be offering my body to them – my long slender legs and perfect breasts – but they just couldn't get over the formerly-a-guy thing. Had a real girl walked in dressed as I was, then leaned across the pool table and flashed them so much flesh, then you can bet they'd have already been fucking her senseless. She wouldn't have had to spell it out in so much detail, so it was lucky for them that I was used to working extra hard.

'Fancy trying something new?' I asked, speaking mainly to Tom, since I could tell he was the alpha-male. I was almost issuing a challenge to his manhood. Daring him to take a risk.

He stared at me, then back at his friend, an I-will-if-you-will glint in his eye. I turned my attention to Ed now, knowing it was vital to convince them both. Neither of them would have had the balls to fuck me without his friend there, but if they did it together, it would be like sharing an exotic erotic adventure. More importantly, it would be like making a compact between them. If just one of them did it, then the other might gossip. But if they had me together, then the secret would be shared and kept.

'Why not bolt the door?' I suggested to Ed, my blue eyes twinkling up at him. I could tell he liked my blond hair, legs and breasts by the way he couldn't stop staring at me. I had noticed his dick getting stiff, as well. He already had a semi on, so it was no surprise that he did as I said.

As he walked to the door and fixed the bolt, all three of us knew it was going to happen. There was no need for me to sell myself any more, or do all the usual lines about chicks with dicks giving the best head ever, because they've got dicks themselves so they know how to treat one; and we don't have pussies, so it's anal guaranteed; and you don't have to worry we're faking it, because we squirt out sticky stuff just like you!

I would have done whatever it took to get laid, but these guys hadn't needed much persuading. With the door secured, Tom walked nearer to me, grinning as I rubbed the front of his crotch. Then Ed came and joined us, so I started manhandling them both at once, just stroking their dicks through their trousers and pants. Already Tom was eager to kiss me, but I didn't let him have all the fun for too long. I was aware of the compact that had been made between them – the secret they would share forever – so I quickly transferred my attentions to Ed, getting them both in equally deep.

Quiet guy Ed was a beautiful kisser, his tongue flicking in and out of my mouth. I unzipped his flies, as his passion mounted, then pulled his prick out of his boxer shorts. It was fully rigid, which gave me such a high, because I love it when I make a straight guy stiff. It proves I look and know how to behave just like a genuine woman. It shows my powers of female seduction are as good as those of any real girl.

'Sit on the table,' I said to Ed, then I turned and faced his louder friend. More confident than his pal, Tom reached out and grabbed me, kissing and groping me both at once. His hands slipped down the back of my skirt, his fingers cupping my naked arse cheeks. With me only wearing a tiny thong, there was plenty of bare flesh for Tom to get to grips with, although the way he started fingering my arse-crack suggested he was more interested in finding where I'd hidden my cock.

But I'm not well-hung, so I don't hide my cock. It barely creates a bulge at all. But the same could not be said for Tom, who was growing bigger and bigger with each passing moment. I could feel his hardness digging into me, so I undid his flies and pulled out his dick. I had a condom in my handbag, which I then fixed to his swollen cock, less for protection and more for the lube that he'd need to penetrate my arse.

Tom was so aggressive, the alpha-male, so I'd already decided to give him my arse. Meanwhile, Ed was sitting on the pool table, his manhood gripped within one hand. I leaned towards his rock-hard cock and took the head within my mouth, which made my bum stick up in the air. My pleated skirt rode above my stocking tops, then above my thong, as I consumed Ed's length.

I pursed my lips around his helmet, then thrust them all the way down his shaft. My nose ended up in his pubic hair, and I was pleased to know I could take his full length inside my mouth. Having seen the size of Tom's erection, I was less convinced I could handle that, but at least the condom was highly lubed. He stood behind me, then tugged aside the strap of my thong, before pressing his helmet against my ring.

Tom gripped his hands around my waist and then powered his manhood between my cheeks. I would have yelled, but I was too busy sucking, so I internalised the sexual tension and then took it all out on the prick in my mouth. I thrust my lips up and down Ed's stem, my tongue flicking here, there and everywhere, while Tom drove his cock in and out of my arse. He'd probably never fucked an arsehole before, so I could forgive him for being over-excited, and the speed and power of his passionate thrusting certainly suggested he was just that!

Unconcerned by the tightness of my orifice, or the extreme degree of friction, Tom hammered his manhood back and forth. I could hear him heavy breathing as he struggled to maintain his rapid tempo, but with a cock in my mouth, I couldn't tell him to slow down, and anyway I was starting to enjoy the high-speed fucking. The greasy lube on the condom had made my anus wet and pliable, meaning I could handle whatever he threw at me. And better still, his bulbous cockhead seemed to have located my anal G-spot, my prostate gland, and every time his helmet went surging past it, a spasm of pleasure shot through my arse.

I gazed up at Ed, still with his dick between my lips, then noticed him staring towards his pal. They were smiling at each other, like they couldn't believe how lucky they were, each balls-deep in a clinging wet orifice. My lips were locked tight around the base of Ed's phallus, then again Tom thrust his full length between my cheeks. It left me plugged from both ends at once, the two dicks inside me validating my gender choice. There, right at that moment, I could not have been more female. I even sensed my two strong lovers had forgotten I was a T-girl. I was now just a slut! A total whore! A fantasy fuck from their wettest dreams!

In fact, even with my dick now hard, I still felt utterly, deliciously femme. The cock slamming in and out of my rectum was making my tits bounce up and down, and I could feel my nipples starting to throb. I wanted one of the guys to touch them, so I tugged down my top, then waited to see who'd get there first. They both made a move, but Ed was quickest, taking my curves in the palms of his hands and then tightening his fingers around my teats.

With cocks in both my mouth and butt, and now my nipples being played with, I was in danger of experiencing a sensory overload. The guys were pleasuring all my erogenous zones, except for the one they were probably too afraid to touch, so I stuck a hand inside my thong and took care of it myself. My cock was already alive with tension, electric tingles shooting through my head. It hadn't been sucked like Ed's had, or fucked an arsehole like Tom's, but it was as close to a climax as either of theirs.

I jerked my phallus hard and fast, while thrusting my lips up and down Ed's cock. I could feel the spasms surging through him, telling me I'd soon be tasting spunk. Tom's dick was still thumping in and out of my anus, then a sudden, final forward charge brought his rapid thrusting to an end. He jammed his helmet deep inside my body, groaning as he spilled his seed. His pulsing made my anus throb, my muscles convulsing around his length.

I lashed the fuck out of Ed's hard helmet as the throbbing in my arsehole sent me wild with lust. My hand was clutching tighter to my prick, the tingle in my cockhead now almost there. Anything could have set off my climax right then – a kiss on the lips or an arse-numbing spank – but it was the rich shower of spunk bursting out of Ed's helmet that finally tipped the balance.

I gripped my lips around his helmet, then pressed the tip of my tongue against his slit. I felt the climactic pressure as his come spewed out, multiple jets of creamy jism splattering against the roof of my mouth. With Tom's dick still spitting out spunk in my arse, I was now being creamed from both ends at once, the thought of which was enough to make a lava-rush of semen spew from my head. I felt the warm waves of come gushing over my fingers, as the double-entry penetration took me there, then my wank grew noisy, the come on my fingers squelching with each new jerk of my wrist.

I spat out Ed's dick, now desperate to scream, but swallowed as much of the scream as I could. Back out in the bar, the jukebox was playing, but I still couldn't afford to make too much noise. So, to gag myself, I took Ed's helmet back between my lips and then slid them right along his shaft. His cock was still alive with orgasmic excitement, as was the rigid length in my arse.

But the biggest tingles were within my hand, which was still wrapped tight around my satisfied cock. Knowing I'd made both Tom and Ed climax had given me a thrill like never before, since both were such robustly heterosexual men – the type who could only ever be satisfied by a genuine girl. It wasn't like they were tranny-chasers, which made it so much more special for me, because I don't want to be somebody's fetish. I'd pulled two men who only liked real girls. Sure, I might have had to work that little bit harder, but my efforts had got their just rewards.

– *Lesley, Burnley, UK*

Under New Management

It happened on a Friday evening in the office after an interminable day. I work as secretary at the local branch of a nationwide firm in the construction industry. As soon as the computers crashed I waited for a couple of hours and then sent the rest of the girls home, telling them that nothing was going to happen until Monday morning. I hung around, just in case the IT manager was able to resolve the problem, but I figured it was going to take forever. So much of the office work relies on computers that I had nothing to do as I waited for the IT manager to call and say the network was back online. By the time the clock was pushing 5:30, I was bored out of my mind and more than ready to go home and have a relaxing weekend. I'd just reached for my coat when George, the boss, popped his head through my door.

'Can you get those invoices onto the purchase ledger before you leave?' he asked.

'No,' I told him. 'The computers are down.'

He frowned and then shook his head. 'They're not,' he insisted. 'IT got them back online at lunch-time. Didn't you get that message?'

I was angry that he hadn't passed on the message and annoyed that he expected me to stay late on a Friday evening. 'I'm not staying to do it now,' I told him. 'Not even if you get down on your knees and beg me.'

'Is that what you want?' George asked.

Before I knew what was happening he had fallen to his knees and was clasping his hands together. Pretending to beg he said, 'Oh! Please, Tina. I need you to do this for me. I need you to do this for me.'

I glared at him and said, 'You'll need to grovel a damned sight better than that.'

He stared up at me uncertainly. Whilst he'd been joking before he now looked less confident. 'What do you mean?'

I was wearing a pair of four-inch heels with black stockings. Seeing George on his knees was not something I had previously fantasised about but I have to admit, the reality got me excited. Sexually I've always been dominant and, although I never mix sex with work, I figured it was close enough to the end of the day for me to make an exception on this occasion. 'If you're really going to try begging,' I told George, 'you'll have to start by kissing my shoes.'

He didn't move. Instead he stared up at me with obvious disbelief.

'Kiss my shoes,' I shouted. 'Do it now.'

Immediately George lowered his head and began to kiss my shoes. There were wet smacking sounds coming from his lips. He placed one hand around my ankle as he lowered his head and I instantly understood that he had done this before.

'Good boy,' I encouraged. 'Is that making your dick hard?'

When he looked up at me an understanding passed between us. I knew that he had done this before and he clearly knew that I was used to dominating servile men. He nodded eagerly.

'Kiss these shoes properly,' I told him, 'and I might let your dick go soft before I go home for the night.' I turned my back on him and returned to my chair. I'd spent a day sitting there, playing computer solitaire and being bored out of my brains. But when I slumped in it this time, I felt none of the previous boredom. I sat with my legs apart, allowing George a glimpse up my skirt, and beckoned him with a nod of my head. 'Come and kiss them properly,' I told him. 'If you do it right I might think about putting those invoices on for you.'

It's hard to describe the thrill that came from watching the manager crawl toward me on his hands and knees. He kept taking sneaky glances up my skirt, which I'd half expected, but I figured I would make him pay for those indiscretions before the evening was over.

He lowered his mouth to my left foot and began to kiss the pointy tip. I placed my right foot on his back, between his shoulder blades, and pushed the heel against him until he groaned.

'You were looking up my skirt, George,' I whispered.

He stiffened and said nothing.

'Did I give you permission to look up my skirt?'

He shook his head.

I tut-tutted and pushed my heel harder against his back. He groaned again but made no attempt to pull away. 'Why were you looking up my skirt? Did you want to see this?'

I inched the hem of the skirt higher and revealed the crotch of my panties. I'd worn black to go with the stockings. When I exposed the crotch to George I could see that he was straining to get a better look at me without struggling too much against the foot I had against his back.

'Is this what you wanted to see?' I asked. 'Or did you want to see what's inside these panties?' I lowered a finger to the edge of the crotch and began to tease it to one side.

George groaned. I could almost feel the pain of his straining neck as he tried to see what I was revealing without fighting too forcefully against the pressure of my foot on his back. His eyes were wide with desperate hunger and I savoured the thrill of having him grovel on the floor at my feet. Slowly, I eased the crotch of my panties aside and exposed my pussy.

This time, George whimpered.

I stroked my index finger against the split of my pussy lips. I hadn't realised I was so excited until I felt the warm dew of wetness that oozed from my sex. Allowing the tip of my finger to slide inside a little, making sure my finger was soaked with my juices, I continued to touch myself while George watched.

'Would you rather be kissing this than kissing my shoes?' I asked.

'Yes.' He said the word with such intensity I wanted to laugh at him.

'Then you can do those damned invoices yourself.'

It took him a moment to understand what I was saying. I continued to stroke my finger back and forth, exciting tiny ripples of pleasure from my pussy. All the time I was watching his face as the meaning of my words slowly dawned on him.

'You can put the invoices onto the purchase ledger,' I told him. 'And if you do it all properly, I'll let you slide your cock into this sweet pussy of mine.'

The hope on his face was almost comical.

'But,' I went on, 'for every mistake you make, you'll move yourself further away from having this.'

It's hard to explain how much pleasure I got from watching him sweat with disbelief. He shifted on his knees and I knew he was struggling with an enormous erection in his pants.

'Make three mistakes and you have no chance of feeling this pussy around your cock. For every mistake you make after that, I'll have you bent over my desk and I'll stripe your arse as punishment.'

He agreed to the arrangement. His head was nodding eagerly up and down. I took my finger away from my sex and smoothed the tip against his lower lip. He was so eager to taste me, he suckled against the finger as though I'd slipped a stiff cock between his lips and told him to swallow.

'Now get on with those invoices,' I cried, snatching my hand from his mouth.

He jumped as though he had been struck. Going to one of the spare workstations, working with surprising competence, he started to docket and enter the invoice information onto the computer system.

I watched with more than a little interest. The thrill of dominating him suited me perfectly. But the idea that he might manage the task without a mistake was a little unnerving. I didn't particularly want his cock inside me – not when I could get so much pleasure from dominating him – and so I walked over to his chair and stood behind him.

His fingers faltered against the keyboard. When I pressed my breasts against the back of his head I could feel the nervous heat emanating from him. I placed my warm, pussy-scented fingers under his nose. 'Is this what you're thinking about now, George?' I asked.

The computer beeped a complaint and I made a mental note that he had now made one mistake.

George cursed.

'I'm sorry,' I whispered. I lowered my hand to his groin. His erection was close to bursting through his pants. A circle of pre-come darkened his trousers where the tip of his erection met the fabric. 'It must be very difficult for you trying to type while you've got this bulge in your pants.' As I spoke I squeezed and kneaded his cock.

George stiffened in his chair and then slammed his hands against the keyboard.

The computer's second beep of complaint told me I only had to distract him once more and then I could have the pleasure of striping his bare backside without worrying about having his cock enter me. 'That's a lot of mistakes you're making,' I murmured. 'If I didn't know better I'd say that you were desperate to have me spank your arse.'

119

'More than desperate,' he muttered. Without any cheating from me, he went on to make the computer beep three times in a row.

I laughed and continued to squeeze his cock. I was leaning over him, my breasts pressed against his ear and my voice lowered to a husky whisper. 'Get all those invoices done in the next half hour,' I said, 'and I'll give you a dozen stripes.' Squeezing him a little tighter, grinning when I heard him suppress a sob of desire, I added, 'And I might let you wank off whilst I'm punishing your arse.'

He swallowed and then set about typing with renewed ferocity. His fingertips were a blur against the keyboard as he input the information for each invoice. I eventually let go of him and returned to my seat, teasing my clit as I watched George hurrying to obey my instructions. Having worked for the bastard for the best part of five years I had no idea he had such a submissive streak. And, relishing my moment's authority over him, I savoured the pleasure that came from telling him exactly what I wanted him to do.

'I've finished,' he told me.

I didn't bother checking his work. I told him to stand up and take the belt out of his trousers.

His hands were shaking as he tried to do as I asked. I'd removed my skirt whilst he was typing, as well as my blouse. I was sitting at my usual desk wearing only heels, stockings, panties and a bra. George's gaze was fixed on me with a horny eagerness that was almost comical.

'Take off your trousers,' I told him. 'And show me your cock.'

He did as I commanded, tearing his pants open and dropping them to his ankles. Because he wasn't wearing underpants his erection stood out from between his shirt tails. It was a modest size – not minuscule – but certainly not the monster I'd been expecting.

'Bend over the desk,' I demanded. 'And you can wank

while I'm striping you.' I raised a warning finger and added, 'But you'd best not come until I give permission.'

George was so painfully obedient it was almost funny watching him. He bent over the desk, wanking himself carefully, and presenting his backside for my discipline. I took the buckle of his belt in my hand, wound it twice round my wrist, and then prepared to take my first strike against his rear. Before taking the first blow, I reached between his legs and cupped his balls.

George sighed.

I squeezed his sac, making sure he knew my firm hold could get even firmer. 'I know you've done this sort of thing before,' I told him. 'And you probably guessed that I've done it before too. So I think we're both sufficiently familiar with these games to know that we need to have a safe word.'

He nodded. I could see, from the sweat trickling off his forehead, he was struggling to hold back a mighty eruption.

'The safe word is: you can have a pay raise, Tina.' And, before he had a chance to register what I'd said, I gave his balls a sudden, sharp squeeze and then slapped the belt across his rear.

George's howl echoed through the empty office building.

I delivered all twelve blows in quick succession. George continued to stroke himself as his backside became redder and redder. His arm moved backwards and forwards with increasing speed and I knew he was enjoying his submission as much as I was enjoying my domination. When I'd delivered the last blow I threw the belt down and collapsed in my chair.

'Get down on your knees and stroke it, George,' I demanded. 'Get down on your knees and watch me wank myself to climax whilst you stroke yourself off.'

And that was how we both came. George was on his knees, staring reverently at my gusset as I fingered myself to climax. I was sprawled in my chair, teasing the crotch of my panties whilst I watched the area manager tug off his surprisingly small cock. Once we'd both recovered I told him he could get dressed and I began to retrieve my own discarded clothes. I saw him looking slyly at my backside as I eased my hips back into their skirt and I snapped my fingers for his attention.

'George,' I said.

He lifted his gaze to look at my face.

'I'll be checking those invoices on Monday morning, just to make sure you've done everything properly. And, if I find there are too many mistakes in that batch, I will come up to your office and punish you again.'

His eyes grew wide and he nodded eagerly.

Since then, I've found myself looking forward to late Fridays at the office and some very satisfying starts to the working week.

– Tina, Otley, UK

Hard Candy

Danielle and I had always enjoyed a healthy and adventurous sex life. Just minutes into our first date, at a tapas bar, she told me she liked the black olives I had ordered. Popping one into her mouth, she added that their taste reminded her of come. We once took advantage of a large divan in a show home, as the nervous Sales Rep rustled her contracts downstairs. We played with love toys and plastic handcuffs. While studying for her Biology PhD, she had been required to teach at the university and openly admitted to staging deliberately provocative lectures whenever the syllabus allowed. I had even pretended to be a student of hers who, driven to obsession by her teasing, had decided to burgle the house and force himself upon her.

I watched her flirt with waiters before she left her flimsy panties screwed up inside a linen napkin, along with a £20 note. This game developed so that one of us would go back to collect a mobile phone also left behind, just to see the lucky guy's face. The twenty would sometimes be 'scented', having been folded inside her gusset for most of the evening. Later, as we made love, we would conjure images of what the finder might be doing with his treasure trove. Were they in his mouth, round his shaft, or soaked in his come while he desperately tried to recall the face of their donor? Would he try and trick his girlfriend into wearing them, along with crimson lipstick and a Dita Von Teese wig until she began to resemble the mystery customer he would never forget? Would he spend the money or treasure it forever in a clear ziplock bag?

This game became known as Candy Tipping, then just Candy, and the name just stuck with her. I felt as cool as shit back in those days, a lover so secure he could share his wife's intimates with strangers, and help her get off on the thought. Relaxed and confident, I could always make her come once, twice, maybe three times without reaching climax myself. The games were a little dark but always healthy, I thought. Better to let our inner sluts out to play sometimes, rather than locking them away in a place where they might grow bitter and start tunnelling.

She mostly liked to sit astride me and, when our love was young and new, she would say 'Baggsy top bunk,' then giggle, whenever we climbed into bed. Later as our love soured, she claimed that it was simply because I had neither the size nor the skill to make her come by myself any more. The shift between these two states was a sudden one, and I clearly recall the moment of transition.

She was a slight girl but deceptively strong, at least sufficiently so to make the pretence of her holding me down fun. As she positioned herself above me in bed that night, I looked up at her face. Holding down my wrists, she increased the pressure, digging sharp thumbnails into the pulse points, as though my passion could be both increased and monitored through them. I raised an eyebrow as if to say, 'This looks like it could be fun.' I was expecting her expression to say in reply, 'Don't worry, it will be,' and perhaps for her to wink. This was, after all, a game that we had played before.

She hovered her tiny puss just above my tip of cock. I have never known a girl so small down there. Outside, two lips as beautiful as those on the face of any cover girl formed a perfect little pink canoe. Inside, a soft and inviting sleeve that gently squeezed my entire length.

As she slid down onto me, however, her face began to change unexpectedly. She began screwing up her eyes and clenching her jaw. Those perfect crimson lips – so red she was often wrongly chastised as a choirgirl for breaching the 'No make up' rule – narrowed. The woman she had become resembled my girl, but after she had lived an entirely different life, the damaged waxwork of a twisted twin. I could barely recognise her as the one with whom I had walked on deserted beaches, collecting shells and dreaming of a happy home together.

Her rhythm escalated from a gentle grind to a steady pounding, as she worked her hips downwards and backwards, testing the root of my erection to its physical limits. Despite the discomfort, I swelled and reached a hardness I'd not felt since my trembling young hands first turned the weathered pages of a magazine found in the bushes during a long-distant summer holiday.

Words began to hiss from her lips, syncopated with her downward thrusts. 'Don't-you-dare-come-in-side-me!'

Of course, this had exactly the opposite effect, and I now realise it was what she truly desired. We rarely used condoms as she liked to feel me come directly onto her clitoris, the small of her back, or occasionally into her mouth. And if she did get pregnant, well, we had decided to leave it up to fate, or so I thought. My sac tightened and an orgasm surged through me.

Sensing my ejaculation, Candy lowered her face towards mine, and puckered her lips. I expected a gentle kiss and I raised my mouth to hers. Instead, and with the accurate hatred of a school bully, she fired a large plume of foaming white spit across, and partially between my own lips. Lowering her head further she whispered, almost inaudibly, into my ear.

'Do you honestly think I want your regressive fucking loser-gene germinating inside me?'

Her words delivered an exquisite sting and for the first time I understood the neat rows of scars on a self-harmer's forearms. This was new territory for me. The physical sex was over but there was none of the usual post-coital malaise. I had touched down in a frightening paradise and wanted to stay a little longer, as much as anything, to see how far this woman would go. Was it even a game still? We weren't pretending to be other people. A thrilling tingle passed through me and I knew that I would soon be hard again.

She began to climb off and looked down at our uncoupling with disgust. Shuffling forward on her knees, she continued. 'If your sperm are as useless as you are, they're probably swimming in the wrong direction.' Another sting but I was already feeling a tolerance to this new narcotic. She lowered her wet puss closer to my face. 'We can't take any chances though. Suck out what you can.'

I opened my mouth to receive her. She slumped down onto my face like a wrestler trapping an opponent. The jolt released a thick string of backflow, making me a little proud at having delivered such a payload. Closing my lips around hers I did as I was told and began to draw nectar from the flower.

'Do you like it?'

Unable to speak I tried to nod.

More spit, this time on the forehead, the only part of me now visible to her. 'That's it. Get your tongue right in.'

A slow gyration told me she was becoming more aroused. Slipping down between her legs, a delicate hand began to rub gently. She shifted herself forwards and I was presented with her ass. It was, until now, the one taboo in our love life. Never once had she allowed me to see it or touch it, let alone taste it. Her weight came down again and I began to run my tongue around her tight asshole.

'Give it a good clean. Make it shine.'

I got to work as she coaxed herself to a sobbing orgasm. As she rose to climb off me, she released a little 'phut' of gas, almost soundless and odourless, causing the faintest warm draught on my face. In the four years that we spent together I had never heard her break wind before.

Lying next to me, she reached across and curled her cool fingers around my shaft. 'Who's a big hard boy then?'

I was relieved that the game was over. She'd had her fun, and now I was going to get mine. Her insults were still ringing in my ears as I plotted a rough vengeful fuck.

'Sorry I was mean to you, honey. I just got carried away. Tell you what,' she said, moving her gentle grip up and down, 'I'll let you put it in my ass. I know you've always wanted to and quite fancy something new myself.' My erection stiffened and throbbed in her palm, eager to plunge inside her. 'But there is one condition.'

'Which is?' I asked.

'All you have to do is stay hard. Unfortunately, I don't think you'll be able to. *I* don't think you're up to it.'

As though a strange spell had been cast upon me, upsetting the delicate mystery that controls the tides of a man's ardour, I immediately began to wilt.

'See, you're already going soft on me, you nancy boy.'

It was true, and all efforts to sustain my hardness were as futile as those of a swimmer in too strong a current. Within a minute I lay cold and flaccid in her hand.

'Oh, bless,' she said, as though she was looking at a crippled child trying to climb stairs. 'I knew you didn't have it in you.' She gave my drained cock a final tug to ensure that all vital signs were absent. 'Now, get dressed, go find a chemist's that's still open and get me a morning-after pill.'

Still reeling from the cruel turnabout I had just suffered, I climbed into my clothes and set off on my errand. In the only place still open, I had the ignominy of being served by a girl I went to school with. She politely explained that they could not serve a man with the product I required, while several other members of staff eyed me with suspicion.

I was expecting a tirade from her when I got home, but Candy simply laughed out loud when I explained my empty-handedness. 'Yeah, I thought everyone knew they only give those out to girls. Otherwise every bastard that got his girl into trouble would be slipping them into her food. It must have been embarrassing, so I'm sorry. You still look a little red now. Thanks for trying, though.'

The events of that single evening brought imbalance to every aspect of our relationship. New roles had been cast for us both; one adored, the other despised. What had felt like three years of consecutive Valentine's Days came to an abrupt end as twelve months of Halloween commenced.

One year later

The staffing rota of our local supermarket seemed designed to ensure a surfeit of cheerful chatterboxes when the store was at its quietest, and the fewest and least competent staff during busy hours. It was in the latter of these situations that I found myself amidst a serpentine queue that led to the 'Express Checkout'. I glanced nervously between my watch and the groceries in my basket. Fretting that the shop did not stock the exact items requested, I tried, but failed to summon calming thoughts. 'No point in worrying if I got the right stuff. She usually changes her mind by the time I return anyway. I am late. She will be doubly displeased.'

'Would you though? Isn't she like 50 or something?' The sound of two scruffy students horsing brought me back to reality. One of them was waving a CD case around. 'Yeah, but she's still fit and she's loaded.'

They seemed without a care in the world as they looked forward to a Friday evening of drinking and carousing, and I envied them for it. As the queue shuffled forwards

I saw the same CD askew in the rack, still with a circle of condensation on the case where a hot thumb had been pressed against it. The cover showed the artiste sprawling in burlesque underwear – *Hard Candy*, by Madonna. I thought of the students, and how they didn't know shit.

An hour earlier I had returned from work to find a familiar scene. Candy, wearing her silk dressing gown, was upstairs in the study working on her beloved laptop. She was almost always logged on to Facebook, Myspace, or catching up with her other online friends via the webcam. Her friendship network seemed to consist entirely of men who hoped to be her lover, men who wished they still were, or her ugly girlfriends who all wanted to be like her. Either way, she seemed to draw great strength from the steady stream of adoration the internet supplied.

'Hi, honey!' I announced my arrival. She cautiously closed the lid of her laptop whenever I strayed into a vantage point. Evidently, I winced.

'It's for your own good. You know how you read too much into everything.'

It was true that her online obsession bothered me. On the few occasions I had glimpsed the screen, the messages were punctuated with xxxxxxxxs, mwahs, and winking smilies. If I ever challenged her about it I was dismissed as paranoid.

'Jim is like my little brother. There's nothing for you to worry about . . . Here.' Her arm snaked out sideways, passing me a list and sending me off with a dismissive flick of the hand. 'And, get me something to drink, something nice, you know what I like.'

When I returned, she was in the bath. 'George is picking me up at eight, and now I am going to have to rush. We're going to go over my finances, see if he can get me out of the mess you got me into.'

It's true that money was a worry for us, and my meagre salary as a carer for the local authority was usually to blame, never her burgeoning collection of heels or overflowing lingerie drawer.

Fucking George! She knew I hated the guy. He obviously had a crush on her, was a wealthy investment analyst, always tanned, full of confidence, and usually cited as the one person she wished I was more like. He owned several properties around the country, and even employed a French chef, and gardener.

'Fix me a drink, honey,' she purred.

I poured her a glass of the Cava I had just bought, ice cold and dry as a bone, just how she liked her fizz. I handed over the glass. She took a sip then wrinkled her little nose to convey disappointment. 'What is this, anyway?' she asked. 'It's Cava, it's like Spanish Champagne'. You know I only like the real thing.'

'Sorry, Candy,' I replied, crestfallen. 'I'm getting near my overdraft limit and couldn't quite stretch to Champagne.'

'Never mind,' she said, rolling her eyes. 'George always stocks an excellent cellar. He's even got a '66 Bollinger, tucked away for a special occasion. Maybe I can persuade him to crack it this weekend?'

The colour obviously drained from my face, earning me a pitying smile from my wife.

'Still, you can help me with something you are good at'. She stood up in the bath, her body slick with foamy suds. 'Here.' She produced her Lady Luck bikini line trimmer, still new in its box, a recent present from me. She was quite hairy down there, but liked to keep herself tidy, especially before sex. Before things changed, I used to do all the tidying for her, and once she even wrote 'To Mr Topiary, the only one for me. xxx' in a Christmas card.

I hadn't been allowed to see her naked since the face sitting, and was surprised to find that she had become quite overgrown. Lady Luck was supplied with four plastic stencils: a small triangle, a narrow Brazilian, a downward pointing arrow, and a heart. 'You choose,' she said. I chose the heart, held the stencil to her mound and buzzed away until the desired shape had been achieved. I clicked the guard onto the trimmer and took the remaining hair down to a nice even Number 2. She handed me my own razor and said, 'Neaten her up.' I felt so privileged to be this close to her again and dutifully set about removing the field of stubble the electric trimmer had left behind.

'Now around the lips,' she whispered. I could see her becoming swollen, but did not dare caress her as a lover would. Knowing my place, I maintained instead the practical touch of a nurse preparing someone for an operation. When I had finished she was completely hairless except for the little heart, and I have never seen a more beautiful sight. The excitement of being allowed to shave her was tempered with a deep sadness and shame. That delightful little puss would never be mine again. Although she had driven me to suspect that I was preparing her for another, I had been so desperate to see it once more that I could not refuse.

'Thanks, honey. Now go and pick some things out for me to wear this weekend.' I shuffled out of the bathroom but left the door very slightly ajar, feeling a defiant determination to see a little more of her through the crack. Unaware that she was being watched, Candy didn't disappoint. Making it look like a sensual act of foreplay, she stood up and shaved her legs, then hosed herself down with the shower head. Widening her stance a little, she pressed her hips forward and urinated like a man, straight into the bath, taking a satisfying swig of the Cava as she did so. Finally she lowered the half-empty glass to between her thighs and refilled it a little, with the last few drops of pee.

I was summoned back to the bathroom. 'Don't worry about the packing, I'll do it. The water is still warm, why don't you hop in and I'll give you a wash.' I undressed and stepped into the water. 'Just lie back,' she cooed. As I lay in the tepid water she proceeded to wash me with a large natural sponge, taking particular care of my face, head, and limp penis. 'Mustn't forget this sleepy little fella, must we?' Despite the humiliation, I was willing to take any attention, any form of contact from her.

Indicating that the wash was over, Candy gently tossed the wet sponge so that it bounced harmlessly off my head. Then she offered me her glass. 'Here, you can finish this off too. It's more your sort of thing. Go on, drink up.' Watching me drain the glass, she began humming an old Stone Roses tune to herself, knowing full well I would recognise the song: 'The past is yours but the future's mine, you're all out of time.'

The taste of the wine faded on my tongue. Only the faint aftertaste of her piss remained.

Leaving me to lie in the cooling water, Candy moved to the bedroom to do her hair and make-up. I tried to put images to the sounds of her preparations. The voom of a hairdryer, the scrape of a hairbrush, the click of a lipstick tube, the plick-plick-plick as she loaded a mascara brush. I also took a quick shower, wrapped myself in a towel, then ventured into the bedroom. Overflowing with enough outfits to last a month, her weekend bag was sat on the bed. My blood ran cold as I saw what was next to it. Laid out, as if the reclining girl wearing them had simply vanished, was a set of matching bra and panties, lace-topped hold-ups and a pair of killer heels. All presents from me, all unworn, owing to a lack of occasion.

Although I had never found concrete evidence of her infidelity, she tortured me daily with a drip feed of hints, half-clues, and suggestions that amounted to nothing but a gradual unpicking at the seams of my sanity. I had hoped, optimistically, that her weekend at George's would be spent walking his precious Salukis across the estate, or pawing over spreadsheets and sums. Now my cruel imagination was spiralling into a perilous descent.

I looked across at Candy as she stood in front of a full-length mirror, moisturising herself where she had been shaved recently, taking particular care around her heart-shaped muff. She finished off by gently cupping her puss whilst making a few little circles with her hips. 'All nice and smooth,' she breathed to herself. 'He'll be here any minute. Help me dress.'

As I handed her the items one at a time, I recalled the words of a Japanese girl from back when I taught English in Tokyo. She once explained that a beautiful sadness at the fleetingness of life lies at the core of their aesthetics. These words, left in a long-forgotten archive of my memory, suddenly began to resound as the cool fabric of her underwear – gauzy, lacy, silky, soft, then gone – passed through my hands. Next, the shoes, simple but stunning black heels. Finally she stepped into her favourite black cocktail dress, letting me zip her up. Although it was bought on the high street, seeing her in that dress always induced a brief daydream of Candy as the muse to a Parisian master dressmaker.

In all she looked simply perfect. I doubted if the natural and man-made had ever been combined to such devastating effect as my wife and her attire that evening.

Candy's impatient voice brought me back from my delirium. 'Are the seams on these stockings straight?' They were, but I knelt down and took the opportunity to work them out of, then back into line. The feel of her smooth legs through the lightest of nylons made me shudder.

A sound of a car horn heralded George's arrival. I peered through the window and saw his convertible Audi TT purring away on the drive. Glancing across at my battered Vauxhall Corsa, I thought I detected a slight shake of George's head. Gliding out of the bedroom and down the stairs, the bag over her shoulder, Candy mumbled something about 'Sunday evening'. A powerful slam of the front door interrupted my meek goodbye.

I sat in the oppressive quiet of an empty house. Almost silent except for a faint sound . . . the steady whine of a laptop! Running late, Candy had forgotten to shut it down. My pulse launched itself into a sprint as I moved into the study, still feeling the lingering presence of my tormentor. Several windows still remained open on the screen, all logged in. Feeling rebellious, I scrolled through her inboxes, but found little more than some flirty messages.

One window, however, seized my attention. It showed a live stream from a tastefully furnished bedroom, the sort you might find in an expensive hotel. I was sure it was George's place, knowing they caught up via the webcam. After a few minutes a young Asian maid entered the room, made the bed, then began fussing around a small table next to it. The resolution of the picture was extremely clear, indicating an expensive camera. The maid momentarily disappeared; the picture jolted as the camera, obviously a wireless model, was picked up and carried across the room to the table so as to afford a closer view of the bedside. Glued to the screen, I was unable to avert my gaze for a second. After four hours nothing had happened, save for me filling two of Candy's empty coffee cups when I needed to pee.

At a quarter to midnight, the maid returned, closely followed by my darling wife. Despite my best efforts, I could not get any sound so had to be content with pictures alone. During my wait, however, I had fathomed out how to save the footage. Moving the cursor over the red icon, I clicked record. Stood on the far side of the bed, Candy began by taking the maid by the hair and giving it a good tug. She released her, and began pointing viciously. I'd seen this first hand, and now Candy was snarling instructions to the Asian girl who promptly began to strip. When her subject was completely naked, Candy spun round and said something over her shoulder. Responding immediately, the maid helped Candy out of the cocktail dress, knelt down, then slid her tiny panties down. Placing her hands on the far wall of the room my wife, wearing just a bra, hold-ups and heels, assumed the position of someone about to be strip searched. The maid crawled forwards and began licking between the smooth white buttocks in front of her. After little more than a minute, Candy turned around and pushed the maid back onto the bed until she was lying face up, head pointed towards the camera. Clambering onto the bed after her, my wife straddled the maid's face and offered a new delicacy for her to taste. I could just make out a little pink tongue darting around at the base of the heart shape I had created earlier. Stirring under the towel across my lap, I felt my first erection in months spring to life.

Shadows in the background indicated that someone else had entered the room. When the picture began to jerk wildly I became quite disorientated, making me realise how utterly engaged I was in the unfolding spectacle. I had never felt so alive. Someone was carrying the camera, and I assumed the cameraman was George. He targeted the lens on the maid's mouth, affording a clearer view of the licking Candy was receiving, before panning up. Her face filling the screen, my wife's dreamy-looking eyes and gently nodding head told me that she was reaching orgasm.

The camera must have been dropped onto the floor at that point, as I had to endure a few minutes seeing nothing more than the ceiling. After a clumsy handover that sent the scene tumbling, I guessed that the maid was now holding the camera. She steadied the view. Candy was on all fours, being pounded from behind by a tanned, thick-set man who looked like he worked outdoors. Could this be the gardener, I wondered? My wife's head, meanwhile, was overhanging the end of the bed where George stood, stroking an impressive erection. He really did seem to be the man with everything. Stepping forward, he guided his cock into Candy's open mouth. I was watching my wife being spit-roasted, and I felt a disgusting euphoria at the sight. She really was a cheating bitch after all.

The camera began to move around, closing in on the penetration of Candy's mouth and pussy from every imaginable angle. Eyes half-closed, she was clearly drunk and revelling in the attention of the two men. Loitering just above her backside, the image settled on the fat erection sliding in and out of her puss. The cock popped out, rubbed vertically between her ass cheeks, then shot come onto her lower back. George then took hold of the camera and filmed the maid cleaning Candy's back with her tongue.

Finally, Candy crawled off the bed and knelt in front of George, cupping his balls with one deft hand, slowly working the other up and down his shaft. I watched her slender fingers treat George's cock expertly. She broke off and lowered herself a little, so that her open mouth was directly under the tiny aperture at the end of his erection. Knowing what was about to happen, I stood up and cast the towel off.

Tiny tugs of her hand released thick gobs of come from the cock above her. Through parted red lips, her tongue extended to receive his semen. At that precise moment, and without needing to touch myself, I felt a pulsating orgasm burst out of me with such force that my legs almost gave way. Thick cords of come launched onto the screen and across the keyboard. My first ejaculation for months gave a sense of immense release that was matched only by its volume. Turning her head, Candy narrowed her eyes and blew a kiss from her glazed lips towards the camera. Realising that the laptop had been left running deliberately, that I had been meant to witness the entire spectacle, that my observation was actually key to her pleasure, I folded the screen down and slumped back into the chair.

'Where the fuck do I go from here?' I said aloud.

* * *

Survival instincts finally kicked in and I began packing. After an hour or so, I had stowed the essentials, at least, in the boot of the Corsa. During a last check around the house an alarming odour, something like the plastic burn smell that emanates from industrial estates, led me into the study. Fused out and gently smoking away, Candy's precious laptop lay on the desk. Opening it up, I found the screen black, the wet keyboard unresponsive. I felt that the karmic balance had been at least slightly redressed. With the relieved agony of someone who had at last extracted a rusty fish hook from beneath their own sternum, I headed out of the door.

In my weaker moments, I sometimes regret leaving the laptop behind. Perhaps I could have somehow retrieved the footage? No, it would have only prolonged the harm and slowed my recovery. Two years on, I still miss her, but only in the way a reformed smoker sometimes pats his pockets down after a few drinks.

— *Alexander, Manchester, UK*

Dubbel

I like a taste of beer every now and then. It's hardly a crime, is it? A good malty flavourful body and a decent creamy head – you can't beat it.

The trouble is I can't drink a whole pint because it's just not sweet enough for my palate. I stick to shorts when I'm out drinking, and just steal a mouthful or two from Craig's pint. Yes, I know it's the sort of thing that can piss a husband off – like women who refuse to accept a portion of chips but help themselves from their bloke's plate. But honestly, what a thing to make a fuss about.

So when we went to stay the weekend with Katie and Damien after they'd returned from Belgium with a whole crate of mixed beers, I declined a bottle of Trappist *Dubbel*. But when Katie went out to help her mother with some shopping I wandered into the sitting room where the two men were talking and watching the Kerrang! TV channel – some things never change no matter how many years go by – and I grinned at Craig and asked, 'Can I try some of your beer?'

For once Craig didn't roll his eyes. He patted his thigh and invited me to sit on it, so I snuggled up in his lap, one arm around his shoulders and neck, and reached for the bottle.

'Do I get a kiss?' he asked. 'A kiss for a beer?'

'So I look like the kind of woman whose favours are for sale, do I?' With a grin I planted a kiss on his lips, tasting malt.

'And so cheaply too,' he smirked, letting me take the bottle. The beer was rich and soft, not nearly as harshly flavoured as its aroma promised.

As I returned his drink, my eyes drifted to the music video, where some Emo woman in torn lace was writhing around in a dark forest. I didn't know the band but Damien was able to tell us all about them and the three of us discussed the subject idly. Craig and Damien have been friends for years – ever since college in fact, where they'd formed their taste in music. Katie and I both came on the scene a few years later, but we all get along just great. And while we were chatting I felt Craig's hand slip surreptitiously under my top and stroke my skin. I didn't mind that at all. I didn't object to his hand framing the swell of my bare breast. It was only when his fingers wandered up to tweak my right nipple that I squirmed and clamped my arm down, pinning his.

'Hey,' he whispered very softly in my ear. 'Do what you're told.'

I quivered, inside and out. Those were Bedroom Words. They meant we were starting on the obedience game – and there were only two possible responses to that phrase. I could use our safeword to chicken out or I could do what he told me to. Suddenly I was hot all over.

Craig had never done this in public before. I wondered what the hell he and Damien had been talking about before I came in, and I cast a wary look at our friend sat in the armchair opposite. Damien's eyes were on the screen, an open bottle cradled at a casually suggestive angle in his lap. I'd always fancied him quite a bit; he's pretty good-looking in his way, with thick backswept red hair and intense eyes. Don't let anyone tell you that women don't assess all their husband's friends.

Deliberately I relaxed against Craig, letting his fingers continue their work on my breast. He showed his approval by kissing my flushed cheek and nuzzling my ear, his tongue-tip tracing its whorls, his breath hot, his teeth nibbling my lobe. I had to force myself not to squirm visibly with pleasure. His thumb and finger tightened to a pinch on my nipple, and I squeaked under my breath.

Damien's eyes flicked in my direction. His expression stayed neutral. If it was obvious that I was looking flustered he didn't acknowledge it. Under the tight stretchy cotton of my clothing, Craig's fingers played vigorously with my nipple.

Damien turned back to the screen. 'Bet she's a wild fuck, mind,' he said dreamily. He was talking about the singer, of course. He had to be.

God, this was turning me on. It was years since the early days when Craig and I had been wild-horny enough to mess around in public. Did Damien count as 'in public'? Who was Craig trying to tease more?

The music changed. The new video was *The Pretender* by the Foo Fighters. I really like that song. Craig wasn't about to allow the fact to remain a secret.

'Now *this* is Rhiannon's song. She loves to fuck to it.'

I opened my mouth to protest but my poor tortured nipple got a pinch that sent electricity jumping all over my skin.

'Does she now?' Damien looked faintly amused.

'Fast and rough.'

Damien ran the tip of his tongue over his teeth, thoughtfully.

'And if I start shafting her when it starts, she comes dead on the final lines.'

Damien lifted an eyebrow and I squirmed against Craig. He was exposing my intimate secrets, and the humiliation felt horribly, unbelievably good – because, I supposed, it was Damien, and deep down I'd always wanted to bare myself to him and get a response. Or maybe just because it was so dirty a thing to do. After all, the point of the obedience game is to see how far I can be pushed – and to see how horny I get on the way.

For a moment the three of us watched each other silently, half-listening to the pounding chorus. Then Craig bent his lips to my ear. 'Want to sit up on my boner?' he whispered.

I caught my lip in my teeth, but nodded, and he let go of my breast in order to pull me into his lap, facing outward. I kicked off my shoes and tucked my feet behind me before I relaxed back against his torso. I guess I was obscuring his view of the TV a bit, but he didn't seem to mind. From this position, once he'd set his beer aside, he could slide both hands up under my top to cup and squeeze my breasts; my right nipple was burning from his earlier attentions and it was a relief to have the left one tormented too. I could feel Craig's cock hard against my bum-cheek and I writhed my hips to make sure of his arousal. Damien sat back in his armchair, his eyes resting on me even while he tilted his bottle to his lips.

'I think you should pull down your top and show Damien your pretty tits, love,' Craig murmured. My pussy pulsed, warm and wet, and I obeyed, lifting my breasts out into view while he transferred his hands to the outside of my clothes and resettled them. The cooler air made my nipples stand out harder. Yet our friend showed no sign of emotion, even when Craig pulled at my swollen teats, tugging them out then flicking them cruelly before stroking them in soothing circles. But he was watching carefully. I groaned as the stimulation became too much for me.

'Just you watch the telly, love,' I was instructed. But I couldn't; I couldn't take my eyes off Damien, though my lids were heavy and I had to gaze at him from under my lashes. Was he properly enjoying the sight of my tanned, pert tits being played with? His free hand rested in his crotch, hiding any sign of arousal.

Then Craig moved one hand down to my pussy and rested it between my open thighs, sending a whole new

141

thrill through my body and saying, 'I think he'd like to see your snatch too, love.'

'OK,' I whispered, because his hand on my pussy was making it soften and open and I couldn't think any more about anything except how much I needed to be touched there.

'Pull your skirt up.'

I used both hands to draw it right up my thighs, revealing the gusset of my lacy panties – which Craig's tickling fingers instantly discovered to be soaked through. He stroked my clit through the cloth, scratching with his fingertips, then pushed the moistened fabric aside to get his fingers into my wetness. I squirmed even more, both self-conscious and helplessly needy. The fact that Damien was looking at my swollen pink pussy-lips was incredibly arousing. The fact that my husband was making me do this for his best mate was even more dirtily delicious and made me unable to resist the waves of heat surging through me. Forget about needing a good shafting; it took only one hand mauling casually at my breasts and a single finger on my clit to bring me off there and then, as the last lines of the song roared out through the room. And I didn't hold back on the gasping and crying out either.

I was rewarded by Damien's unblinking attention, and the slow slide and squeeze of his hand on his thigh.

'Kneel up,' Craig urged, when I'd recovered from my spasms. I put my hands on his knees and lifted my backside up: giving him room, it turned out, to tuck my skirt up into its waistband and wrestle his cock out of his fly. He guided my bottom back into his lap, spearing me with his thick prick and sliding it right the way into me.

'Hold on,' I gasped, head spinning. 'Give us a drink first.'

'Ask Damien.'

I groaned as he pushed deep inside me. 'Please Damien . . . Could I just have a sip of your beer?'

Damien stood then, and the bulge in his jeans made it clear at last how much he'd been enjoying the show. He came forward to stand in front of me, and put the mouth of his bottle to my dry lips. 'How deep can you take it, Rhiannon?'

So I deep-throated the brown glass bottle, to his obvious satisfaction. But when he pulled it out again and tipped it over my open lips, only a tiny trickle of beer ran out and splashed my chin.

Craig was settling to an unhurried rhythm by now.

'New bottle needed.' Damien fetched another from the box and returned to face me. His hand played with his belt-buckle. 'A kiss for a beer?' he wondered, deliberately echoing Craig.

'Oh yes.' I couldn't think of anything I wanted more right now; Craig was filling me over and over with his meat, working me up and down on his shaft, and my mouth wanted to be filled too. I watched as Damien shook the bottle, then prised off the cap with his penknife. The creamy foam gathered, hesitated, then surged from the neck – not squirting like canned lager but heaving up and pouring down with swift grace. Even quicker, though, was Damien's hand, untying his belt and buttons, yanking down his fly, hefting his erection into the open. It was every bit as big as I'd hoped for, and just as hard as the glass.

He caught most of the foam on his cock, letting it run down the dark shaft just as it had run down the bottle's neck, coating himself in the malty beer ejaculate to his big balls. And I bent my head and took his cock in my mouth, slurping down the Trappist ale, finding his heat under the cool foam. There was so much head to the beer that some of it escaped me and dripped on the carpet and ran down my throat onto my breasts, but no one was caring by then.

He wrapped his fingers in my hair and made me take his cock right down. I moaned with pleasure. Then Craig and Damien fucked me front and back, pussy and throat, and when my husband came deep in my wet cunt his best friend filled my mouth with his own creamy foam. He tasted beery and sweet: just right. I lapped it all up greedily.

I don't suppose the monks ever intended their beer to be drunk that way, but I've never enjoyed any beer so much as that Trappist *Dubbel*.

— *Rhiannon, Middlesbrough, UK*

An Older Man

I didn't decide I wanted Ted the first time I saw him. I only thought of him as a challenge when he'd told me he was one hundred percent faithful to his wife. As soon as he said that I knew that I had to have him, even though he was old enough to be my father.

I suppose you'd say I have a reputation for being a bad girl. I'd taken a creative writing class to try and do something productive with all my energies. I've read a lot of erotic stories and, while some of them are fairly arousing, I knew they were nothing compared to the sorts of stories I could tell if I learned how to get the words on paper. So, to that end, I'd enrolled on the local college's creative writing course, which is where I met Ted, the tutor.

At 54 Ted was old enough for me to barely consider him as a potential conquest. I'd seen his wedding ring glinting as he taught lessons on style, character and narrative. But I'd been too busy checking out the other students to properly notice him. It was only when we were having a one-on-one discussion, and he was asking about character motivation, that our conversation shifted onto sex and Ted said something that caught my interest.

He asked why the hero of my story had screwed around behind his partner's back. I said it was because the hero was a man and all men did that. Ted laughed and shook his head and said that wasn't true. He said he'd been married for thirty years and he'd never once cheated on his wife. I told him he'd probably never had the opportunity and Ted assured me he'd had plenty of opportunities, but he'd never acted on them. As soon as he said those words I knew I had to have him and prove myself right.

It was a powerful erotic fantasy at first.

I could imagine Ted bending me over his knee. I thought about his large, weathered, manly hands spanking my pert, eighteen-year-old buttocks. And I fingered myself to a climax as I imagined myself calling him 'Daddy'. As I said before, I'm something of a naughty girl. But the whole idea of calling Ted 'Daddy' as he spanked me to orgasm was so outrageous I came in a hot, wet and very sticky rush.

But, for me, it wasn't enough as a powerful erotic fantasy. I wanted to experience the reality and I wanted to prove to Ted that I was right about all men being unfaithful. I made a vow that I would have Ted before the year was over.

I made a point of producing the raunchiest stories I could write for Ted's lessons. I never read them out in class. But I'd hand them to him – just before break – and ask if he could give me his opinion on what I'd written by the end of the lesson. Then I'd join the rest of the class for a quick coffee and leave him alone to enjoy the story.

He had a hard-on after the first one.

I wasn't surprised. It was a true-life story about how I'd done a double-header with my ex-boyfriend and his brother. It had been a very arousing and satisfying experience. The content was very explicit and I'd made it as exciting and graphic as possible.

Ted put his jacket on and fastened it so that the hem covered the bulge in his pants. I smirked at that. I asked him what he thought of the story at the end of the lesson. He coughed with embarrassment and described it as 'a stimulating read'.

A week later I handed him the story of my first taste of pussy. I'm not lesbian. I'm not sure even if I'm bi. But I'd licked this girl out at a party and then she'd fingered me to a climax, so I suppose I must have some same-sex interest in my make-up. The story was as explicit as the first and I left it with Ted just before the class break.

Again, Ted had a hard-on when I returned. He made the same attempts to hide it but I could see that my stories were having an effect. And I was growing more and more desperate to see what his cock looked like when it was hard and unhidden by his pants and the hem of his jacket.

After the lesson I asked him if my second story had been as stimulating as the first – I waited until the other students had left the class – and he said it had read a little too much like a fantasy. I shrugged at that and said I'd written it exactly the way it had happened. I told him that all my stories were autobiographical.

He went bright red when I said that and shifted his position so I couldn't see his crotch.

We continued like that for a couple of months. I'd leave him to get horny in the break. We'd chat after the lesson and I'd watch him get hard again and grow embarrassed because of it. We were having another one-to-one discussion when he asked if I was content with the way my writing was progressing. I'd been expecting this question and I said I was happy with the way I could shape my stories but I was having difficulty with one particular piece.

Ted asked what the problem was and I told him I was trying to write a fantasy story about an older man spanking a younger woman. I told him that I thought the idea would be outrageously exciting, but I couldn't get it down on paper. When he asked why I wasn't able to write the story I said, 'Because it's not something I've done yet. I've never had an older man spank my bare backside while I scream, *"I'm sorry, Daddy!"* for him.'

Ted's reaction was priceless. Judging from the expression on his face he was nearly coming as he thought about the image I'd suggested. I could feel he was on the verge of offering his services when I whispered, 'It's something I've always wanted to try. The idea gets me really hot and wet.'

'Is that all you'd want from an older man?' he asked.

I raised an eyebrow and considered him in silence for a moment.

'You'd just want an older man to spank you,' he explained. 'You wouldn't expect more, would you?'

I gave him my most coquettish smile and said, 'If I'm being spanked over the knee of a man I have to call Daddy, it's up to him to tell me what I can expect.'

Watching his face, I saw him make the decision in an instant. 'Come back to mine,' Ted grunted.

I reminded him that he was married. I was tempted to remind him that he was also one hundred percent faithful to his wife, but I didn't want to spoil his mood. Ted said his wife was out for the evening, and we had two hours to ourselves, if I was interested.

I took his hand, said, 'That sounds like fun, Daddy.'

And then I let him drive us back to his house.

It's hard to describe how exciting those two hours were. My pussy was sopping on the drive to Ted's house. I felt triumphant because I knew that I'd managed to seduce him, despite his claim to being such a faithful husband. When we arrived at his home I asked him if I'd been a naughty girl for writing such rude stories in his class.

His eyes sparkled with excitement as he picked up on the game I was suggesting and he said I'd been a very naughty girl. I said, 'I'm sorry, Daddy,' and Ted said that I needed to be punished. He settled himself down in a large armchair, called me over to him and said he needed me bent across his knee.

'Are you going to spank me?' I asked.

'It's what you need,' he told me.

I shivered as I bent over his lap. I could feel his good-sized erection poking at me through his pants as I assumed the uncomfortable position across his legs. 'You've been a very naughty girl,' he said gruffly. 'Be thankful I'm not making you take your knickers off for this spanking.'

I glanced up at him, trying to contain my grin. 'I wouldn't be able to take my knickers off,' I told him, 'because I'm not wearing any.' Flicking up the back panel of my skirt, exposing my bare buttocks to him, I watched his eyes grow wide with tortured pleasure. The good-sized erection that poked into my hip began to throb as though he was having an orgasm. My own excitement was riding a new high at that point and I think I could have climaxed there and then.

Ted chose that moment to slap his hand against my rear and the shock was astounding. My backside was suddenly ablaze with the red heat of smarting flesh.

'Tell Daddy you're sorry,' Ted demanded.

'I'm sorry, Daddy,' I whispered.

Ted's hand slapped down again. The sound was like a thunderclap. I heard it first. Then I felt the abrupt sting, followed by the glorious spreading heat. 'Say it louder,' Ted insisted.

'I'm sorry, Daddy,' I told him.

He struck again, this time with more force. His fingers struck the same spot he had hit before. The bruised flesh was already growing sensitive. Every new slap of his palm took the intensity of that sensation to a new extreme. Each time he struck me he demanded I make my apology louder. And every time I shouted the words back to him, he hit again and with more force.

It was everything I'd hoped it would be.

After half a dozen slaps of his bare palm I was screaming, 'I'm sorry, Daddy,' so loudly I expected his neighbours to burst in and come to my rescue. The pressure of Ted's erection against my hip was a constant and I wondered if he was as close to coming as I felt.

Ted paused after the first six slaps and let his hand rest against one of my arse cheeks. The tips of his fingers were dangerously close to the molten heat of my pussy lips. I wondered if he might finger me to climax. The idea was gloriously exciting and, if I hadn't thought he would take offence at the suggestion, I would have begged him to do that for me. The idea of saying, 'I beg you, Daddy,' was not unappealing and I had opened my mouth to say that when he struck me again with a seventh, stinging blow.

'You've been a very naughty girl,' he said.

'I'm sorry, Daddy,' I whispered.

'You've caused me unnecessary frustration in classes,' he told me. 'And you've made me seriously contemplate being unfaithful for the first time in thirty years. I think you need to make amends.'

I glanced up at him from my position over his knee. Trying my best to look naive and innocent I asked softly, 'How can I make it up to you, Daddy?'

He pushed me rudely from his lap and unzipped his pants. His erection sprouted through the open fly, looking monstrous, large and totally irresistible. 'You can start by sliding your pussy onto this,' he said.

And, because I was trying to be a good girl for him, I did as Daddy asked. The two hours sped past with alarming speed. I'd ridden Ted to climax within moments of him penetrating me but he only had to spank me again and his erection was suddenly rigid and ready for action and I was able to ride him to my satisfaction. I was on his doorstep and thanking him for the lesson as a car turned the corner of his cul-de-sac. His wife parked on the driveway and greeted me with polite suspicion as Ted explained I was one of his students and he'd been helping me with a story I was working on.

And then I was left to walk home, with Ted's come still running from my pussy and my arse cheeks still burning from the spanking he had administered. My thoughts whirled with how best to put Ted's story down on paper and, as soon as I got back, I thought about writing it all down. Instead, I went to bed with a dildo and spent a gruelling night achieving climax after climax.

I haven't been back to Ted's classes since that night. I don't think I've yet learned everything I need to know about writing but I do think Ted's taught me everything he can. However, to show him that I'm grateful for all that he's taught me, I've sent him a signed copy of this story.

– Fiona, Leeds, UK

Prime-Time Viewing

This confession is about my first life. My London life. I used to love and hate it in roughly equal proportions, before the incident happened and swept everything away. I've tried to leave all the power, the adrenaline and the excitement of those times behind me. 'Draw a line and move on,' Dom says, 'try to fit in, this is the sticks, things are different.' And I know he's right. But now and then I let myself remember, and revel in it for a moment. Until the inevitable shudder of shame and embarrassment courses through me and I have to try once more to forget.

It's like getting out the teenage 'rock chick' clothes that you've kept hidden in the loft for twenty years. You only have to look at them, all studs and laces and tiny scraps of leather, to remember that you were once utterly fearless and entirely uninhibited. But then you recall everything that went with it, the self-hatred, the puking in doorways and the ill-advised blow jobs in bus shelters, and feel like the worst kind of scum.

The incident happened six years ago. I had just been hired as a regular anchor on the breakfast news, which was the culmination of ten years of scheming and drudgery; associating myself with anyone or anything successful and sucking up to whoever had the power to promote me. Having slaved variously as an intern, researcher, travel presenter, and reporter, I felt as though the clouds had finally parted and it looked like clear skies all the way to *Newsnight*.

My first few weeks in the job passed in a dreamy haze. A car would materialise outside my house at 4 a.m. and transport me into the hands of Katriona, an expert stylist. She would set about me with brushes, powders and glossy slicks of this and that until my face was positively creaking under the weight of make-up. I felt almost clownish, but through the lens of a TV camera it looked flawless and magical. I called the look 'headmistress glam'; it was sexy but still authoritative. 'The hot mom at the school gates that all the dads fancy and the other moms hate' is how Dom describes it.

The wardrobe was similarly prescribed, and I didn't mind in the least. I had a range of beautiful and boxy little suits to choose from every day, in various colours selected to avoid clashing with the set. All were lined with satin and fitted snugly against my compact hourglass figure. The final touch was the hosiery.

The hushed reverence with which Katriona introduced me to her hosiery box made me smirk. She was the custodian of a vast collection of stockings, hold-ups and tights. All the finest brands in every conceivable shade. Access to the box was the sole preserve of the breakfast anchors, because from 6 a.m. to 7 a.m. every morning (the sofa hour) our knees and lower legs were on display. To complete the immaculate grooming, she would ensure that my toes, calves and thighs were coated in an ultra-sheer second skin. The stockings had to shimmer enough to give a healthy glow, but not so much as to cause a nasty glare under the harsh studio lights. I had never been a frequent stocking-wearer, so it felt like I was pulling on a new personality whenever I rolled them up my legs. With hindsight, that might have been a problem.

A couple of months passed, and I began to feel more and more confident in my new role. I got to know the other anchors and some of the staff, and would joke around with the library boys now and then. The other anchors, mostly women, kept me close. More due to jealousy and distrust, I felt, than affection. It was at one of their boozy networking lunches that I first met Dom. He was the Head of News back then, and cut a very slick and intimidating figure. His status was immediately apparent, and so I hung on his every word and nodded my head vigorously whenever he expressed an opinion. It didn't go down well. He saw right through me, much more than I ever realised. Still does.

Dom became the focus of my career ambition, but my erotic ambition found a rather different target. His name was Andy and he was a cameraman. Not one of those socially inept techies that usually man the lenses, but a real alpha-male with a powerful torso, smooth tanned skin and a primal air about him. God knows how he made it past the undead in human resources, I think they hired him to meet some kind of 'opportunities for the disadvantaged' target.

In the beginning, I knew him only by the cut of his jeans and the gold chain around his neck. His face was always obscured by his camera, which he operated with just his right arm, the way swaggering young men drive their cars. The other arm would hang at his side, or slip casually into a pocket to play with some loose change.

It seemed to me that his camera spent more time pointed in my direction than was strictly necessary. And I wasn't the only one who noticed. On my way out of the studio one day, Dom approached me surreptitiously and slipped a disc into my hand. It was labelled 'Andy's cam' with the day's date written underneath.

I watched it as soon as I got home. It started boringly enough, just shots of the back of my head during an interview, then a few close-ups of my eyes looking fascinated by something Jim (my moronic co-presenter) said. But surely enough, the angle began to slip slowly downward. I watched, a little breathless, as the lens traced the contours of my profile. The shot lingered on my breasts, focusing on the small creases in my satin blouse where it strained across my cleavage, before following the buttons over my tummy and down to my waist. After thoroughly investigating the curve of my bottom, he zoomed right in to pick out the little bumps my suspender belt clasps made in the fabric of my skirt. These clearly fascinated him as the camera remained in that position for a good twenty minutes at least.

I suppose I should have been creeped out, but I was actually quite flattered by Andy's attentions. Perhaps if I'd been a bit less fixated on building my career, I might have had a lovely boyfriend to distract me from his charms. But as it was, I was terminally single and had a frustrated sex drive which would have given my male colleagues a run for their money.

So when I woke the next morning with an urgent feeling in my pussy, the temptation to put on a little show for Andy was far too strong to resist. Instead of reaching for the functional black bra, knickers and garter belt that I usually wore, I put on my date underwear. The bra cups were completely sheer and stopped just south of my nipples, leaving them to stand naked and erect in the chilly air. My knickers were slight and silky, with the thinnest ribbon of material covering my pussy. The garter belt was barely there, just a thin band around the narrowest part of my waist with four clasps suspended on slim laces.

Later, when Katriona had finished working her magic on my face, I stripped off my linen trousers and flip-flops to put on the pink dress and barely-black stockings she held out for me. She looked me up and down as I stood almost naked in the dressing room. 'Oh my God! Are you moonlighting at a girly bar?' I tried to laugh it off, but she must have known something was up. Maybe I was too turned on to really care what she thought.

On set, the adrenaline pumped through my body a lot harder than usual. I could see Andy's camera pointed right at me, his left hand tapping out a drum rhythm against his hip. My hands were fidgeting too, either flicking out my bottle-blonde hair or brushing across my hard nipples where they pushed out the pink fabric of my dress. It was just impossible to make myself concentrate and I lost my thread in at least two interviews. Thankfully Jim stepped in to save me from looking a complete idiot. I guess male colleagues do have their uses now and then.

During an ad break, I spotted Andy's cam sliding right down until it was level with my knees. He had to crouch down to operate it, and ended up kneeling, his left hand still drumming, only now it was against the floor. The dirty bastard's trying to look up my skirt! A surge of wetness coated the lips of my pussy and I ground myself against the sofa to try and assuage my nagging clit. I really wanted to make it easy for him. Hitch up my skirt, put my heels up on the table and open out my slick pussy for his delectation. Maybe he'd come crawling over and eat it out. Then get out his thick cock and ... owww, it was too much!

I needed some pretext to open my legs and give him a quick flash. As if she could read my mind, Katriona chose that moment to come on set and do a make-up check. Seizing the opportunity, I twisted and beckoned for her to come over and powder my face, wriggling my skirt up and parting my legs as I did so. The little hairs on my inner thighs pricked up as the cool studio air hit my skin, warm, white and naked above my dark stocking tops. I could feel the ribbon of my knickers pulling sideways against the outer swell of my lips, leaving my pussy bare and very visible. I kept my legs apart for as long as I dared, whilst Katriona caked me in porcelain dust, then reluctantly twisted back to face the cameras, crossing them as demurely as I could manage.

Jim was still busy doing a crappy link to the sports round-up, so I flicked my eyes in Andy's direction to check for a reaction. What I saw made me feel faint. The zoom lens was out about a mile, and his free hand was now tucked inside the belt of his jeans. Could he just be rearranging? No, not for that long. Not with such a steady rhythm. I could even make out the little circles his thumb was making over the head of his cock. Oh God. Oh my God.

His body gave a series of little jerks and he withdrew his hand swiftly as though it had been bitten. Having climaxed in public, his body was clearly flooding with shame, and now I was the only one still playing. A cold sensation seized my groin, turning off the urgency and excitement like the flick of a switch. You bloody idiot girl, where's your professionalism?

Back in the dressing room, I struggled to pull on my casual clothes as fast as possible in case Katriona noticed the damp wreckage of my knickers. As soon as I was decent, I raced out of the building and into the coffee house over the road. With a calming herbal tea and a skinny muffin inside me I began to perk up. What had I done wrong after all? Just flirt a little bit with an attractive guy. Nothing to feel bad about. And anyway, he was the one wanking in a room full of people, not me.

I was about to get up when I spotted Andy's torso hovering above me. My eyes swept upwards and we made eye contact for the first time. And right then I knew. Knew that he realised I was complicit in this thing. That I'd put on a show for him deliberately, and that I'd enjoyed watching him get off on it. What I said, however, was 'I'm just going actually, so you can have this table.'

'Oh I'm not after a coffee.' His voice had a soft northern burr. 'It's a bit pricey in here, I get my breakfast in the caff over the road.' I laughed, then realised he wasn't joking. How quaint.

'I just wanted to say sorry for earlier.' He touched the back of his neck, which was flushing pink. 'I know I took it a bit far. It's just that you're so distracting, like my ultimate fantasy woman, the way you dress on set and everything.' He laughed. 'Dunno what you make of me?'

Poor darling, I thought. He's gorgeous, but absolutely not relationship material. Why are some guys programmed to fall for the kind of women who will never take them seriously? But I said, 'Oh don't worry about it, really. I totally played along with it so it's not just your fault!' He looked relieved and pulled up a chair.

'Thank you so much, I was really worried.' And I could tell he had been, there were beads of sweat on his golden-brown forehead, mingling with soft blond hair. I smiled magnanimously. 'It's just that it was so hard to get this job, and that head of news bloke, is his name Dom?' – I nodded – 'He's noticed my thing for you, and he's not impressed with me.'

I sighed, 'He's a bloody hard man to impress, believe me.'

'I know, I know,' he said, 'but I really want to do well here, cos this job means everything to me.' His eyes began to gleam. 'I'm really passionate about news and journalism you see. I want to be a reporter actually, but doing the camera was my only way in since I didn't go to a redbrick uni or anything . . .'

I surreptitiously looked at my watch, wondering when the life story was going to be over.

'. . . and I've had some ideas, about the format and how we use the idents, which I reckon Dom might really go for.'

My ears pricked up. 'Oh really? Well, you know I have a one-to-one with Dom every week . . . why not tell me your ideas and I'll put in a good word next time I meet him?'

'Oh my God, would you? That would be amazing!' He was almost bouncing, like one of those excitable, shivering dogs. Bless.

'Sure,' I said, 'just note them down on a bit of paper for me.'

As he wrote, I admired his clean-shaven jaw and powerful forearms. I may have also eyed the tantalising bulge in his jeans. Even if I'd never consider actually dating him, I couldn't see the harm in having a bit more fun. I established that he was working again the following Tuesday, and arranged to meet him in the studio at 3 a.m. that day. A full hour before the staff usually arrive. 'We can work on your transferable skills . . .' I said, pushing my manicured hand into his crotch and thrusting my tongue into his mouth. He looked terrified, but compliant.

Meanwhile, I had my one-to-one with Dom, at which I presented all of Andy's ideas as my own. It turned out that they were rather good, to my surprise. And, just to make sure, I dropped a hint that Andy's inappropriate attentions were making me feel uncomfortable and that I wasn't sure I could continue sharing the newsroom with such a perv. I wish I could say I felt some remorse about the whole affair, but honestly I didn't. TV is a brutal business, and without the right contacts he didn't stand a chance anyway. The sooner he learned that, the better.

I put it out of my mind, and concentrated on preparing for our assignation. I could see no point in going to bed the night before, so I went out on the town with some of the other anchors and downed a bottle or two of Pinot Noir. By 2 a.m. I was seriously pissed and horny as hell. I got a cab from the club straight to the studio and collapsed into a giggling heap in my dressing room.

Katriona had laid out make-up, knickers and stockings, ready for my arrival. But I spurned the subtle shades she always made me wear, slapping on thick black eyeliner, huge false lashes, and bright red lipstick instead. And I discarded the flesh-coloured hold-ups in favour of glossy black seams and four-inch Cuban heels. The room was swimming around me, and it was a struggle to stay on my feet. Finally, I buttoned a suit jacket over my bare tits, stepped into a tiny pair of sheer black knickers, and tottered on set.

It was completely silent, but for the echoing click-clack of my heels. I set down the bottle of wine I had liberated earlier from the hospitality fridge and poured myself a generous glass. 'Camera boy?' I hollered. 'Come out, camera boy.' Still no sound, but in the corner of my eye I saw the red light flicker on camera 5. Sure enough, there was Andy's delicious torso, bare and gleaming. His jeans were riding low, low enough to expose his thick, hard cock which was pumping through his left hand. The other arm, as ever, operated the camera and his face was completely obscured.

I spun around and heard him extend the lens to focus on my ass, which wiggled with every step I took. When I reached the sofa I paused, took another big gulp of wine, and then half-sat, half-fell, onto the seat.

'Good morning and welcome to *Morning Breakfast*. Today's top story is that Emma Davies has a really wet pussy and she wants everyone to see it.'

My head lolled back on the cushions as I reclined, stretching my legs right up in the air. With my heels pointing skyward, I took hold of my ankles and spread them apart. Then pulled them right over my head until I could lick my knees with my tongue. I remembered that in yoga the position is called 'happy baby' which made me giggle.

I knew the camera was focusing in on my pussy, which was starting to swell with excitement. He must have been so desperate to fuck me – how could he stand to just watch it? I began to ease off my knickers, teasing them over the bare cheeks of my bottom but keeping my pussy slit and pink little anus just about covered. I looked out, between my legs, into the studio where Andy was pulling on his balls to hold back the inevitable.

With knickers still at half-mast, I rolled over onto all fours and then struggled up onto my knees. 'In other news,' I pouted, 'Emma Davies also has really big tits.' I popped one out of my jacket and gave it a squeeze just to illustrate the point. 'And sources close to her say that she wants them sucked, really hard and right now.'

That was the final straw. As if called to heel, he came running and stumbling across the floor to the sofa, losing his jeans and shoes en route. I reached up for the back of his head and forced his mouth down onto mine, fucking his lips with my tongue and grinding my pussy against his cock.

'Get this jacket off.'

He fumbled obediently with the buttons and then took my nipples in his mouth. I pushed them together and thrust them out into his face. 'Don't bite, just rub them properly with your tongue, that's it, that's right.' I had my fingers around my clit now, flicking and stroking it. And then they were entwined around Andy's cock, thick and pulsing in my hand, ready and desperate to shoot all over my tits.

'I want to fuck you, Emma, I want to fuck you,' he moaned. Yeah? You and half the nation, I thought, as he dropped to my feet and took the heel of my left shoe into his mouth. I prodded his balls with the right heel, pushing it deeper and deeper as he angled himself to try and get it up his arse.

'Get up and lick me out.' He clambered up onto his knees, a little reluctantly I thought, but he was still as hard as a chair leg so I didn't really care. I sat back down on my bottom and yanked my knickers all the way down and over my feet, where they snagged on one heel. My pussy was pink and almost foamy with excitement. With my fingers at the back of his head, I guided his tongue down onto my clit and held him down at just the right pressure as he licked and lapped. I could feel all my thoughts draining away, just leaving the primal urge to fuck and mate, and come hard on a big new cock.

My hand crept down his torso to find it, still hard and beating and full of hot spunk. I groaned, pushed his head away and lifted my legs back over my head. My hands gripped my ankles to brace them. 'Go on then, camera boy, get on with it,' I snarled, and Andy obeyed with one hard thrust which nearly took my breath away. It was so thick I felt like something in my pussy had snapped to let it in. But the next few strokes were softer, and soon I was riding wave after wave of pleasure as he pounded rhythmically into my womb.

'Can I come inside you?'

Just the suggestion of it pushed me over the edge. 'God yeah, get it really deep,' I yelled and let my clit flutter into climax on the frantic pulsing of his cock.

As we came, we clasped each other like drowning things, kissing and nuzzling at each other's ears, lips and necks. 'You're amazing, you're amazing,' he whispered.

I just giggled, and then pushed him off to take another well-earned swig of wine. 'You'd better clear off,' I said, catching a glimpse of the studio clock. 'We need to make it look like this never happened.' I was sobering up now, and just wanted to get on with my day and put my depravity behind me.

'But I'll see you again, right?' Andy was looking anxious.

'Oh . . . yeah, yeah,' I said, in the full knowledge that I was hoping to get him sacked for misconduct within the week.

He sloped off, looking a little dejected, and I downed the last dregs of wine from my glass. Hair of the dog, you know. I lay on my back, contemplating getting up, when a loud bang made me leap into the air, followed swiftly by the sound of men's shoes thundering against the floor, getting closer and closer. I whimpered and cast about looking for my knickers, or the jacket, anything to make me feel a bit less naked. But it was too late, the wearer of those thundering shoes had already seen me, and it was bad news.

'Dom! Oh my god. I can explain. I know this must look terrible, but you see –'

162

'Shut the fuck up.' His voice was too quiet; it made me nervous. He picked up my jacket and knickers and threw them out of reach. I tried to cover up my pussy and crossed my arms over my tits, much good that it did.

Dom sat down on the sofa next to me, staring straight ahead. Then, too fast for me to stop him, he took hold of my shoulders and pulled me roughly over his knee. My face was buried in the cushions and my bare bottom was thrust up in the air. It was all desperately humiliating, but at that point I would have done anything to save myself from getting a P45. I kept quiet.

His hand came down gingerly on my bottom and rested on the fullest part of my cheeks. It vibrated a little, like the dance floor in a club. I realised his whole body was shaking, with rage I assumed . . . and possibly something else.

'Emma, you and I need to get a few things straight.' Again the unnaturally smooth voice. 'Point one, you are a talentless little bitch, with no ideas of your own, whose only skill is in tearing down the careers of far better people.'

'Now hang on!' I strained against the arm which was pinning me down by my neck, but it wouldn't budge. He ploughed on, getting louder now.

'Point two! You don't know the first thing about journalism, and you don't deserve to lick the boots of half the people in this studio.'

The pressure on the back of my neck was even firmer now, and with a mouthful of sofa all I could manage in response was 'Mmnff!'

'Point three! You have consistently appropriated the ideas of others, treated your colleagues with disrespect, and, point four!' He was shouting now, and his hand was airborne. 'You are leaking spunk out of your nasty pussy onto a very expensive suede sofa.'

I could feel it as well. Andy must have deposited half a pint deep inside me and it was coming out like a dirty secret. But it wasn't just the sofa, I'd made a wet patch on Dom's suit trousers which was getting bigger and bigger. He must have felt it too, seeping through the material onto the skin of his own cock. As if in response, it suddenly jerked into life, making a sudden, urgent pressure against my close-cropped mound. His breathing became erratic.

'You dirty bitch, look what you've made me do now.' Much as I hated this onslaught of criticism, my clit was recovering itself, sensing a cock in close proximity and wondering if round two was on the cards. And my rational brain was wondering if fucking Dom might actually save my career. After all, if he disgraced himself too his credibility would be completely blown.

'Oohhh.' I gave an encouraging moan, and kicked my nylon-clad legs up in the air. 'Go on, baby, that's it, why don't you take me if you have to, if you need it?' My pussy opened up skyward, as I arched my back catlike and parted my thighs. His cock gave a desperate pulse against my tummy. But instead of loosing his grip on me, he redoubled it, fisting hair at the nape of my neck and shoving my face once more into the coarse material.

Unsure how to react, I kept my bottom up high, still open and inviting. But a volley of handslaps beat it back down, where it tensed up again in shock. The force of each stinging blow filled my eyes with tears, but there was a strange comfort in it. In a way, my work was done. He'd lost control, and I needn't think at all from now on, just play along like a willing doll.

'Do you seriously think I don't know what you're playing at? You don't want me, you've never even looked at me!' Dom emphasised the first syllable of each word with a spank.

'It's true,' I whispered, 'I don't even fancy you, I'm just trying to save myself.' The slaps got faster again, and harder, a grunt of effort accompanying each one. It was all I could do not to cry out. But eventually the ferocity subsided, and his hand began to relax and explore the cleft of my cheeks. His grunts became groans and breathy sighs. The pressure on my neck finally abated too, his fingers releasing my hair and moving underneath me to paw at my breasts.

'OK,' he whispered, 'it's a deal. I'll take the bait.' I crawled obediently off his lap and onto the table, my head still bowed in submission and my legs spread wide. I heard the belt of his trousers clank against the floor, and then the slap, slap, slap of a cock beating through a strong hand. The anticipation set the nerves in my pussy jangling. I thought it might not be such a chore after all to take this powerful man's cock. My pelvic floor relaxed in the hope that there might be a lot of man to accommodate.

Instead of a cock though, the next sensation was the rough surface of a tongue. It probed upwards along my slit and then took a deep, long lick around my anus. My tummy lit up with electricity. I'd never felt anything so good. He moved away but I wanted more, so I clasped my cheeks in my glossy red nails and pulled them as far apart as I could, making myself completely accessible. Andy's spunk still coated me down there, making me all salty and sticky, but it didn't prevent Dom from pushing his tongue hard against my puckered skin, so hard I thought it might pop inside.

I was on the verge of coming, and he must have felt my clit contracting under his chin. Resolved to deny me, he pulled away and climbed up my back like a big panting bear. Then his weight descended and crushed me into the polished wood. My anus briefly became a burning point of broken glass, but then something gave way and it was as if my rectum were sucking him in. I forgot to breathe. An impossibly big shaft filled me up completely. He slipped it in and out ... in and out, agonisingly slowly. My hips shuddered with every inch of deep penetration, flooding and swelling with endorphins. I twisted and writhed on the huge phallus, trying to feel the whole length, every pulsing vein and ridge. Lying prone and empty-headed, I let my boss pump himself into my deepest regions like a cheap hooker doing it for crack.

I don't think I ever made it to orgasm. It's hard to recall. I just know that eventually the nips and licks against the back of my neck turned into one long suck. His climax, when it came, was almost silent. Only the ropes of spunk spooling into my tummy gave him away.

The studio speakers suddenly thrummed into life with a deep electronic drone, then emitted a sound like someone falling off a chair. Finally a disembodied voice whispered 'Fuck, turn it off!' I froze. Blood began to bang in my ears and the ground seemed to buck and roll under my feet. Dom sprang up like a meerkat, his ears straining to identify the source of danger.

'It came from the edit suite, someone's in there, they must have seen.' His mouth formed a soundless O.

Panic gripped my stomach and drained the strength from my legs. I heard Dom start to run, his feet pounding out of the studio doors towards the edit suite. There were a few moments of silence, and then, 'Bastards have already gone. Fucking bastards!' He staggered back into the studio, panting heavily, then stood gently swaying with both hands pressing against his furrowed brow.

'Dom?' I whispered.

He was silent.

'Dom . . . One of the cameras was on.'

He wouldn't speak.

'Dom, what if they recorded it?'

I suppose I should just be grateful that the tape never made it onto YouTube. But it did pass through at least four hundred hands in the 24 hours it took Dom to track it down and destroy it. By then the damage was well and truly done. I don't know. Maybe we could have built up our credibility all over again, given time . . . but I just didn't have it in me, and neither did Dom. I lasted a week before handing my notice in. Dom lasted almost a month.

I guess he and I were pretty much forced to shack up together. It was that or give up all prospect of a normal family life (no one else in our media set would date a loser whose career is in the toilet). We set up a business selling organic yoghurt, down here in Cornwall. The farm was in Dom's family, I think . . . I forget. I do know that I fucking hate yoghurt. And the people around here are so stiff. Mind you, some of the local boys can be quite amusing.

Andy's the Head of News now. Apparently his career is really taking off. Bit of luck really, having the two biggest obstacles to your advancement taken out in one blow. And we never quite managed to establish the identities of those edit-suite lurkers. Still, live by the sword . . .

– Emma, Cornwall, UK

Strap It On

I was round at my friend Danny's and we were watching porn. We always did it every Friday night. Danny would rent the DVDs from the obscene sex shop in town, or we'd watch the latest downloads from his ever-growing porn collection. It was something of a joke between us, and we made a night of it – popcorn, beer, comfy cushions. Because Danny was gay, I could snuggle up against him and jokingly sneak pieces of his popcorn, in a way that just isn't appropriate with straight male friends.

Sometimes Danny would get aroused by the films. He tried to pretend that he didn't, but I could hear his accelerated breathing and he wouldn't let me cuddle up against him. I knew it was because his cock was hard and he didn't want me to brush up against it. I was sure that the moment I left he would masturbate in front of the TV, the slap of taut male flesh on taut male flesh driving him to orgasm.

I won't lie to you – the thought turned me on. Danny is as flamboyantly gay as they come. He grows his hair long at the back and dyes it pink. He whips out ridiculous moves on the dance floor. He even calls me 'darling'. But he isn't one of those gay men who treat the vagina as some sort of voodoo horror object which they would never dare go near. I'm not saying he sexually interacts with them, but the thought of them doesn't turn him off, as such.

I was glad of that, on these Fridays, because, boy, did I fancy Danny rotten. Wrong, eh? – a single girl getting off fantasising about her gay best friend. I didn't care though. In fact, it almost didn't bother me. Almost. Danny was the ultimate shirt-lifter and there was very little chance he'd return my amorous feelings. So, I kept them hidden and contented myself with our shared porn-watching experiences on Friday evenings.

But on this particular Friday, everything changed. Tonight's choice was *Rim Reapers Three*. We were intrigued: *Rim Reapers*, the original, had been spectacular. *Rim Reapers Two*, not so. Would the third instalment bounce the Rim Reaper brand back up into the lofty heights of our good opinion? Or would it mean that the forthcoming part four would never grace the screen of Danny's television? It was a gamble.

As the film got underway, I assumed my customary position curled up against Danny's side, his arm around my shoulders. Our hands brushed as we reached into the bag of Doritos at the same moment and I glanced up at him, always hoping that something in his face would register the spark of electricity I felt between us. Nada. I wish I had a cock, I thought savagely, watching the screen. A big, thick, juicy cock that I could fuck Danny with, until he was sore.

And before you judge such a rude thought jumping into my mind, please remember that the very thing was happening in front of us in vivid technicolour: a multitude of clean-shaven jaws bumping, nipples being bitten, and well muscled arses penetrated by the enormous purple-veined cocks that all the men in the gay porn industry seem to possess.

We lay there for a while, munching on the cheese Doritos. There were a couple of hardcore scenes – chains, balls in mouths, pain inflicted in ways that made me wince and bury my head in my hands. *Rim Reapers Three* was obviously trying to make up for the errors of part two and was doing so via an onslaught of S and M that so far only *Gang Bang No. 5* had ever delivered.

Danny was breathing a little more heavily now, and he didn't wince when I did. He was staring at the screen, eyes wide, and he angled his body a little further away from mine, wriggling slightly. I took the opportunity to look at him, rather than the screen.

He's so hot, Danny. Lynx-like eyes that shine when he delivers one of his customary sarcastic remarks. Shapely cheekbones, dimpled chin, eyelashes way too long for a boy. God, do I fancy him.

I could feel him shifting his pelvis slightly against the floor cushions. There was some spit-roasting taking place now, and I knew Danny loved that. I looked up at him again, but he had zero interest in me whilst *el spitroast* was taking place, so I got up, disgruntled, and went to the toilet.

I rubbed my clit miserably once I was in there, but I couldn't be bothered to make myself come, which was what I normally did on a Friday evening. Sometimes it was depressing, you know, being sexually infatuated with someone you were totally inadequately equipped for.

I stayed there for a little while and then I told myself to get over it. When I went back into Danny's room, the film was just winding down, so I amused myself poking about in his bedroom, nosing around his stuff.

I idly opened one of his desk drawers. And was confronted by a huge black rubber dildo. It was *massive*. It had some faux balls at its base – big like a fucking *horse* would have – and was attachable by a series of straps. The packaging beneath it stated that it was for those who 'loved dark meat'.

An idea began to worm its way into my head. I leaned in, grabbed the dildo, and messed about trying to attach it to myself. Danny was still watching the film.

It was tricky to get into, that strap-on. A bit like a harness. Eventually I stepped into it and secured it all, feeling a bit like I had when I'd gone abseiling on an activity holiday. Just with a huge bobbing appendage affixed to the front.

'Danny,' I cooed, waving my hips from side to side so that the cock waggled. 'Danny!'

He turned his head, took one look at me, and burst out laughing. 'Take that off, you!' he said. 'Things like that aren't for nice little girls. They're for *men*.'

'Oh really?' I said, arching an eyebrow. I walked over to him and started nudging the side of his face with the dildo.

'Stop it!' he said absent-mindedly, swatting it away. His eyes were riveted back on the porn action unfolding before him. I didn't stop, and continued to gently nudge at him. Instead of the hollow of his cheek, I aimed the tip of the dildo at the corner of his mouth. It was somewhat hard to operate, seeing as it was about two metres long.

'Quit it, mate,' he said, with a flash of irritation, still looking away.

'Why don't you suck it like the guys on the telly?' I said casually. He looked up at me, annoyance and faint disgust etched on his face. Then he caught my eye and fell silent. Slowly, an expression of interest filtered into his dark eyes.

'You want me to suck it?' he said slowly. Then, to clarify: 'You want to watch me, sucking this?' The slow way he formed the words, the sudden huskiness seeping into his voice, sent a thrill buzzing through me.

'I want you to suck it,' I reiterated, matching his slow tone. 'With me watching you.'

'You fucking surprise me sometimes, Anna, you really do,' he said, shaking his head. But he didn't say no, he didn't look away. I'd piqued his interest. And then his pink tongue darted out, tentatively, and licked the end of the cock. Experimentally he pursed his lips around the tip of it and sucked gently.

Heat was starting to spread through me, slowly but exquisitely. Watching Danny do this was nothing like

171

watching the exaggerated sucking and fucking on the TV. The way that he was moving his mouth was beautiful. He looked up at me to gauge my reaction, and I could see that his pupils were beginning to dilate, his eyes dark.

'How does it taste?' I asked, my voice a whisper. He eased the cock from his mouth.

'Rubbery,' he said. And then he smiled a wicked smile. 'But it *feels* amazing.' He enclosed his lips over it again, his tongue winking at me as it snaked and swirled and lapped at the huge cock. I could barely keep it still in his mouth now. My cheeks were fiery and my hips were trembling.

'I wish I had a cock,' I said in that whispery voice, low with excitement. As the words fell out of my mouth, his eyes widened with shock, his gaze fixed on mine as he continued to love the strap-on with his mouth. The floodgate opened and suddenly the words started to spill out unstoppably. I knew there was no going back now. 'If I had a cock, I'd make you get on your knees and suck it like you're doing now. I'd make you suck me until I was rock-hard. I'd ram myself into the back of your throat and when you had sucked me for long enough, I'd turn you over.'

He'd got onto his knees now, kneeling in front of me as if I really was a man and he was giving me head. He'd taken the dildo deeper into his throat, but when I paused, he stopped and withdrew again. His eyes were still penetrating mine and the expression on his face was one of intrigue and growing arousal. With a little thrill, I saw the bulge at the front of his jeans – a bulge that, at last, I'd been the cause of.

'And then what?' he said eventually, his voice hoarse. 'After you turned me over, Anna, what would you do with me then?'

'I'd fuck you.' There was a sweet release within me as I said it. Months and months of pent-up sexual tension had built inside me and with those three words I relieved myself of it. A throbbing began within me, in the place between my legs, and a slithery wetness began to seep into the hidden slit.

The words that came from my mouth shocked me. 'I'd fuck you. I'd spread lube all over my great pulsing cock and just as your arsehole started widening for me, I'd ram it right in, and screw you until you came.' Riveted by my words, he'd stopped working on the cock.

'What then?' he demanded urgently. 'What then?'

My mind scrabbled around for the right words, trying to express exactly what I wanted to do to him, to let him know *how much* I wanted him.

'You'd come. You'd come hard, your muscles clenching around my cock until I came too, my hot semen spurting inside of you, running out of your battered arsehole, dripping onto your balls, which I'd suck till they were raw . . .' My breath was coming out in little gasps now, the dildo attached to me quivering as I shook. Danny's mouth was slack and a rosy colour was spreading on his high cheekbones. When he reached down with one hand to massage his cock through his jeans, lust trickled through my groin.

'Do it then,' he whispered. 'Do it. But take your clothes off first.'

I was shaking like a leaf. I couldn't believe my fantasy was coming true, and for a second neither of us moved, unable to believe what we were about to do. And then Danny wriggled out of his jeans and boxers, giving me a tantalising glimpse of his velvety cock springing up from a thatch of wiry hair, before he turned away from me and bent on all fours.

I stripped my clothes off in seconds, my nipples screaming and my clit desperate for stimulation. I ignored them as I put the dildo back on, the harness tight around the naked cheeks of my arse. Finding a jar of lube in Danny's top drawer, I scooped some out and slathered it on, making the cock shine. Hot and determined, I turned back to Danny and his vulnerable, waiting arse. I could see my reflection in his window – God, I looked good with a cock. I could get used to it.

'Anna,' he said, almost pleading. 'Anna, put it in me.'

I teased his arse with the dildo as the sounds of the men fucking on the television chorused in the background. He strained back against it, trying to spear himself on it. With one hand he held himself up and with the other he stroked his dick with long, measured movements. His breathing was harsh and he was evidently trying to keep himself in check.

Aware of how desperate he was, I teased him for a little while, nudging his entrance. I was *loving* the control I had over him. He whimpered and I eventually took pity and slid the cock into his arse a little way. Lubed as it was, it slipped in easily, and with that all reason and constraint gave way. I plunged in, and the rush of power as I ravaged his arse with that enormous cock was unbelievable. I plundered the long slippery tunnel of his arse again and again, his body convulsing in front of me. His hand on his cock was a blur, and eventually with an agonised shriek of 'Fuck, Anna!' his arse clenched and seized up around the dildo, semen spurting through the air as he came violently. I withdrew, blood pounding in my head and in my pussy.

Both of us were breathing hard and Danny lay in front of me, the last vestiges of his orgasm sending quivers through him. Then slowly, he turned to face me. His face was flushed and his eyes were glazed with arousal.

'Your turn,' he growled, and a rush of thanks and desire went through me. Finally, I was going to get the fucking I had been hungering after. If he – or I – didn't touch my clit soon, I was going to *die*.

I held the moist dildo up suggestively, and he shook his head.

'No no, darling,' he said. 'I'm going to fuck you myself.' I practically dissolved. Christ, I'd been longing to hear those words for a long time. His hand was on his dick again, massaging it back to life.

'Your arse or your cunt?' he said, with that dirty sexy smile.

I wanted his cock in me everywhere, *anywhere*, but there could only be one answer.

'My arse,' I said, and his eyes lit up. I eased the harness from my body, and mimicked his earlier actions, bending on all fours on the floor. I was so worked up, even the carpet under my hands and knees felt good. My cunt was dripping, and my untouched virgin arsehole was splayed, waiting for him to fill it.

God, those few moments waiting for him to fill me were the most horny of my life. I've never felt such anticipation as I waited for someone to do something so filthy to me. He came up behind me and slipped one hand around my waist, locking my body into his. Everywhere he touched was like the sun coming up over my body and sending its rays straight into my pussy. His cock was stiffening again already, and as he began to tease the outer rim of my hole, as I had his, I could feel it swelling even further.

With one hand he brushed my pubic hair, delicately enough to make me want to scream, and with the other he reached into the pot of lube and with a cold squelch slapped it onto my quivering arse. Then he pushed a finger in, pressing against the resistant muscles before breaking through into my most private hole. He put another one in slowly, then a third. I was in an agony of delight, squirming against his restraining arm. My arse and my clit felt like they were connected by a rope of fire, and any minute the whole thing was going to melt.

'Darling, I love it,' I heard him say behind me. 'You are just *so* fucking *tight*.'

And with that he withdrew his hand, nuzzled my slippery, lubed entrance for a nano-second with his huge hard cock, and then slammed in as if he were fucking for his *life*. I yelled with the impact and pain flashed through me, subsiding quickly as he filled my arse again and again. With each thrust he drove deeper and I gasped and writhed as the point of his cock forced wave after wave of pleasure to roll through my body.

Just as I thought I couldn't take any more, stuffed and impaled again and again, he moved the hand that was holding my waist, and started to stroke my swollen clit through the saturated lips of my cunt. The attention was so welcome, my clit burst into orgasm almost at once. My hips bucked and my breathing went crazy, as I strained for it, teetering on the edge . . . And yes! There it was! The most intense orgasm I'd ever had pulsed through me, my pussy and my arse squeezing and burning with pleasure as it fizzled through my system. He kept his cock in me the whole time, sunk to the hilt, groaning with pleasure as my muscles spasmed and contracted around it. When eventually the tremors subsided, he withdrew from my aching hole, and we both lay there, dripping with juice and semen and sweat. I looked at his cock, red and sore.

'Danny, you've got yourself all dirty,' I said.

He looked me straight in the eye. 'We just need a few minutes and then you're going to lick me clean.'

It was the best fuck I've ever had.

Fridays were never the same after that. I guess you're asking the obvious, aren't you? Why would a gay man be fucking a straight girl? Don't think the same question didn't cross my mind. So I asked Danny about it, later that same evening. And was more than satisfied with the response.

'Darling,' he said, 'I wouldn't want to live in Brighton. That isn't to say I don't enjoy the occasional day trip.'

– Anna, Sussex, UK

Upskirt Cravings

It didn't surprise me when I found out that my husband had a secret stash of pornographic magazines. I'm a woman of the world, so I've always assumed that most men keep a stash of porn hidden away somewhere. But what did surprise me was that the mags were all dedicated to a particular fetish. It seems that my husband has an abiding passion for legs, bottoms and upskirt pictures, for tantalising glimpses of frilly knickers, suspender belts and stocking tops. Since I'm very busty, I had always assumed that my husband was a tit man. It was a shock to find out that his interests lay elsewhere, but an even bigger shock was to follow.

In an attempt to understand my husband's fetish, I spent an entire afternoon flicking through his stash of mags. I wanted to know what it was that he found so arousing about staring up a woman's skirt and seeing her panties. And, to my amazement, as I gazed at the upskirt pictures, I felt a moistening sensation between my legs. My knickers began to stick to my sex lips, because the pictures were genuinely arousing to me. I could see quite clearly what my husband liked about the magazines. Most of the girls were amateurs, or girl-next-door types, and many of them had been photographed unawares. Glimpsing up their skirts without the girls knowing seemed so naughty and so dangerous. I was able to see what they thought was kept hidden. I was gazing into their most intimate areas and I couldn't help liking what I saw.

It was ever so strange, because it's not like I wasn't used to seeing women in various states of undress – in the changing rooms at the gym, for instance, or trying on clothes with friends. Over the years I must have shared hundreds of changing room cubicles with my friends and not once has it led to any feelings of lesbian desire. But this was different. The girls in the mags were total strangers, and yet I was getting to view them so intimately. The girls had gone out feeling safe and secure in their dresses and skirts, but the cameras had still managed to take a sneaky peek into their private worlds. The cheap thrill I got from getting to see what I wasn't meant to see made me start to look at the female body in a whole new way. I liked the soft, smooth flesh, which looked so different to my husband's hairy skin. Even more, I liked the way the girls' silky knickers hugged the peach-like contours of their lovely bottoms.

I liked it all so much that I went back to the magazines every day for a week. I masturbated while looking at the upskirt pictures, but even more worrying was the way that I began to behave in public. I started going out in skirts and dresses that were far too short and slutty for a woman of my age (37) to wear. In the past I've always dressed quite conservatively, but the magazines made me change. Suddenly, I wanted other people to look at me in the same way that I looked at the girls in the magazines. I wanted a gust of wind to blow up my skirt, so that everyone would get to see my knickers. Better still, I wanted someone to secretly photograph up my skirt and put me in the magazines, so that strange men could wank over pictures of my arse.

I even found myself turning into something of a stalker. When I was out shopping and I saw a girl in a short skirt, I would follow her around for ages. I would be waiting for the moment when she went up some stairs or an escalator, then I'd stand at the bottom and try to look up her skirt. Sometimes I'd see just the tiniest peek of her bum cheeks, but it was always enough to make my pussy get wet. Actually, it was only enough until the day came along when I was no longer content just to look. Eventually, I wanted to touch as well. I wanted to push my face up a young girl's skirt and plant kisses all over her arse and pussy.

For a month I tried to resist the urge, but the depth of my desire was too extreme. So I went along to a local bar that I knew was popular with gays and lesbians. It was terrifying walking in there that night, in case somebody saw me. My husband still had no idea what effect his secret stash of mags had had on me, so I was taking a real risk by being seen out in public. Anyone could have spotted me and told him about the way I started sniffing around the sexy young dyke in the red pleated miniskirt. There was a disco taking place and the girl was dancing in a way that made her skirt keep riding up her smooth slim thighs and reveal the tops of her stockings. I couldn't take my eyes off her and I know she saw me looking. She even smiled at me a couple of times. I felt sure that she was attracted to me, but I was too scared to make a move.

So for ages I just stood there watching the girl, all the while imagining what it would be like to push my head up her skirt. Then I noticed her going to get her coat and I realised that she was leaving. I made a snap decision to hurry after her, then I stalked her until she got to her car. It was parked down a quiet alleyway, so there was no one around but her and me. Her dancing had made me amazingly aroused, so I ended up doing something crazy.

I ran up to the girl as she was unlocking her car, then I knelt down behind her and pushed my head up her skirt. She froze to the spot as I pressed my lips against her stocking tops. She almost screamed, but she held the scream inside, then I heard her start to speak to me.

'You nearly scared me to death,' the young dyke said,

then she mentioned how she'd spotted me in the club and asked why I hadn't tried to chat her up.

'Don't speak,' I said, then I placed my hands upon her gorgeous thighs. 'I need you to pretend that you don't know I'm here.'

It must have been a confusing comment for the girl, but she did as I said and fell completely silent. I wanted her to be silent for the simple reason that I wanted it to be just like in the upskirt magazines where the pictures are taken without the girl's knowledge. I suppose I wanted to imagine that I was a hidden camera getting a sneaky peek up the lesbian's skirt. As a hidden camera, I'd be free to explore every nook and cranny of the young girl's body, and she wouldn't even know I was there.

With the young girl silent, it was just like I was trapped inside my own private world. The pleats of her skirt kept me hidden away as I ran my fingers up the sides of her legs. As my fingertips enjoyed the feel of her nylon stockings, I kissed the bare flesh just above her stocking tops. I kissed upward and upward, until I reached the lower curve of her buttocks. Her knickers were red and made of silk. I pressed my face against the back of them, then pushed my face between her soft, warm cheeks.

The lesbian sighed as I stuck out my tongue and licked the back of her knickers. My tongue jabbed back and forward, pushing the silky panties deep inside her crevice. I gave her a wedgie, then I pulled down her knickers just far enough to uncover her hole. I had never seen a woman's arsehole up close before, so my excitement got the better of me. With my tongue fully extended, I licked the girl's ring, lubricating her orifice with my saliva and gradually burrowing my way inside her anus.

It would be hard to describe the taste of the girl's asshole, but it would be easy to describe the effect that it had upon me. My cunt grew wet and my insides started to spasm. Added to that, my nipples grew hard, so I undid my blouse and pressed my tits up against the back of the girl's thighs. My tongue was still exploring her rectal cavity and soon my hands had found their way towards her clit. I poked her sex-button with one middle finger, then penetrated her gash with the other. Her labia were already overflowing with sticky juices. The dyke might have been shocked by the way that I had approached her, but my perverted upskirt fantasy had definitely turned her on.

The first of many intense groans burst out of the girl's lips, as I rammed the whole of my middle finger right up her cunt. I gave her delicious arsehole a long, lusty lick, then I took several deep bites out of her pert little buttocks. I wanted to explore every inch of her upskirt area, to uncover all the secrets that her pleated skirt was supposed to conceal. So I licked my way back down her thighs and stared at her stockings tops, then I kissed the flesh either side of her lace suspenders. Next, I withdrew my finger from her cunt and moved around in front of her. I stared at her hairy bush, then pulled her knickers right down, before pressing my mouth against her sweet-tasting hole.

As my tongue pressed deep inside the dyke's wet pussy, I placed both of my hands on her arse cheeks. The finger I'd withdrawn from her sticky quim was sopping wet with cunt juice, so I forced it against her ring and then pushed it well inside her back passage. The girl screamed out loud as her anus got pierced, then a thick stream of juice poured out of her pussy. My cheeks and chin got covered in her come, while loads more come gushed into my mouth. The anal fingering and the labial licking had brought the dyke to a very juicy climax. I kissed her pussy and her clit, as the juice just kept on spewing out of her slit. My finger pushed repeatedly in and out of her anus. The girl could not stop squealing with delight, because I was causing her so much pleasure!

The girl yelled and panted for over a minute, then she managed to speak some proper words. She told me to get up, so that she could drop to her knees and lick me out, but there was no way that I was going to leave the place where I felt so happy – up her sexy pleated skirt. Still licking her out and fingering her anus, I reached between my legs and began to strum my cunt and clitoris. I was so turned on that it only took a few quick strokes for me to make myself come. I didn't even have to take my knickers off. I just rubbed my crotch through the fabric and, in seconds, I was climaxing.

And what a climax it was! An ocean of juice came teeming out of my pussy, the insides of which were churning around like mad. The whole of my flesh had turned into goose bumps, while my most sensitive parts, my nipples and clit, seemed to have turned into mini-vibrators. They were pulsating wildly and sending out shock waves that ricocheted here, there and everywhere upon my body. The dyke must have thought I was a total sex maniac, because I was roaring my head off with pleasure and really rubbing my face all over her upskirt area. I brushed my cheeks against her cunt, her clit, her thighs, her stocking tops and especially her pubic hair. I loved pressing my skin against her most secret intimate areas. For me, it was the ultimate high. That's why I drenched my knickers so badly.

In fact, my knickers stank so much when I got home that night that I had to stick them straight in the laundry basket, before my husband guessed what I'd been up to. I often wonder how he'd react if he knew that I had developed an upskirt fetish even greater than his own – a fetish so strong that it's even made me develop lesbian tendencies. My guess is that he'd love it, so maybe I'll test him out one day. Maybe one day he'll get home to find me bending over the kitchen table in my shortest skirt and my sexiest underwear. I'll pretend he's caught me unaware, as he kneels down behind me and licks my arsehole. It's sure to lead to some amazing sex. I'm getting sticky right now just thinking about it!

– *Gail, Kent, UK*

SouthWestMa'am

Before I start, I need to make one thing clear. I really am not a lesbian. I'm not even the kind of girl who will kiss her mates for a laugh after a night on the Breezers, checking for the reactions of any males in the vicinity and fumbling drunkenly at spaghetti straps. No, I am fully heterosexual. I like the physical contrast of a man's body – its flatness, its hardness, its latent power. I am the only woman I know who positively relishes stubble burn, and one of the most delicious moments in any new relationship for me is the inevitable playful arm-wrestle. Woe betide the man who is still pushing at my small hand after five seconds.

'Thanks. See you around.'

So how I ended up on the back seat of a car with my skirt hiked to my waist, knickers around my ankles and a woman's hand exploring my pussy and even my virgin arsehole is a story requiring a certain amount of explanation.

All my life I have fantasised about taking a fully submissive role in a relationship, and yet the prevailing sociodynamics have conspired to make this almost impossible for me. The eligible men of my sphere were all serious-minded, earnest types who expressed strong beliefs in equality. Which is fair enough – I would never argue that men and women are anything but equal. But it does make it very difficult to ask for a good spanking.

I tried it a couple of times, but my partners were uncomfortable with the idea of striking a woman. They did not, they said, need to act like a caveman to assert their masculinity. *But what if I want you to?* I felt like whining. But there was clearly no point. I had to cut my losses and try to embrace the vanilla.

And embrace the vanilla I did, to the point of marriage to a wonderful man who is my partner and my best friend. Perfect in all respects, except ... Well, you can probably guess. Our sex life is pedestrian. He has tried to indulge me on occasion but never repeated the games, confessing that he finds them a little ridiculous and he doesn't enjoy play-acting. So there was the stark reality made plain – live the rest of my life able to climax only by fantasising that I am tied down and writhing on a sore, hot bottom. Or ...

Adultery was out of the question. There was no chance of anything like that. The idea of all the sneaking around and having to act normal was enough to raise my blood pressure. And besides, it was not so much an emotional connection I craved. I began to surf BDSM internet sites and briefly contemplated a visit to a professional disciplinarian, but I surmised that even that would involve baring my private parts to a strange man, which went against my conscience.

For weeks I tried to put the idea from my head, to douse the red hot chilli that persistently intruded into my vanilla masquerade, but it just kept on burning a hole in me, deeper and darker and hotter, until one day it occurred to me: what if I met a new female friend? Perhaps one I could pass off as a former colleague or university acquaintance? One that just happened to be a domme? In my confused and frustrated mind, exposing my body to a woman was no more wicked than using the communal shower at the gym. I suppose I might have thought further and reconsidered, but I just didn't want to. I refused to be diverted from this new and excellent plan.

My excitement was so intense that I just had to log on to a BDSM personals site and make myself a profile straight away: *'Wayward young woman requires strict female disciplinarian to keep her on the straight and narrow. Discreet older woman preferred, natural authoritarian with a keen desire to improve my behaviour by means of humiliating punishments and generally shaming treatment.'* Other more personal information about my age and appearance followed, though for obvious reasons I did not post up a photograph.

I was not sure whether I should expect any response at all, but I was pleasantly surprised to find a good half-dozen replies in my inbox the next morning. Most could be discarded for geographical reasons, and of the two local respondents, one sounded slightly weird. Which left Lucinda. Not that she revealed her true name quite so early in the proceedings; for the first week of exploratory emails, I knew her only as SouthWestMa'am. Little by little, information was drip-fed. She was an experienced domme and a lesbian, with a partner who did not mind her playing away now and again. She was in her late forties and worked as a barrister, which was thrilling to me; actually the thought of a severe lady in black silks and a wig rather turned me on. As the level of trust between us increased, we began to test each other in little ways. I sent her my fantasies, and she responded with tasks for me. Once I had to spend the day at work wearing stockings, suspenders and no knickers beneath my skirt. Another time I had to buy some curtain tie-backs and restrain my wrists and ankles with them, prior to masturbating and giving her a full report. She was always pleased with my reports, and referred to me as 'Good Girl', which made me quiver inside.

Then, one morning when I had emailed her to say my husband was out at rugby practice, she got straight back to me with a mobile telephone number and an order. I was to undress to bra, knickers, stockings, suspenders and high heels, then to call her on the number provided. When she picked up, I was to pleasure myself over the phone to her, obeying any and all instructions she might give. My entire body trembled at the thought of this – actually *speaking* to her, and in such intimate circumstances too! – but I shot up the stairs to clothe myself as she required, and my fingers were so nervous I had to punch the number into my phone three times before I got the ring tone I needed. My stomach was in knots and I seriously thought about pressing 'End Call' before I could get any deeper into this, but as soon as she picked up and I heard her voice, I knew I could not withdraw now. Such a voice. Calm, crisp, clear and with the aristocratically clipped vowels of a 1950s newscaster, she sounded every inch the fantasy headmistress.

'Hello, yes?' she said in a tone that could be construed as terse, though I know now that this was her natural manner. I took a deep shuddering breath, and before I could speak, she cut in with, 'Ah, this is my girl, isn't it?'

'Yes, Ma'am,' I squeezed out.

'And are you appropriately dressed, girl?'

'I am.' I was made to describe what I wore in detail, then commanded to climb onto the bed, pull my knickers down to my knees, spread my legs and masturbate, describing my actions to her as I did so. I cannot convey to you the incredible rush; the mix of mortification and submissive rapture I experienced that day. I was a girl who had trouble speaking up in staff meetings without blushing, yet here I was, telling a strange woman over the telephone that I was fingering my clit in circular motions and thinking about how much better it would be if she were watching me.

'Good girl,' she encouraged in that brittle undefiable voice. 'You're doing very well. Keep those thighs wide, dear, and imagine I have you tied up and I'm watching you with a riding crop in my hand. Because dirty girls like you need a good whipping, don't they? They need to

186

learn to keep their fingers clean and their thoughts pure, and the way to do that is to have a stern mistress who can keep them in line. Believe me, girl, I am going to show you the meaning of obedience and respect, and if it takes a regular good hard thrashing, then so be it.'

That was what it took. I came enormously, wailing into the phone, bucking up and down on the bed, and ending it all with a whispered, 'Thank you, Ma'am.'

'It was a pleasure, girl. Now I really think it's time we talked about meeting face to face, don't you?'

I had seen a photograph beforehand, but when I saw her waiting for me, elegantly cross-legged in the hotel foyer, I nearly bolted. I couldn't really be doing this, could I? But before I could make good my chicken-livered resolution, she glanced over the top of her *Telegraph*, fixing me with the hardest of stares through her gold-rimmed glasses until all I could do was cross the room on somewhat uncompliant legs.

'Gail, I presume?' she said, standing and thrusting forward a hand for me to shake. She was rather taller than I thought, and slender to the point of bony, dressed in an elegant trouser suit. You would never have called her beautiful, but she certainly had a striking presence; all those years of holding forth in court had given her the air of one who cannot be argued with. I had to fight back an urge to curtsey, though maybe that would come later. 'Better than your photograph,' she said brusquely as I sat. 'Not carrying as much weight. A decent haircut goes a long way too.'

I had no answer to that and I just half-laughed lamely, but she had moved on already and was ordering two gin and tonics from a waiter. I had never told her I liked gin and tonic; it was simply assumed, and somehow that gave me a thrill. She had assumed command from the very start.

At first conversation was brittle, covering our respective journeys and our previous experiences of the hotel, but over lunch her manner changed; if you can imagine steely flirtation, then that was what she was doing.

'I must say, I like your dress,' she said. 'Clings in all the right places. Nice deep V-neck. I suppose you are wearing a bra?'

The fish was like a solid obstruction in my throat before I could croak out, 'Well, yes, I am. So I'm what you expected?'

'More or less.'

'Do you do this . . . you know . . . often?' The polite cliché sounded so ludicrous in this context that I was hard pressed not to laugh out loud with nerves.

'I've had a number of submissives over the years. The girls usually go on to find somebody they can have a live-in relationship with; my position makes that impossible, of course. I suppose you will do the same one day. Hopefully in the distant future.' She flashed me a smile that was genuinely warm and a twinge of conscience pricked me. I had not told her I was married; somehow I couldn't bring myself to disclose that detail. If I did, then it would seem like genuine cheating. The conversation moved on and remained largely unsexual; this was a no-strings meeting and if either of us decided we didn't want to pursue the liaison, we would be free to walk away. However, I very much wanted to dip my toe further into the waters, and it seemed that she did too.

She paid the bill and gave me a hard stare over her gold rims. I swallowed. This was serious. She had expectations of me, and she didn't want to be disappointed. More than this, it was suddenly very important to me that I didn't disappoint her.

'So then. Gail. I haven't booked a room or anything. Didn't want to be presumptuous. So can I give you a lift home?'

'Oh . . . thanks. Yes, thanks for lunch and everything.' Was that really it?

'And perhaps if you know of any secluded beauty spots on the way . . . .'

My heart thundered. All I could do was nod.

We drove to a woodland spot I know, her well-manicured hand on my thigh all the way and *The Archers* playing incongruously on the radio.

'You're nervous, of course,' she stated baldly, putting the gearstick into neutral and patting my thigh with that hand, as if I were a skittish pony. My breathing was shallow, and I half-nodded half-grimaced my reply. 'Only to be expected the first time. But there is nothing to be nervous about, girl. All you have to do is what you're told. It's really very easy. Do you trust me?'

I nodded again, because oddly I did.

'Good. Now lift that skirt up so I can see that you have been a good girl and worn what I told you to.' She had stipulated stockings and suspenders, and I had complied, to her obvious approval. She ran her hands over my white thigh-tops, twanging the suspender straps so that I gasped, which made her chuckle. 'Well done; you've passed the first test. Now recline that seat and we'll have a good look at you.'

I fidgeted with the mechanism until the smooth leather seat tilted backwards, leaving me lying at a slight angle, not quite flat.

'Dress all the way off, I think. That's good. Lovely underwear; is it Janet Reger? Now then, pull down the cups of your bra so I can have a look at your nipples. Oh yes, nice and stiff and red – are you cold, dear? No, I thought not. And a gorgeous pair. What size are you?'

'36C,' I said meekly, feeling a heady sense of surreal arousal, especially when her hands descended on my exposed breasts, stroking and squeezing, brushing the nipples deliciously and then pinching them so that I squirmed.

'Keep still, girl. I think you're a lusty little minx, aren't you? Thoroughly enjoying your examination, aren't you?

Hmm?' She twisted a nipple so that I yelped my assent. 'Very well. On to the next area. Knickers off now, and spread those legs nice and wide. Good girl.'

It can't have been comfortable for her, hanging over me from the side, but she did not register anything other than utter composure as she peered avidly into the apex of my V-shaped legs. Her commentary on what she saw there was mortifying and yet so perfectly attuned to my fantasies that I hardly knew what to feel. 'Oh, plenty of juice here already. I thought there might be. Does it make you wet to be laid down and intimately examined, girl? I know it does. Look at that luscious little clit, standing up to say hello.' Her fingers pulled at my labia, spreading them even further apart and massaging them in the process so that a damp slicking sound was produced. There was no mistaking how wildly turned on I was. She circled my vulva for agonising minutes before inserting one finger – I tensed against it, worrying suddenly about the length of her fingernails and the potential for injury. She slapped my thigh sharply and barked an order for me to let her in. I could not resist, and allowed her to push two and then three fingers all the way in. 'Oh, you're tight, Miss,' she hissed, thrusting and penetrating me so that I had to lift my bottom from the seat. 'Very tight and very wet. A very wicked little madam. And I believe I told you not to move.' By now I was arching my back, rotating my hips invitingly, wanting her to persist with the attentions of her fingers, while her other hand had just introduced itself to my hungry clit.

'Oh no!' I moaned, propping myself onto my elbows in protest at her sudden and cruel withdrawal.

'You disobeyed, girl; I'm afraid you must be punished. Open the car door and get out.'

'What?'

'Don't make it any worse – do as you're told.'

I stared down at myself, aghast for a second or two, naked but for stockings, suspenders and a bra with wrenched-down cups – and then reluctantly opened the door and stood beside it, my feet cold on the grass. She came around to stand behind me, still every inch the professional lawyer, not a hair out of place.

'Bend over and place your palms on the car seat please. Now!' The 'now!' was like a pistol shot, and I pivoted at the waist as fast as I could, standing with my naked bottom presented in all its glory, vulnerable and unshielded in the open air. Before I could even worry about observers or unwelcome guests, I felt a sharp hard smack to my bare backside and I cried out. My disciplinarian friend was not going to be diverted by any amount of protest, though – she spanked away at my poor arse until it was bright red and the skin felt stretched and burning hot to the touch. All the while, through my indignant ouches and aahs, she scolded me and lectured me on the necessity of submission and obedience. After a while, my moans softened, extended, became lower in timbre and I pushed my bum out to meet her hand as it fell, falling into the sensation, revelling in my soreness and heat.

'Well, my dear,' she said, laying on the final stroke after a good five minutes of this, and moving her hand between my legs. 'If I had any doubts, I don't now. You are genuinely submissive. Aren't you?'

'Yes,' I whimpered, rubbing myself gently on her palm as she pressed it against my clit.

'I think we will get along famously. But you must address me as Ma'am. Don't forget.'

'No, Ma'am . . . I won't.' I groaned, feeling her fingers poke their way back up my greedy passage.

'Lovely. I might allow you a little orgasm now, girl. What do you say?'

'Thank you, Ma'am.' Oh, her hands were like magic; their refinement of touch quite unlike anything I had experienced with a man. Pushing down on her, grinding my hips, I pictured how this would look to a passer-by and the thought almost made me come then and there –

my soundly spanked bottom thrust out while my mistress fingered my spread, nude pussy. Suddenly an even filthier element was added to the tableau, as she began to circle my virgin anus with her thumb, prodding it harder and harder until she broke past the ring of muscle. Oh, God, what was that feeling? I felt plundered, taken, owned, crazed with the intensity of it all, and when she said, 'You really are a dirty little whore, aren't you?' I came like a roaring monster, thrashing around under her firm hands until she let me go and I flopped helplessly down, face in the leather, knees on the grass.

When I had recovered, she had me kneel and lick her until she reached her own climax, then I dressed and she drove me home. We did have plans to meet again, but when it came down to it, I felt too guilty. It was, after all, proper adultery and I realised I could not trust myself not to get emotionally involved with her. So I confessed my marital status and she retired gracefully. It remains, however, the single most powerful sexual experience of my life, and I often fantasise about what might have been.

– Gabrielle, Southampton, UK

Hard-Earned Cash

The most exciting thing I've ever done, sexually, was getting paid to fuck a stranger. It happened because I was talking to my best friend Claire. I knew she was working as a prostitute – she called it being an escort but I knew Claire fucked the clients she escorted – and she asked me if I'd be interested in helping her out on a job.

I have to admit the idea had a lot of appeal.

I've always thought Claire's life seemed pretty glamorous. She was able to work whatever hours she pleased, she got to dress in pretty clothes and sexy lingerie, and she never seemed short of money. But, because I've got a boyfriend, Ricky, who I knew would not approve of my doing such things, I'd never explored the possibility. However, when Claire asked if I would be interested in helping her with a job, I asked her to tell me more.

She explained that one of her regulars wanted a double. Then she explained that a double was when a customer paid to have two women, who both serviced him and put on some sort of lesbian show for his entertainment. I don't know why, but the more Claire told me about it, the more I found the idea irresistibly exciting.

'Tony's decent enough, for a client,' Claire said. 'And he's willing to pay us a grand each for four hours, tomorrow night, from eight until midnight.'

The money sounded astronomical – almost like a lottery win. At the time I would have to have worked for more than a month to earn that much cash, and then there would have been tax to take off. Even if the idea hadn't been so sexually stimulating I think I would have been tempted. Because I could feel the familiar rush of warmth spreading through my loins, it was inevitable I would say yes. Instead of immediately blurting agreement, I said I had three questions that she needed to answer before I committed myself.

'Will this Tony wear a condom?'

'Of course.'

'Can we keep this secret from Ricky?'

'I won't be telling him.'

'Are you going to be all right pretending to do lesbian things with me?'

Claire laughed at that question. 'Will I be all right with that?' she repeated. She licked her lips, eyed me up and down, and then said, 'I've been waiting for a chance to do that since we first met at college.'

I told Ricky I was off to have drinks with Claire the following night. He didn't suspect anything and, because I was dressed down in jeans and a T, he didn't have any reason to be suspicious. I arrived at Claire's and she ushered me into her bedroom and told me to pick whatever clothes I wanted from her wardrobe. An hour later I was looking ultra-glamorous and sitting beside Claire in the taxi as we sped toward Tony's hotel room. My stomach was tied in knots that were part nervousness and part excitement. When Claire put a hand on my bare knee, squeezed and told me it would all be all right, I could feel my excitement grow more obvious. The crotch of my thong was sodden.

Tony was not what I expected. I had thought men would pay for sex because they were ugly and weren't able to get laid through regular means. As it turned out Tony was a fairly attractive man who explained, later in the evening, that he didn't want to go through the rigmarole of getting into a relationship. Being able to pay for the sex he wanted helped him satisfy his needs without any emotional complications.

But that conversation happened later in the evening.

When Claire and I first walked into his hotel, he greeted us at the door of his room wearing only a towelling bath robe and holding a bottle of champagne in his hand. He greeted Claire with a light embrace and a kiss to her cheek. And then he appraised me with a smile that was pure lechery. I loved that.

'Is this the girlfriend you were telling me about?' he asked.

Claire introduced me as Mandy – not my real name – and suggested she and Tony should sort out the finances whilst I poured drinks. I watched him hand over a fat roll of notes to her and Claire counted her way through it before putting the money safely into her purse. I walked over to them both with glasses of champagne and realised that now the money had changed hands there was no going back. That thought made me even more excited.

'Why don't we give you a massage?' Claire suggested. 'Get you relaxed and ready for the night?'

Tony thought that was a good idea and slipped out of his bathrobe.

I'd been going out with Ricky for the best part of three years and this was the first time since going steady that I'd seen another man's cock. Tony was already partially hard and his cock looked a few inches longer than Ricky's and a lot thicker. Staring down at him, I couldn't help but grin as I thought how good it was going to be to have that length slide inside me.

I smiled approval and followed Claire's lead as she ushered Tony to the bed. My heart was beating real fast, I knew I was moments away from cheating on Ricky, and a part of me kept screaming that I should run out of the hotel room and never talk to Claire ever again.

But, instead, I said, 'Does anyone mind if I slip out of these clothes and make myself comfortable?' Without waiting for a response, I unzipped the dress I was wearing and stepped out of it to reveal myself in just boots and a thong.

Both Tony and Claire looked at me with obvious hunger.

'How about we massage her?' Tony suggested.

And that was how the evening began.

Claire had brought some baby oil with her. She put some into her own hands as well as Tony's, and I was sprawled on a stranger's bed while he and my best girlfriend massaged my near-naked body. My boobs and nipples received the most intense massage from Tony but it was Claire who slipped off my thong and started to stroke the oil against my pussy lips. I was already on the brink of climax by the time she started doing that. How I made it through the massage without coming is a mystery I shall never know.

Occasionally, as I lay on the bed, I reached out and stroked Tony's erect cock. And, when I was feeling a little more daring, I reached out and touched the swell of Claire's breast. The atmosphere in the room was charged and thick and almost unbreathable. When Claire said to Tony, 'Do you want to watch us fuck?' I don't know which of us was most aroused.

I had thought it would feel strange to be kissing my best friend but Claire made the experience seem as natural as anything. She leaned over me, teased me for a moment with the threat of her lips, and then she was crushing her mouth against mine in a sultry, passionate exploration. Her tongue struggled against mine; I felt her fingertips sliding against my inner thigh, and I realised, as we were kissing, she was also starting to finger my pussy.

Tony groaned and ejaculated.

I barely noticed his climax. I was too busy enjoying my moments with Claire. I don't know how long we spent entwined on the bed – kissing, touching and growing more intimate – but I do know the time passed far too quickly for me. Claire went down on me, licked me to an orgasm, and then she presented me with the sight of her freshly shaved sex as we settled into a 69 position.

Tony was hard again – probably from watching us – and Claire said she would go and get the condoms from her purse. Whilst I was alone with Tony I began to play with his impressive cock.

'Do you want to suck it?' he asked.

I grinned at him. I'd been wanting to suck it since I'd first seen his cock. Now that I had the opportunity I told him nothing was going to stop me from getting my lips around his shaft. I managed to restrain myself until Claire had returned with the condoms and then, when we'd managed to roll one down Tony's thick girth, I placed my mouth over him.

Tony made all the sounds to indicate he was really enjoying my mouth. Claire made the moment even more memorable by fingering my clit as I sucked Tony's cock. When I glanced up from his erection I realised we were linked together with Tony lapping at Claire's pussy.

The evening was torrid and sweaty and has stayed in my memory ever since. We coaxed three climaxes out of Tony but he got a lot more out of me and Claire. I sucked his balls whilst he held his cock inside Claire's pussy. And, when he came, Claire and I put on a finger-fucking show for him that got his erection rigid again.

When we were going, as Claire was getting her coat and checking that the money was still in her purse, Tony gave me an extra hundred pounds and told me that was a gift because I'd made the evening so special for him. When I kissed him thank you I could taste pussy on his mouth but I didn't know if it was mine or Claire's. However, the combination of the money and the taste was enough to make me horny all over again.

I haven't done another job with Claire since that one. Even if she did ask me, I probably wouldn't do another one. But that doesn't mean she isn't still my best friend.

And when we get together for our occasional girls' nights in, it's good to know that we don't just have to watch a movie to keep ourselves entertained.

– 'Mandy', Rotherham, UK

Wet Paint

Never interrupt an artist at work. They get really crabby.

I discovered this the day I went to the special place I have. Of course, it's not really my place – it's owned by some business corporation and managed by the Royal Society for the Protection of Birds, I think. Anyway, it's got public access. It's called Dove Mere and if you pick the right time – not first thing in the morning when the dog-walkers are out, or at the weekend when there are dinghy-sailors and kids messing about on the open water – you're pretty much on your own down there. A few fishermen are always around at any time of day, but there's a long footpath right round the lake and little branching paths down to bird-hides at the edge of the water, among the tall reeds. I go there because my own back garden is overlooked by all the neighbours and I like to sunbathe topless. I take a magazine or a paper-back and find somewhere secluded to lie back and relax. And I always know if there's someone coming down the path toward me because the wooden walkways bounce slightly to the rhythm of footfalls; there's just enough time to whip a top back on and look absorbed in my reading.

I'll admit, I always take my Rabbit vibrator in my bag on these little outings. There's nothing like the sun on my skin to make me feel good and horny. That summer afternoon, wearing just a crop-top and a miniskirt and flip-flops, I went with a copy of *The Da Vinci Code* to my favourite spot. It's right down among the tall rushes, hidden from the bank, and the platform itself is shielded from the water by a woven screen of sticks, so as not to let any of the birds on the lake see that you're there. There's an eye-slit for bird-spotters to peer through, though personally I've no interest in the wildlife. But this time I found the bench where I'd hoped to sit occupied by a painter. He had a little easel and a case full of tubes of paint, and was staring through binoculars out across the lake, sometimes daubing at the paper in front of him, or rinsing the brush in the jar of water at his feet. He'd been there a while too; laid all around him were bits of paper on which he'd been sketching or painting.

I was a bit put out. This was supposed to be my place, I thought. And I have a wicked streak. 'Hello!' I said as brightly as I could. 'What are you doing?' I intended to be irritating; it seemed to work. He cast me a brief dismissive glance.

'Painting.'

Oh, a sarcastic one. He was just a skinny little bloke, not exactly unattractive but geeky-looking and a bit dishevelled, with unkempt curly hair and gold-rimmed glasses. I came in closer and picked up one of the loose sheets of paper. It had a pencil sketch of a duck on it. 'Hey, this is pretty good,' I told him.

That did wind him up. 'Thanks,' he sneered, holding his hand out, and I gave him the paper back. Only so I could squint closer at his easel though, which had a proper painting on it of the lake, with the big stems of reed mace and a couple of golden ducks.

'That's pretty. Are you using watercolours?'

'Acrylics.'

I gave him a beaming smile. 'So what sort of birds are they?'

'Mandarin ducks.' He looked irritated. I guess curvy young women didn't make a habit of chatting him up and he didn't know how to take it. I moved some papers and sat down on the bench right at his shoulder.

'Go on, keep painting.'

He grunted sourly. Then he turned his attention back to his picture. I let him paint in an area of lake before I spoke up again.

'Do you like birds especially, or do you just like painting anything?'

'Well, today I'm painting birds,' he said quietly. 'Trying to, anyway.'

'What about painting a pair of Great Tits?' I grabbed the hem of my top and hoiked it up, revealing my big firm breasts. Give the man credit; his reaction was more collected than I'd have expected. After a brief hard stare he slapped his paintbrush into the paint on his tray and daubed it onto my left nipple. The paint was thick and cool and stood up in a tiny peak from my flesh.

Cerulean blue, I believe it was.

'You'll find they're just Blue Tits,' he remarked snarkily. 'Very common.'

'Well you could at least even them up,' said I, pulling my top right off over my head. He saw the delight and the challenge in my face, and something changed in his. His mouth softened.

'OK.' He dipped the brush in water and gathered blue paint again, more carefully this time. He applied it carefully too, swirling the brush-hairs over both my areolae until they puckered, coating my nipples which hardened to stiff nubbins with the pleasure of the cold, soft touch. I sighed in appreciation. He sat back and regarded his work critically.

'Are you going to –?' I started. He popped the long brush handle between my lips, sideways, like it was a horse's bit. Or a gag,

'Hold this.' He waited until I'd taken it obediently between my teeth, then instructed me: 'Lean back.'

Eagerly I adjusted my seat on the bench, straddling it with my legs and leaning back on my arms, so my torso was drawn out and my tits upthrust, wobbling gently with each breath. The painter nodded approval. I wondered how he was going to manage without his brush, but it turned out he wanted a different one anyway; one with a fatter shaft and a big square-tipped head, the kind used for putting in big areas of sky. With this he began to paint me, starting with my breasts, and it turned out he had a bit of a talent for abstract art as well as for drawing birds. I became his canvas; a warmer, more rounded one than he was used to maybe, but generously sized. He painted swirling lines of bright colour, following my body contours, mostly in greens and yellows like I was some strange jungle reptile. He painted down the line of my chest and stomach, then turned my navel into the centre of a sunburst. He worked quickly, with an expression of great concentration. I'd never seen an artist in action close up like this, and it was fascinating. The tickle of the brush was tormenting because it was so concentrated when every inch of my skin wanted to feel it at once; it was like a cold wet tongue lapping at me.

I started to mew with arousal around my wooden gag. He ignored me. On top of the background colours he layered paths of spots in blue and white, using a narrower brush and undiluted paint. If I've ever seen anything like it, it's Australian Aboriginal painting.

He got all the way down to the waistband of my skirt. 'Take this off,' he ordered, so I shimmied awkwardly out of it before resuming my position. He stared at my tanga briefs. 'Open your legs.'

I spread my thighs for him.

'Are you shaved?'

I nodded.

He didn't even ask me to do it this time. He just took hold of my panties and pulled them down, tossing them aside before crouching to look at my plump bare pussy. His nose twitched as he inhaled the scent of my sex. I could smell myself too: I was wet with anticipation.

He painted my mound, turning it into a madly-coloured tropical flower. He painted my velvety outer lips until the flower began to open all its petals. Then, 'Get your knees up,' he said: 'I want to see everything,' and I did, lying back along the hard wooden bench to do it, bringing my knees up to my chest and hoisting my ankles over my head.

He cleaned his brush and manipulated my swollen pink clit with the cold tuft, making me moan. My pussy was so overflowing with juice that he could wet his brush in me and use it to mix his paints. He dyed my inner lips in bright crimson and then coloured right down my crack to my bum-hole, the brush-tip swirling like a tongue around my puckered little entrance until I squealed, feeling it dilate.

'Quiet.' He lifted his brush, showing me. Then he reversed it in his hand. The wooden shaft was, oh, about as thick as a middle finger; he slid it into my arse, jiggling it about to make sure I felt it and groaned at the invasion. Then leaving the brush hanging out of me like a skinny tail, the painter stood. Slipping his trouser-buttons he unzipped his flies to release an erect cock that wasn't nearly as weedy as you might think from the rest of him. His glasses glinted as he stared down at me, jacking himself with one hand, hefting his ball-sac with the other. The eye of his cock winked at me as he pulled his foreskin up and down.

I reckoned that lying there holding my legs up to display my open slash, I wasn't really in much of a position to argue, even if I'd wanted to. Which I didn't; I was so turned on by this artist's attentions that all I wanted was to get my cunt stuffed full with that cock.

I wriggled my arse, making the paintbrush wag. He obliged by straddling the bench and dropping down onto me, slipping his prick into the wet gape of my hole with a couple of good hard shoves. Then he banged me good and proper, practically bouncing up and down on my thighs. I grabbed my clit with one hand because he wasn't going to be paying it any attention, and rubbed frantically as he rammed me. His face was scrunched up in a grimace and sweat ran down his temples. The paint from my belly got smudged all over my legs, and the crimson around my pussy went mostly on his trousers and hairy belly, but I guess art isn't everything. In fact soon art was nothing, and the only thing in my world was his cock squelching away in my cunt, pulling right out then slamming back in again until I saw stars.

Bright rainbow-coloured starbursts then, as I came. He followed up soon after, pulling his cock out and squeezing it like a tube of acrylic, painting my stomach and tits with his spunk. It's my favourite colour of all.

And while I lay panting he managed to stagger away a pace and take up his jar of dirty paint-water, which he poured all over me, slowly and ceremoniously, from tits to throbbing cunt. It was cold on my burning skin, and I spasmed again in aftershock as the torrent hit my pussy. His voice was hoarse as he demanded, '*Now* will you let me get on with it?'

All in all, it was a filthy, degrading fuck. Next week I think I'm going to see what happens when I annoy a fisherman.

– Beverley, North Wales, UK

204

The Factory Floor

I told everyone that I had two dozen women working under me during the summer. The truth was, although there were two dozen women working at the factory, I was pretty much under them.

I got the job to cover my expenses during the summer holidays from university. At 19, I thought I'd landed really lucky getting a management position at a well-known local factory. When I discovered my duties were mainly working as a supervisor, and covering for staff who were away on seasonal holidays, I figured I wasn't quite so lucky. But the money was better than using up the last of my grant and, when I was away from work, I got to brag about all the hot and horny women I had working under me.

Not that they were really that hot and horny. Most of them were typical mums or grannies just doing their daily grind at the factory for a minimum wage although there were a couple of girls, Sandra and Gillian, who were extremely hot. However, I was still pretty shy around all the women and trying to cover my embarrassment by acting like I owned the factory. I think that was what riled them all in the first place, and was probably why they took their revenge on me in the way they did.

It was an early August nightshift, I was on the shop floor with the rest of the girls and, because of the weather, the conversation had moved on to the factory's policies about uniforms – a nylon coat that had to be worn over regular clothes.

'It's too hot to wear this stupid coat,' Doreen complained. At 54 she wasn't the oldest of the factory workers but she was considered the most senior by the other girls. If the management had allowed the girls to have a union, Doreen would have been the shop steward. 'I'm taking mine off,' Doreen announced.

'You can't do that,' I told Doreen. 'It's against factory policy.'

Even though the noise of the machinery was loud I think everyone heard our exchange. Doreen complained that she was sweating cobs in her uniform, and she didn't like the fact that I was able to work in just a T-shirt and jeans. The rest of the girls were on Doreen's side and complaining that it wasn't right that they were expected to work in such conditions. Because there was no one from senior management to resolve the conflict, it was down to me to make an executive decision.

'I'll put in a report if you take off that coat,' I warned Doreen.

She laughed at me. Some of the other girls laughed too and I should have realised then that I wasn't going to win. But I was young and stupid and I figured they would fear the wrath of my superior position.

Doreen walked over to me and stared me in the eye. She pulled off her nylon coat and tossed it to one of the other girls. Plucking at my T-shirt she said, 'What right have you got to put in a report about me when you're not wearing the regulation uniform?'

I spluttered to find an answer. The management's policy said all women on the shop floor had to wear the nylon coats but it made no mention of men, and the overcoats were designed for women. Consequently I'd not really thought about my wearing jeans and T-shirt as being anything out of the ordinary. But, as Doreen plucked at my T-shirt, and I noticed the surge of support for her from the other factory girls, I began to realise I was in no position to argue.

'I'll have a word with the MD tomorrow morning,' I told Doreen.

'That doesn't change anything for tonight,' Doreen snapped back.

A circle of the girls were gathering around us. Work on the floor had ground to a halt. I was growing very nervous but I tried to hide it with a show of bravado. 'There's nothing that can be done about it tonight,' I said firmly. 'I suggest you all get back to your jobs now – wearing your uniforms.'

Doreen shook her head. She nodded at someone behind me and I felt hands grabbing my arms. I was uncomfortable with the idea of striking out. I've always been appalled by the idea of violence toward women, but I did struggle to break free. Unfortunately there were too many of them.

'Why don't you try wearing the uniform?' Doreen smiled.

'Pass me one and I'll put it on,' I told her.

She shook her head again. 'We're not cruel, like you,' she told me. 'It's too hot to be wearing one of those nylon things over your clothes,' she went on. 'So we'll let you undress and wear one.'

I understood what she was suggesting and I struggled even harder to escape the women that held my arms. My struggles were pretty pointless though because the factory girls were now laughing with manic glee. My T-shirt was wrenched upwards and strange hands stroked and scratched my bare flesh. I could feel hands on my trainers and tugging at the belt on my jeans. Within moments, and to the sound of lots of cheers and hilarity, I was stripped down to my boxers. They came off almost instantly and I was left standing naked amongst a circle of the factory girls. My clothes had disappeared before I could think to keep an eye on where they were going.

'He must like the rough treatment,' someone said. 'He's getting a stiffy.'

I glanced down and, to my horror, I could see that I was getting hard. I don't know if it was from the exertion of fighting against the factory girls or if something about the struggle had excited me. But, whatever the cause, I was starting to sprout a modest erection.

'He's getting a stiffy because he likes bossing women around,' Doreen laughed. 'Let's see how much he likes it when the women take control.' As she said the words she took a firm hold of my balls.

My erection stiffened.

'You'll finish the nightshift like this,' Doreen hissed. 'You'll not complain that we're not dressed in regulation uniform and, if you say one word about this to the real bosses, I'll put in a complaint about you being naked on the shop floor. Do we understand each other?'

Her fingers tightened against my sac. I had no idea where the arousal had come from but my erection throbbed with a need for release. Feeling the pressure of Doreen's fingers firm against my sensitive flesh I could only nod agreement at her terms. 'We understand each other,' I whispered.

She released her hold on me with a sneer of contempt.

I was surrounded by a dozen women and, even though my cheeks were burning bright red with embarrassment, I don't think any of them noticed my blushes. Every face seemed to be tilted downwards and I realised they were all looking at my cock. I put my hands over myself to protect my modesty but – naked and surrounded by twenty fully-clothed women – I still felt acutely vulnerable.

'Take off your uniforms if you want, girls,' Doreen called. Cackling nastily she added, 'Our supervisor has relaxed the dress-code for this evening.'

I don't know if that was the best or worst night of my life. I do know that there has never since been another one like it. Half a dozen of the shop-floor girls crowded around me. Although I was trying to keep myself covered up fingers kept pulling at my arms and I wasn't able to keep my hands over my groin. As soon as my erection was exposed to them I was aware of nylon-covered bodies sliding against me and fingers touching and teasing my stiff flesh. One girl asked me if I was embarrassed to be caught in such a position. I was trying to stammer a flustered response when I realised she was just distracting me whilst one of her friends cupped my balls and another one pressed a finger against my anus. I tried to back away but there were so many of them surrounding me escape was impossible.

And my cock had never been harder.

A handful of the women went back to the assembly line and continued with their work. But the majority seemed fascinated to have a naked male on the shop floor and the chance to tease was clearly irresistible. I noticed that Doreen had returned to her work but she kept glancing toward me and smirking.

'Wank him off,' someone whispered.

I don't know who made the suggestion but the idea spread like wildfire. The hand around my cock began to slide up and down and other fingers began to stroke and caress my body. I tried to see who was touching me but I was locked in such a tight crowd of women I couldn't work out who was doing what. And, in truth, it didn't matter who was doing what because I was in a blissful situation. There was one hand around my cock, another touching my balls and another pair teasing my buttocks. When I came, spurting hard and surprised by the force of the climax, I heard a cheer. I was even grinning, stupidly, when I heard someone say, 'Wank him off again.'

The night turned into a marathon of masturbation.

My cock, sensitive after that first climax, was tugged and pulled until it was coaxed back to hardness. Mouths were pressed against my ear and lewd phrases were whispered to me.

'I want to watch you come and then drink it.'

'I've always wanted to see your cock in action.'

'Do you need me to suck it hard for you?'

Even without the physical stimulation, I knew I would have been instantly erect from the lewd tone of those phrases. But with the nearness of so many women, and the fact that they were teasing my foreskin back and forth, tugging at my balls and doing everything they could to excite me, it didn't take long before I was rock-hard again. And, a moment later, my length was quivering as another eruption spat from my cock. Even before I had a chance to fall limp another set of hands were stroking and teasing and trying to get me hard again. And, although my cock felt sore from exploding twice in such quick succession, I was thoroughly enjoying the attention.

'Let me make him come,' one of the girls cried. I recognised the voice as belonging to Sandra.

As she said the words I could feel myself pushed beyond the limits of personal restraint. For the third time in a matter of minutes my shaft was pulsing and a less than impressive stream of my ejaculate was spitting onto the shop floor.

'Not fair,' Sandra complained. 'I wanted to bring him off.'

'No one's stopping you from getting him off again,' Doreen told her.

I wanted to groan and protest but I could see that none of them were listening to me. My hyper-sensitive flesh was grabbed again and Sandra began to vigorously try and tug me back to hardness.

'He's not going to be able to get it up a fourth time,' someone behind me sniffed. The comment was crushing.

'I can make him hard,' Sandra insisted. She pressed her mouth against my ear and said, 'Get it hard and I might take you in my pussy before the night's out.'

This time I did groan. But, despite the fact that she was

tugging and rubbing my sore cock, there was no sign of an erection.

Sandra's best friend on the shop floor, Gillian, joined us. There was still a circle of women around me, all laughing and coaxing me with words of encouragement that went from the suggestive ('Should we all take a turn at sucking him hard?'), to the daunting ('Let's see if he gets hard with a broom handle up his arse'). But when Gillian stepped in front of me the chattering stopped.

'Would the sight of these make you hard?' she asked. She lifted her T-shirt and showed me a pair of large, ripe breasts. Her bra was a sheer fabric that was virtually transparent. I could see the cherry-pink colour of her areolae. Her thick nipples were fat and erect. 'Does that work for you?' she asked.

'Maybe this will work better?' Sandra said. She let go of my cock and began to fondle Gillian's breasts. With a girlish giggle she pushed her face against her friend's chest. I knew both of the girls from my time on the shop floor. It would have been hard not to notice Sandra's pretty face or Gillian's ample bosom. But seeing them both together, Sandra's tongue darting against the shape of Gillian's erect nipples, was enough to stir my hardness back for a fourth time.

'He likes the look of that,' someone muttered.

Sandra flicked her tongue against Gillian's breast and then clutched my cock. Working me with brutal swiftness she grinned as she wanked me.

'The poor lad's sweating cobs,' Doreen muttered. 'Perhaps we should leave him be?'

I should have been crippled by the embarrassment of Doreen's pity. But her comment made every woman on the shop floor turn and watch as Sandra continued pulling at my cock. And, with everyone watching, I squirted with a fourth agonising climax.

Most of the girls went back to their shift and I was pretty much forgotten about. My cock was sore, I was exhausted and spent and I was no longer amusing to them. An hour before the shift was due to end I had to go to the toilets. When I came back, my clothes and Doreen were waiting for me.

'This won't happen again,' Doreen said as I climbed back into my clothes. 'We've had a laugh and you've learned your lesson. Is that clear?'

I finished working at the factory a week later. As it was only a summer job I didn't mind quitting and I knew, the longer I stayed there, the greater the danger that someone might talk about what had happened and my reputation would be ruined. However, if I'd thought there was a danger of it happening again, I'd still be working there to this day.

– Richard, Corby, UK

Three-Way Therapy

I watched Bernice making breakfast. She was wearing her ratty pink bathrobe and dust-fuzzed bunny slippers, curlers in her dyed-brown hair, half a cigarette dangling out of the corner of her unpainted mouth. The old girl's springs were sagging in back and front, and her chassis was anything but rigid and svelte, her grill requiring a couple coats of varnish before it could be presented to the public. Even so, for a woman of forty-nine years' vintage, she was still plenty attractive. The solid shifter in my own bathrobe attested to that fact.

When Bernice had her hair done up careful as her face, strapped her voluptuous breasts into a bra and her voluptuous body into a nice dress, she could still turn heads. Even after twenty-six years of being hitched to yours truly. But what had really wound down over the long years of blissful marriage – and the even longer years of spiteful marriage – was Bernice's sex drive. She just couldn't get it in gear for me to take her for a spin more than once a month, at the most.

I couldn't blame myself. I'd kept up my end of the bargain. Yeah, I'd put on thirty pounds of solid beer belly and developed a smoker's cough. But I still commemorated all the important anniversary dates with nary a reminder. And spontaneously showered the woman with flowers or candies or tickets to a football match every nine months or so, regular as clockwork. And I was still as randy as a trucker after a long road trip.

So, I'd decided I had to do something drastic to light the fire in my wife's loins again. 'The technical term, I believe, is "ménage a trois",' I remarked to her that morning.

'You on about that again,' she sighed, poking at my sausage – in the frying pan.

'I just think it might be just the thing to put the spark back in our love life, my dear,' I responded, spooning sugar into my tea, and voice. 'Something this dead needs a shock to bring it back to life – like Frankenstein and lightning.'

'Didn't we just have sex?'

'That was last Labour Day!'

'Tell me about it.'

I stood up and wrapped my arms around the whole lotta woman. 'See, that's just what I mean. We need to do something different to get the old juices flowing again.'

'That not good enough?' she said, gesturing with the greasy fork at a can of prunes on the counter.

'Not those juices, my love,' I cooed, pressing my erection into her plush bottom. 'Now how 'bout it – for the sake of our marriage?'

'A threesome?'

I hugged her tighter, keeping my balls crossed. 'A threesome.'

'OK,' she finally sighed.

'Really!?'

'Really.' She poked at the sausage some more. 'I know this bloke down at work might be into it. I'll feel him out on Monday.'

I choked, my best-laid plan taking a header from the frying pan into the fire. 'Wait a moment! I meant –'

Bernice laughed and spun around in my arms and kissed me. 'I'll make the breakfast, you make the arrangements.'

I split open with a grin like the sausage in the fire, raced for the telephone and started dialling. Six months of diligent research meant I didn't even have to look up the number.

She was a stunner, all right. Bernice glanced at me suspiciously as the long, tall, cool blonde strolled through the door and into our home, her black stiletto heels click-clacking over the linoleum floor. Her long hair was braided into a ponytail that trailed down her curved back like spun gold, her grey-blue eyes cold and clear as ice behind a pair of wire-rimmed glasses, her full pouty lips done up perfectly silver and glossy. Her heavy breasts provocatively pushed out her tailor-made pinstriped suit jacket and pearl-buttoned white satin blouse, her round pert buttocks straining the stitching on her short pinstriped skirt, her long trim legs pouring out from under the skirt sheathed in sheer black stockings.

'Like the classy corporate types, huh, dearie?' Bernice observed.

I grinned sheepishly. I'd been dyed-in-the-wool blue collar since my eighteenth birthday – when my parents had thrown me out of the house – but I had always admired those sleek, slender, elegant corporate types in their crisply fashionable skirts and blouses (usually while wolf-whistling from my perch on a construction crane). So, I'd figured I might as well kill two fantasies with one bone.

Her name was Evelyn, and she coolly led the pair of us down the hall and into the bedroom. I was excited as a hunting dog in a cathouse, while Bernice seemed somewhat indifferent. Evelyn was all business, as befitted her gorgeous appearance, casually and sensually removing her jacket, her glasses, unbuttoning her blouse and unfastening her skirt.

I bounced up and down on the edge of the bed, barely stifling an impulse to thrust some hard-earned notes into the lovely lady's garter. I graciously gripped my wife's plump hand in a sweaty vice, instead, staring at the breathtaking blonde, watching open-mouthed and hard-dicked as she turned her graceful back to us and unfastened her white lace bra, silver fingernails flashing deftly.

And when she turned back around and displayed her big, firm, tan-lined tits for our amusement, I squeezed Bernice's hand blue, my boner splitting my bathrobe open. The woman's breasts were simply perfect, ripe and heavy, with coral-pink nipples that jutted out and made my mouth water.

She faced away from us again, and slowly shimmied out of her tight skirt, revealing an equally tight pair of shiny white satin panties. They came down, sliding smoothly over the twin bronze moons of her buttocks. I clutched Bernice's hand to my mouth and bit into her knuckles.

Evelyn strutted over to the bed, juicy boobs jouncing, blonde-tufted pussy glistening pink. I tried to jump into her arms, onto her spectacular body. But she placed a cool restraining hand on my heaving chest and took Bernice's hand in hers and pulled my wife up off the bed.

She looked Bernice in the cow eyes and slid the woman's ratty pink bathrobe off her round shoulders. I watched in awe as the robe puddled at Bernice's bare feet, leaving my wife as lushly nude as the Lady Evelyn. Bernice's pale, plump-curved body formed a stunning contrast with the younger woman's bronze statuesqueness. And when Evelyn took Bernice in her arms and the women's bare breasts came together in a heated embrace, I let out a whoop of joy.

Evelyn kissed my wife. Softly, on the lips, their tits and nips squeezing together. Bernice's face flushed with an impassioned heat I hadn't seen for years, as she returned the woman's kiss. As Evelyn's elegant hands slid down Bernice's back and onto the old girl's butt cheeks, gripping and squeezing the thick pliable flesh, Bernice moaned. Evelyn darted her tongue inside my wife's mouth, entangling it around Bernice's tongue.

I couldn't take it any more, aroused beyond hormonal human endurance by the rod and cone-blasting sight of those two naked women exchanging wicked pleasantries in the hushed confines of our marital bedroom. I sprang to my feet and shucked off my bathrobe, grabbed up my straining cock and started fisting, only one lustful lunge away from the frenching females.

Evelyn glanced at me out of the corner of her eye, at my hand-cranked cock, and sank her sharp white teeth into my wife's wilfully extended tongue and sucked on it. She dropped Bernice's buttocks and picked up the woman's breasts, kneading them with her sure hands so that Bernice shivered with pleasure.

I stroked my hardwood like I meant to start a fire – or douse one – watching Evelyn release my wife's tongue and lower her head down to my wife's breasts, swirl her long silver tongue around first one fat cherry-red nipple and then the other. I rushed in to help – Bernice's knockers being more than a handful. Evelyn allowed me a tit, and I excitedly squeezed and sucked on it, as she coolly tongued my wife's other tit. Bernice moaned, clutching at our heads, her body shaking like mine. My plan was taking flight.

At Evelyn's signal, the two women suddenly went down on their knees at my feet – and dick. The beautiful blonde grasped my beating shaft in her warm smooth hand and started stroking. I jerked with joy like when Bernice had first agreed to the threesome. And then I went haywire, when Evelyn fed my pulsating love-club to Bernice, and she took almost all of it into her wet-hot mouth and held tight. Then pulled back. Then plunged back down again.

Getting a blowjob from the missus was usually as difficult as getting England qualified for an international football tournament. But with Cool Hand Evelyn in control, guiding Bernice's head back and forth, it seemed like the most natural and wonderful thing in the world.

Bernice's nose poked right into my short 'n' curlies standing straight on end, her silky cauldron of a mouth and throat widening to accommodate me like never before. Until Evelyn popped me throbbing and dripping out of my wife's mouth and into hers.

The two lascivious ladies passed my bloated baton back and forth between them like I was in a pornographer's wet dream, sucking, licking, nipping. I started to rattle and groan like I meant to really whetten their sexual appetites, the double-doll dong-sucking pressure too much for me to take. That's when Evelyn expertly capped my boiling desire, just below the hood with her throttling fingers. She and Bernice then climbed to their feet, leaving me practically out on mine.

They moved over to the bed, and Evelyn had Bernice lie up against the headboard. Then she settled in between my wife's legs, grasping and spreading Bernice's thighs and burying her tongue in my wife's pussy. She wiggled her peach-taut behind at me as she licked at Bernice's muff.

I leapt on board, grabbing onto the woman's trim waist and slotting my poker deep into her shaven slit. 'Sweet Ev-el-lyn!' I groaned, the blonde every bit as hot and wet on the inside as she was cool and dry on the outside.

I started churning away, plunging my raging cock in and out of Evelyn's gripping pussy as I watched the lewd lass lap at my wife's jungle pussy like I'd never had the guts to do myself. Bernice stared at me fucking another woman, her eyes glassy, hands working her fleshy boobs, fingers rolling her swollen nipples.

Our terrifically talented marriage counsellor/sex therapist licked pussy from bumhole to clit, over and over, all the while bouncing back and forth on my cock in rhythm to my frantic thrustings. My knuckles blazed white on her bronze skin, my thighs beating up against her bottom, setting the firm flesh to shimmying. The stuffy bedroom grew hot and humid with the smell of wet sex.

I picked up the pace even more, pistoning Evelyn's sweet pussy with my iron cock, the babe rocking in between Bernice's legs but never once letting up the tongue-pressure on my wife's twat. Then she must've somehow latched her pouty lips onto clit, because Bernice's eyes suddenly rolled back in her head and her voluptuous body and breasts shuddered with blessed orgasm.

'God-damn!' I roared, quickly joining my wife in ecstasy. My flapping balls boiled over and my flying cock blew sizzling jizz deep into Evelyn's velvety love tunnel. I came as hard and long and voluminous as when Bernice and I had first started dating back in the day.

That initial threesome did indeed work wonders on our matrimonial sex life. Only, now I can hardly keep up with Bernice. The old girl's become positively insatiable; getting her sexual second wind and then some. I think she might even be helping Evelyn out with some of her 'clients'.

So long as she still has room in her schedule for me every fortnight, I can't complain.

— *Hank, Sacramento, USA*

nexus

The leading publisher of fetish and adult fiction

TELL US WHAT YOU THINK!

Readers' ideas and opinions matter to us so please take a few minutes to fill in the questionnaire below.

1. Sex: Are you male ☐   female ☐   a couple ☐?

2. Age: Under 21 ☐   21–30 ☐   31–40 ☐   41–50 ☐   51–60 ☐   over 60 ☐

3. Where do you buy your Nexus books from?

☐ A chain book shop. If so, which one(s)?

_____

☐ An independent book shop. If so, which one(s)?

_____

☐ A used book shop/charity shop
☐ Online book store. If so, which one(s)?

_____

4. How did you find out about Nexus books?

☐ Browsing in a book shop
☐ A review in a magazine
☐ Online
☐ Recommendation
☐ Other _____

5. In terms of settings, which do you prefer? (Tick as many as you like.)

☐ Down to earth and as realistic as possible
☐ Historical settings. If so, which period do you prefer?

_____

☐ Fantasy settings – barbarian worlds
☐ Completely escapist/surreal fantasy
☐ Institutional or secret academy

- ☐ Futuristic/sci fi
- ☐ Escapist but still believable
- ☐ Any settings you dislike?

_____

- ☐ Where would you like to see an adult novel set?

_____

6. In terms of storylines, would you prefer:

- ☐ Simple stories that concentrate on adult interests?
- ☐ More plot and character-driven stories with less explicit adult activity?
- ☐ We value your ideas, so give us your opinion of this book:

_____

_____

_____

7. In terms of your adult interests, what do you like to read about? (Tick as many as you like.)

- ☐ Traditional corporal punishment (CP)
- ☐ Modern corporal punishment
- ☐ Spanking
- ☐ Restraint/bondage
- ☐ Rope bondage
- ☐ Latex/rubber
- ☐ Leather
- ☐ Female domination and male submission
- ☐ Female domination and female submission
- ☐ Male domination and female submission
- ☐ Willing captivity
- ☐ Uniforms
- ☐ Lingerie/underwear/hosiery/footwear (boots and high heels)
- ☐ Sex rituals
- ☐ Vanilla sex
- ☐ Swinging
- ☐ Cross-dressing/TV
- ☐ Enforced feminisation

☐ Others – tell us what you don't see enough of in adult fiction:

_____

_____

_____

8. Would you prefer books with a more specialised approach to your interests, i.e. a novel specifically about uniforms? If so, which subject(s) would you like to read a Nexus novel about?

_____

_____

_____

9. Would you like to read true stories in Nexus books? For instance, the true story of a submissive woman, or a male slave? Tell us which true revelations you would most like to read about:

_____

_____

_____

10. What do you like best about Nexus books?

_____

_____

11. What do you like least about Nexus books?

_____

_____

12. Which are your favourite titles?

_____

_____

13. Who are your favourite authors?

_____

_____

14. Which covers do you prefer? Those featuring:
(Tick as many as you like.)

- ☐ Fetish outfits
- ☐ More nudity
- ☐ Two models
- ☐ Unusual models or settings
- ☐ Classic erotic photography
- ☐ More contemporary images and poses
- ☐ A blank/non-erotic cover
- ☐ What would your ideal cover look like?

_____

15. Describe your ideal Nexus novel in the space provided:

_____

_____

_____

_____

16. Which celebrity would feature in one of your Nexus-style fantasies?
    We'll post the best suggestions on our website – anonymously!

_____

THANKS FOR YOUR TIME

Now simply write the title of this book in the space below and cut out the
questionnaire pages. Post to: Nexus, Marketing Dept., Virgin Books,
Random House, 20 Vauxhall Bridge Road, London SW1V 2SA

Book title: _____

NEXUS NEW BOOKS

To be published in April 2009

ON THE BARE
Fiona Locke

Fiona Locke's *Over the Knee* has become a cult classic and is considered a definitive work of corporal punishment and fetish fiction. This anthology of short stories is even stronger, portraying the bratty, the spoilt and the wilful as they each get their stinging just-deserts from masterly purveyors of discipline. Full of the authentic and exquisite details her fans adore, these stories are spanking masterpieces for true connoisseurs.

£7.99   ISBN 9780352345158

If you would like more information about Nexus titles, please visit our website at www.nexus-books.co.uk, or send a large stamped addressed envelope to:
  Nexus
  Virgin Books
  Random House
  20 Vauxhall Bridge Road
  London SW1V 2SA

NEXUS BOOKLIST

Information is correct at time of printing. To avoid disappointment, check availability before ordering. Go to www.nexus-books.co.uk.

All books are priced at £6.99 unless another price is given.

NEXUS

☐ ABANDONED ALICE	Adriana Arden	ISBN 978 0 352 33969 0
☐ ALICE IN CHAINS	Adriana Arden	ISBN 978 0 352 33908 9
☐ AMERICAN BLUE	Penny Birch	ISBN 978 0 352 34169 3
☐ AQUA DOMINATION	William Doughty	ISBN 978 0 352 34020 7
☐ THE ART OF CORRECTION	Tara Black	ISBN 978 0 352 33895 2
☐ THE ART OF SURRENDER	Madeline Bastinado	ISBN 978 0 352 34013 9
☐ BEASTLY BEHAVIOUR	Aishling Morgan	ISBN 978 0 352 34095 5
☐ BEING A GIRL	Chloë Thurlow	ISBN 978 0 352 34139 6
☐ BELINDA BARES UP	Yolanda Celbridge	ISBN 978 0 352 33926 3
☐ BIDDING TO SIN	Rosita Varón	ISBN 978 0 352 34063 4
☐ BLUSHING AT BOTH ENDS	Philip Kemp	ISBN 978 0 352 34107 5
☐ THE BOOK OF PUNISHMENT	Cat Scarlett	ISBN 978 0 352 33975 1
☐ BRUSH STROKES	Penny Birch	ISBN 978 0 352 34072 6
☐ CALLED TO THE WILD	Angel Blake	ISBN 978 0 352 34067 2
☐ CAPTIVES OF CHEYNER CLOSE	Adriana Arden	ISBN 978 0 352 34028 3
☐ CARNAL POSSESSION	Yvonne Strickland	ISBN 978 0 352 34062 7
☐ CITY MAID	Amelia Evangeline	ISBN 978 0 352 34096 2
☐ COLLEGE GIRLS	Cat Scarlett	ISBN 978 0 352 33942 3
☐ COMPANY OF SLAVES	Christina Shelly	ISBN 978 0 352 33887 7
☐ CONCEIT AND CONSEQUENCE	Aishling Morgan	ISBN 978 0 352 33965 2
☐ CORRECTIVE THERAPY	Jacqueline Masterson	ISBN 978 0 352 33917 1
☐ CORRUPTION	Virginia Crowley	ISBN 978 0 352 34073 3

NEXUS CLASSIC

--------- ✄ -------------------------------

Please send me the books I have ticked above.

Name   ....

Address   ....

            ....

            ....

            .... Post code ....

**Send to: Virgin Books Cash Sales, Direct Mail Dept., the Book
Service Ltd, Colchester Road, Frating, Colchester, CO7 7DW**

US customers: for prices and details of how to order books for
delivery by mail, call 888-330-8477.

Please enclose a cheque or postal order, made payable to **Virgin
Books Ltd**, to the value of the books you have ordered plus
postage and packing costs as follows:
   UK and BFPO – £1.00 for the first book, 50p for each
subsequent book.
   Overseas (including Republic of Ireland) – £2.00 for the first
book, £1.00 for each subsequent book.

If you would prefer to pay by VISA, ACCESS/MASTERCARD,
AMEX, DINERS CLUB or SWITCH, please write your card
number and expiry date here:

....

Please allow up to 28 days for delivery.

Signature ....

Our privacy policy

We will not disclose information you supply us to any other
parties. We will not disclose any information which identifies you
personally to any person without your express consent.

From time to time we may send out information about Nexus
books and special offers. Please tick here if you do *not* wish to
receive Nexus information.   ☐

--------- ✄ -------------------------------